THE
OUTCAST

Book One of The Hayle Coven Destinies

PATTI LARSEN

ALSO BY
PATTI LARSEN

The Hayle Coven Universe

The Hunted Series
Fiona Fleming Cozy Mysteries
The Nightshade Cases
The Clone Chronicles
The Diamond City Trilogy
Didi and the Gunslinger

and much, much more.
Find your new favorite author at
pattilarsen.com
Sign up for new releases
bit.ly/pattilarsenemail

ONE

I dodged to the left, dipping my head over Max's rough shoulder as the wide-open mouth of our attacker spewed neon green acid in my direction. My shields shuddered under the touch of the potent fluid, bursting into flame and smoke, washed away in the beating of my drach friend's giant wing strokes.

The ball of rainbow magic in my hand sizzled in my palm as I took aim on the nasty critter now winding its way beneath us and tried to focus. *A little lower, Max.* He obliged immediately, banking to the left and dipping his massive, gray scaled head. Right in the path of my throw. *You're blocking my view.*

My apologies. He actually sounded like he was having fun. Imagine. Then again, as he turned his big noggin to the right, long neck snaking his face out of the way, I had to admit the thrilling bubble in my stomach was my very own brand of excitement.

Seriously, Hayle. Get a grip already.

The reptile-like creature slithered through the air, clearing Max's bulk. Shining teeth made up most of its scaled face. Two pinpoints of black eyes and one bare slit just above the glittering fangs were almost lost in the gaping of its mouth. A high pitched squeal assaulted my ears, making it down to my bones, sending shivers through me. Wingless, flying by energy alone, it twisted sideways, thin, ribbon-like body snapping into a multihued coil. Spit sizzled another round of its horrible venom our way.

My shields could handle it. This particular creature might be slippery, but it wasn't all that clever. As though he was reading my mind—and perhaps he was—Max turned on his side, one wing over my head, giving me a nice, clear view of the pale lavender horizon and two suns cresting the distant mountains. And, even better, the monstrosity attacking us.

Perfect.

My arm drew back even as my power built inside the hissing ball of magic. While it wasn't necessary for me to actually throw the weapon, I took great satisfaction from doing so.

With the practiced pitch of long experience, I let the ball of multicolored fire fly, letting out a whoop of success as it impacted solidly in the center of the twisting creature's face. Its squeal was muffled this time, not the penetrating nasty I'd been enduring since this fight began. The rainbow power of my attack split into ribbons, forming a net of magic around the creature's head, smothering it. Tail thrashing, it fell beneath us, plunging to the deep purple lake below, a large splash marking its passing.

My hand swiped at a trickle of sweat running down the side of my face as I patted Max's scaled shoulder. *Nicely done, big man.*

Not so bad yourself, my friend. He turned in a slow arc, both of us watching his people far below. Only a handful or so of the odd creatures remained to be dealt with, a far cry from the hundreds of twisting, vicious whatever-they-were that showed up as a pack last night. At least, I thought it was last night. It was so easy to lose track of time when I was on other planes, fighting with the drach.

Brilliant idea luring them here, I sent as Max hovered in place. His big head turned toward me, one diamond eye spinning with power.

Indeed, he sent. *I had hoped our current strategy of drawing them to an empty plane might make our job easier.*

Did it ever. Hard enough fighting these creatures who crossed over from the other Universe, but doing so in the veil made tracking them all down almost impossible. At least if we managed to lure them to a plane and forced them to cross in our wake or drive them through an opening we created, we could trap them and deal with them in a contained environment. We had, as yet, to discover a species who could use the veil on their own, so it worked most of the time.

Should we do a sweep to see if we missed any? Wow, did I actually sound eager? Max had the good sense not to tease me about it. But, damn it, this was fun.

Yeah, I admitted it. Fun. Sigh. Something was seriously wrong with me.

I believe we captured the entire swarm, he sent, faint amusement in his mental voice. *Your assistance is appreciated, as usual, Sydlynn Hayle.*

Weariness had begun to set in and, as I rolled my throwing shoulder, eyes scanning the drach cleaning up the last of the mess below, I realized I was tired. Tired and sore and probably ready to go home after all.

Any time, I sent as Max raised his head and widened his wings, thrusting upward. A gap appeared in the veil, shimmering around the edges with the glitter of diamonds as he plunged us through. It felt weird to be in the veil again, the muffled darkness hugging me close as the slice sealed shut behind us. Until the next time.

Max grunted in my head. *Is it just me*, he sent, *or does it seem no matter how hard we try, we are unable to eradicate the threats which emerged when the veil between Universes was damaged?*

I didn't want to go there, had actually dreaded the

conversation. Because I knew where it was going. The giant first race of drach were the most powerful creatures in the Universe—in our Universe, anyway—and though their leader was a very dear friend, I still felt uneasy reminding myself all of this mess was kind of my fault.

Okay, so Fate had a lot to do with it. Like my purposeful creation and development from ordinary witch to powerful maji. The discovery of my drach heritage. And the fact everything I went through to get to this point was, as it turned out, fated long before I was born. I suppose I shouldn't have felt any guilt over our present predicament. My son, Gabriel, may have opened the way between the two Universes, but it was Max and his people who divided them in the first place, wasn't it?

Syd. Max's voice was soft in my head. *I'm sorry. I know where your mind is going.*

I shifted on his back, uncomfortable that he knew, though I patted his neck ridge so he would know I wasn't angry. *It's okay*, I sent. And sighed. *We all played a part, didn't we?*

We did, he sent, body effortless in the vastness of the veil, soaring over glittering divisions between planes. Every time I came into the rubbery membrane separating the worlds of my Universe, I was in awe of just how vast this place really was. But it couldn't distract me today, not with my mind going where I'd tried to keep it from wandering. My son's kidnapping and subsequent control by Ameline Benoit could not have been avoided. I still cringed at the memory of the loss of my first husband, Liam. Gabriel's father's death was also fated, damn them. *But you won, in the end, as you always do.* Max's mental voice broke my whirling thought process. *And I know we will succeed now.*

It's been seven years, Max. I leaned forward and rested my forehead on his neck, weariness washing over me in waves. *You would think we'd have made some headway by now.*

Perhaps if Demonicon's Node hadn't fallen, he sent, banking right as we neared my home plane at last. *But the damage done when Meira was forced to rebuild it allowed even more creatures through.*

I remembered. My sister's fight to become true Ruler of Demonicon almost broke her and the entire Universe. But she made it through, was stronger for it.

How long do you think we'll have to keep doing this? Oh, Syd. Syd. So transparent my eagerness, even when weary from this most recent fight.

A while yet, Max sent. *I'm certain there are still many more creatures who escaped the Dark Universe and came here, now hiding among the planes.*

We'd encountered a few that weren't a threat and left them alone on abandoned worlds. But the harmless ones were few and far between. I had no desire to visit the Dark Universe—even if that was possible—if all they bred were violent, nasty and dangerous creatures like the ones we'd fought over the years.

I wonder how many of our own creatures crossed into their Universe? It had been on my mind for a while.

There is no way of knowing, Max sent as the air before him split and gaped wide. His body shifted, shrinking even as we plunged forward toward the darkened basement on the other side of the rift. *Though from the empty planes we've been uncovering, I fear we've lost whole civilizations to the other side.*

I hope they are okay. I leaped from his back as he stepped out into the quiet, my sneakers squeaking on the concrete. Max's diamond eyes glowed as he smiled a little at me, gray toned face softly marked with tiny scales. He bowed his bald head.

"As do I." His deep voice matched the rumble of his mental one, the edges of it touched by the hint of the song of the drach. I hugged him, impulsive, my shoulders aching from the battle, but I didn't care. Max embraced me with his powerful arms, the powder scent of him touched with a hint of smoke from the fight. His gray robe felt soft under my cheek as he spoke again. "We do what we can, Syd."

I nodded into his chest before leaning back and stepping away. Bitterness bubbled and I did my best to contain it, rubbing at the goosebumps that rose on my arms. "Would be nice to have a little help," I grumbled.

Max sighed, a soft sound that nonetheless stirred the

air around me. I wondered sometimes if his human shape actually hid the dragon within, like an illusion. Everything about Max was larger than life. "The maji," he said.

Damned, cursed, wretched maji. "You'd think for once they'd get off their sorry asses and give us a hand." I did my best most times to forget about the pathetic race I'd become part of. But, I shared none of their refusal to act. The second race of the Universe, they feared interference and, no matter the risk facing us, had always refused to assist.

Cowards, the lot of them.

Max's smile was gone, but his gentle presence helped me settle down.

"A time will come," he said, "when even they will be forced to admit their need to act." I highly doubted that, but I was too tired to argue. "For now, we are more than enough." I grinned at him, nodded. Way to make me feel better. "I will let you rest," he said. "Be well, my friend."

"You, too." I waved as he turned and entered the gap, hugging myself when it sealed behind him, leaving me alone in the quiet of the basement under my house.

Well, mostly alone.

I turned to face the one waiting for me, not sure if I should expect a lecture or not.

TWO

The silver Persian stared up at me with his glowing amber eyes, the soft light of morning shining in through the basement window lighting his fur with gold.

"Sydlynn." Sassafras swiped his tongue over one paw before returning to stare at me.

"Sass." I crouched in front of him, exhaling my weariness as I smiled and stroked his forehead. A soft, deep purr rose from him immediately, the pulse of his comforting power reaching out to me in return. One quick scoop and he was in my arms, kneading my shoulder as I scratched one of his fuzzy cheeks.

"How was your trip?" His amber eyes blinked slowly, evenly. Such a loaded question, really. Sassafras so rarely said anything that wasn't either double edged or important—at least, in his mind.

"You know," I said, turning to the stairs and heading

up to the kitchen. "The usual."

"You stink." He sniffed delicately at me, ears flickering.

"Thanks." It was impossible not to laugh. The stairs creaked under my feet as I reached the top and pushed open the door, already ajar from his entry. "No respect from you, fuzzy butt."

Sassafras snorted softly, nuzzling my cheek. "Someone has to keep you humble," he said.

As Max would say, "Indeed."

The kitchen was quiet, the sun just rising, everything still and softly warm. Summer was half way through, the lazy days and nights my favorite time of year. My alter egos stirred within me, now free of the focus of battle. It had taken me a long time to get used to having my demon, the Sidhe princess, Shaylee and the vampire essence coexisting with me in my head. But the longer we spent together, the less I even thought about it. We just were.

I settled Sassafras on the table and crossed the kitchen to the coffee maker. It was just beginning to bubble, the scent of its rich, delicious nectar making my mouth water. The temptation to drink it right from the pot was so strong I had to stuff my hands in my pockets. While I wasn't affected by strong temperatures anymore thanks to my powerful magic and maji status, it was probably best to wait and use a mug.

At least, that's what the watchful stare on Sassafras's face said. I knew him too well.

"You were only gone one night this time." No judgment in his voice. There never was, these days. Still, his comment was enough to tweak my guilt all over again. But this was different. It had nothing to do with who was responsible for the mess in the first place and everything to do with abandoning my family on a regular basis to run around the Universe. I chewed at my bottom lip as I retrieved a giant mug from the cupboard, watching the door swing softly shut on its slow-close hinges. My feet carried me to the fridge, the act of doing things with my physical body instead of with magic helping to ground me. My demon growled at me for my choice of cream while Shaylee asked for extra sugar this morning.

"Quick clean up," I said, my spoon rattling against the sides of my mug as I waited for the coffee to finish.

Sassafras sighed, loudly enough I turned to face him. While I knew he understood my need to assist Max and the drach, I often wondered what his real opinion was. It wasn't like Sassafras to hold back. Still, I'd refrained from asking and he, for whatever reason, hadn't made a point of it.

Until now, apparently.

"You feel badly," he said, voice soft and deep and a little thick. His ears turned to the sides, lying flat, whiskers curving down. I immediately crossed to him and sat, hands stroking his fur. "You think you've abandoned us."

I shrugged, choking up myself. "Haven't I?" I was so mixed about how I felt. After all, I spent years faced with constant turmoil and stress, developed powers no one else had and saved the Universe a time or two. Was it any wonder I said yes the moment Max appeared and asked for help?

And yet, I was coven leader of the Hayle family. And was taught from early childhood the family always came first. My demon hissed softly in protest while Shaylee and my vampire remained silent.

"I've been meaning to talk to you," Sassafras said, tail twitching. "To tell you how proud I am of you, Syd."

Why now? I was so tired he was going to make me all blubbery and stuff.

"I don't know why I left it so long," he said. Cleared his throat, ears rising. "But we all have our parts to play. And, thankfully, you are here to clean up what others can't." I opened my mouth to comment, but he shushed me with a paw on my lips. "Besides," he said, a twinkle returning to his eyes, "all this running off with Max keeps your trouble seeking side happily occupied." My demon chuckled and even Shaylee and my vampire joined in.

"It does," I said, kissing his forehead again.

Sassafras shifted position, head dropping a little, tail twitching again. "It's part of what I wanted to talk to you about," he said, voice hesitant. When he raised his gaze to mine, I could see the troubled look there. "Things are so quiet here."

I nodded, sitting back, coffee forgotten. At the sound of a soft tread of feet behind me I turn around to smile at the beautiful young woman entering the kitchen. Sashenka Hensley paused to hug me around the shoulders before continuing on, her bare feet padding over the tile, light pink silk robe whispering around her.

"Is that a problem?" I frowned. "You're saying quiet is a bad thing?" After everything we'd been through, he was complaining about peace and stability?

Shenka turned toward him, her dark skin catching the morning light, glowing with a faint yellow hue. "What do you mean, Sass?" She crossed to us, handing me my mug of coffee and I smiled up at her as she joined us, slipping into the seat next to me, one hand stroking his soft fur while her dark brown eyes watched him carefully.

The silver Persian's fur ruffled as he shook himself. "I don't know," he said, sounding frustrated. "I've just been feeling... dull. Uninterested in anything." His gaze traveled back and forth between my coven second and me. "Am I imagining things?"

I immediately reached out, Shenka's power joining mine, and searched the vicinity. Were we in danger? Under attack? But I felt nothing and, from the curious feel of my second's magic, she didn't find anything either.

I pushed all the way to the border of my territory, touched the edge of the power waiting there. Just the North American Witches Council, keeping mark as always.

We both retreated at the same time. But even as we did, I realized Sass was right. The weariness I felt was exacerbated here at home. I had simply blamed it on being tired.

Sassafras shook his head as we both emerged from our search. "I know, I know," he said, irritation clear in the set of his ears and whiskers, the thrashing of his tail. "I've looked, too. Found nothing. All is freaking well." He sounded almost angry, so much so I soothed him with a touch of energy.

"Sass," I said, leaning toward him, speaking softly, "I might not be the only one who has a penchant for trouble seeking."

His amber eyes flamed a moment. "You think I haven't thought of that?" He shook his furry head. "Whatever. Never mind." He tried to hop down from the table, but I caught him and cuddled him.

"If you're worried," I said, "I'm worried." Shenka nodded in turn, hands cupping her mug, face serious. "We'll keep watch, just in case."

Sassafras's tension eased. "Thank you," he said. "I'm sure it's nothing."

I let him go, watched him sashay his way out of the

kitchen and into the hall. Shenka's dark eyes met mine when I turned back and smiled at her.

"He's rarely wrong," she said, a frown pulling her black brows together. I really needed to get her to shape mine. Hers were perfect. And shook my head at myself. I was thinking about beauty styling at a moment like this?

Maybe he was right after all.

"There's nothing we can do if there's nothing out there to fight," I said. My coffee was half empty already and I stood to return to the pot. "But we'll pay attention."

Shenka nodded as I filled a second mug. "Just in case."

I turned and winked at her. "For now, I'm off to bed."

She eyed the pair of coffee mugs with a little grin.

"Sure you are." She waved me off as I left the room, blushing.

I might have been going to bed, all right. But I when I thought about the man already between the sheets, waiting for me, my weariness faded away and I hoped he had other ideas than sleep.

THREE

I reached the top of the stairs without spilling a drop, though giggled to myself a little magic was involved to do the trick. Another soft touch of power eased open the first door on the left, leading to my old room. I peeked inside at the tiny girl under the pink covers, one hand curled under her cheek, dark hair spilling over the edge of her pillow. Sassafras perched next to her, licking his paws and blinked slowly in acknowledgment before I pulled the door softly shut behind me with another brush of magic.

The next door down lead to a smaller room, though with the benefit of corner windows. Deep greens and golds were my son's decorating colors of choice and I had no doubt where his desire for earthy tones came from. Gabriel slept peacefully, strawberry blond hair mussed, covers thrown askew, showing off his cartoon pajamas. It was hard to believe he was only seven years old, Ethie six already, my little family growing up around me. The giant black hound stretched out at the foot of Gabriel's bed lifted his head with a soft groan, black eyes reflecting a hint of red fire as he licked his chops.

Sorry, I sent. *Back to sleep, Galleytrot.*

The big dog laid his head down again. *Nice to see you home, Syd.*

I did my best not to wince, backing out of my son's room and turning to the other side of the hall. Shenka's door was closed on the far end, the bathroom entry across from Ethie's ajar. But it was quiet and mostly dark up here still, and I felt my eyelids beginning to weigh down again at the thought of my soft, comfy bed and the warm body I could curl up to.

Quaid was still asleep when I crept inside, muscular chest exposed where he, like our son, threw off the covers in slumber. I sat on the edge of the bed, depositing the two mugs on the side table, and looked down at my sleeping husband. I still felt breathless from time to time, in moments like this, that Quaid was mine at last. Though it was seven years later, I found there were moments when my heart swelled with old grief and worry that I'd somehow lose him again one day.

And I would, eventually. Considering I was maji, practically invincible and definitely immortal. And Quaid... wasn't. But I refused to linger on the fact too often. I would enjoy the time we had together, even if it meant I would someday have to watch him grow old and die. And find a way to live without him.

I should have let him sleep, but I couldn't resist running my fingertips over his tanned skin. The tattoo of a pentagram on his shoulder reminded me of being a teenager again, in lust for him, our power tied together. The first time I saw him without a shirt on… I drew a shaking breath and laughed softly to myself in the stillness of our bedroom.

Oh dear. Maybe I really wasn't tired after all.

I bent over him, lips brushing across his, feeling his power stir as his body woke. Quaid's chocolate eyes eased open, big hands rising to slip up my arms and pull me down, a grin tugging at his luscious mouth.

"Morning," he whispered before kissing me for real, big body turning me over and pinning me to the bed.

Exactly where I wanted to be.

I woke slowly, languidly, one arm draped over the edge of the bed, Quaid's warm body pressed against my back. The clock flashed 8AM as his body flexed and a deep sigh ruffled my hair, tickling my ear with the heat of his breath.

"Missed you," he whispered.

"You, too." My throat tightened, the guilt returning, though I wished it would just go away. I turned over on my side, slipping my arm around his shoulders when

Quaid sat up on one elbow and leaned over me. His lips traced a lazy line down my jaw and to my neck, across the top of my shoulder.

"Nothing damaged?" One eyebrow shot up, a wicked grin on his lips as he tugged on the sheet covering me. I rolled over on my back and shrugged.

"You might want to check and be sure." I winked. "Just in case."

Quaid laughed, kissed me before nuzzling my neck. "You got it." His gaze lifted to the end table. "Is that coffee?" The soft groan of hope in his voice made me laugh.

"Excuse me," I said, poking him in the ribs while he lunged past me and retrieved one of the mugs. "World's Greatest Dad" graced the side of it, a favorite gift from the kids. "You were attending to something important just now."

Quaid's dark eyes glittered over the rim of his mug as he lifted it to his lips. Bubbles emerge from the surface, steam erupting, my demon warming it for him. His lips sipped at the drink and he closed his eyes with a blissful expression.

"In a minute," he said. "It's coffee we're talking about, Syd."

I laughed and sat up, reaching for my t-shirt lying on the floor. A quick tug and it was on, my missing panties joining it. Decent enough just in case, I propped myself up against the headboard and drank my own newly heated coffee, shoulder to shoulder with the man I loved.

"Drach problem solved?" Quaid slipped his arm around me, kissing my temple with his hot lips.

"One, at least," I said, and frowned. "Were you talking to Sassafras?"

"About?" Quaid's brown eyes watched me carefully as I chewed one thumbnail. His free hand rose and pulled my hand away. I flashed him a frown and resumed gnawing.

"He said he's been feeling off lately." His big hand trapped mine, forced me to stop mutilating my nail.

Quaid's frown darkened his handsome face, scruff of beard tightening around the corners of his mouth and casting shadows. "He didn't mention it. But now that you do…" Quaid looked off into the distance. "I know what he means. Everything is kind of… muffled." He shrugged. "I chalked it up to boredom and peace and quiet, Syd."

"Maybe that's it." I stared down into my mug. "We've had a lot of that lately. At least here at home."

Quaid's arm tightened. "Don't tell me," he mock groaned. "You're looking for trouble again?"

I tsked at him and jabbed him in the ribs, but he laughed, lips on mine a moment before he spoke again.

"Syd," he said. "I've learned to trust your gut, my beautiful wife. And Sassafras isn't one to raise an alarm for no good reason." Quaid sipped his drink. "Maybe we should be more careful. We've been pretty complacent lately."

"Not really." I felt the need to defend our actions for some reason. "We're warded, and in touch with other races." One of my promises to myself when the last mess ended was to stay in tune with what was happening around me, on this plane and others. Was I failing? But no, Shenka and I both searched, as did Sass, and we found nothing even remotely resembling a threat.

Still.

"Just saying," Quaid said. "If you think something is off, it's probably off. So, we'll be more vigilant in the next little while. Just in case."

I loved my husband so much.

But I didn't get a chance to show him the way I would have liked. The door to our room slammed open and two squealing children hurtled themselves over the threshold and onto the bed. More magic kept our brew from spilling as Ethie threw herself at her father, snuggling into his lap, a slightly more demure Gabriel wiggling his way between Quaid and me. Sassafras leapt up to the end of the bed, curling up to wait for the kids while Galleytrot padded his soft way into the room, giant head on the edge, eyes locked on our children.

"Mom!" Ethie leaned in and kissed my cheek with a very loud suction sound before repeating her smooch on her father. Gabriel hugged me, leaning his head on my shoulder. "You're home!"

I stroked her dark hair back from her blue eyes and smiled. She looked just like a Hayle, but she had her father's jaw, the shape of his nose. And she tanned way more easily than I ever did. I felt Quaid in her as much as me, despite her outward appearance, and the feeling of her demon deep inside.

Gabriel, on the other hand, was a breath of spring air, sweet face beloved to me and more painful to look on the older he grew. I could see Liam in him, his dead father long gone. Ethie might look like a Hayle, but thanks to the power of the Sidhe and the Gate that controlled the O'Dane family for centuries, my son was literally the exact image of his lost parent.

"I'm so glad," Ethie said with a little huff of air. She reminded me a lot of her namesake, my grandmother. Though much more boisterous and overwhelming. I could only imagine Ethie would make an excellent coven leader one day, if only we could teach her some restraint. "We had a question to ask you." She said it like knowing the answer would solve world hunger.

"Ask away." I grinned at Quaid as Ethie prodded her brother. But Gabriel looked down, shy suddenly, and his sister, as usual, just took over. I held in my need to giggle at her seriousness as Ethie leaned toward me, beautiful little face inches from mine.

"We think it's about time," she said in her piping voice, power rippling around her, "you told us who Gabriel's real father is."

FOUR

I choked on my coffee, staring at her, all amusement gone. Quaid recovered first, tipping Ethie's face up to his.

"Pop-tart," he said. "What are you talking about?"

She rolled her eyes at him while Gabriel looked up, hopeful and quiet. "Dad," she drew out the name, already a mistress of sarcasm at six years old. "Have you looked at him lately?" She jabbed a finger at her brother who smiled just a little, cheeks rosy. "And seriously." She crossed her arms over her chest, tapping her fingers on her arm. "His power is totally different than ours." Ethie looked back and forth between Quaid and me. "There's only one logical explanation." My daughter really was too smart for her own damned good. If she was this intelligent at six, the whole Universe had better watch out. "So, out with it." She tossed her dark curls, sniffing.

"Gabriel deserves to know."

I met Sassafras's eyes and he offered a cat shrug, but no "I told you so". It wasn't that we were purposely keeping the truth from the kids. I just wanted them to be old enough to understand before we told them. I shook my head at Quaid and sighed.

I totally underestimated them, I sent.

We both did, he sent with a warm hug of power that extended around our little family. "Kids," Quaid said, setting his coffee on the opposite end table. "It's true. I'm not Gabriel's biological father."

Gabriel nodded, playing with the hem of the sheets. "I knew a long time ago, Dad."

Ethie made a face. "Did *not*."

Her brother didn't respond. He didn't have to. She pouted and sank against Quaid as I ran my fingers through my son's hair and ignored the fact his sister wanted to be the star of this show.

"We did plan to tell you," I said. "But it's a hard story, baby. Are you sure you want to hear it now?"

He nodded, sparks of green lighting in his hazel eyes. For the second time in a very short period, my throat tightened. I covered my surge of grief by kissing his forehead.

I skimmed most of the details. The bigger story could wait for later. But Gabriel and Ethie both listened, wide-eyed as I told them about the past and who Liam was.

We were all crying by the time I finished, explaining that Fate needed Liam to sacrifice himself so the Universe could continue. I wiped tears from my cheeks with the corner of the sheets, rocking Gabriel against me. "He loved me so much," I said. "And you, my beautiful boy, are just like him. Kind and sweet and with a solid oak tree at your center. The only thing that kept me from falling apart completely when your father died, was knowing I had you."

Gabriel snuffled a bit then sighed. "Thanks for telling me, Mom," he said. "You're right. I needed to wait to hear it. Until I was ready."

Quaid's big hand slipped over Gabriel's fair hair. "You have to know," he said, voice heavy with grief, "how much I love you, Gabe." My son—our son—turned his head and looked up at Quaid. "I know Liam was your real father, but I'm your dad."

Gabriel hugged Quaid, Ethie snuggling between them.

"I know," our boy whispered. "You're the best dad ever."

"Mom." Ethie met my eyes, tears sparkling in her blues. "Is that why Gabriel can open gates?"

Second jaw drop moment, this one massive. "What?"

Gabriel leaned back and met my eyes, guilt flickering over his face. "You know, Mom," he said, steady and sure. "Gateways. To other places."

But… but, I…

Oh. My. Swearword.

I walled up that particular part of his power years ago. To protect him and the rest of us, after Ameline forced him to grow faster than he should, used him to open the way between our Universe and the dark one lying on the other side of the divide.

How did he manage to unblock himself?

Gabriel must have seen the confusion and worry on my face, because he shrugged apologetically. "I know you wanted me to keep that power locked up," he said. "When I first found the wall, I figured it protected me from something. But I had to know what it was." His face crumpled. "I'm sorry."

The last thing I wanted to do was cripple my son's abilities. Or make him feel like what he could do was wrong in any way. I'd seen the result of such control, when my friend Mia had her power walled off as a baby by her mother who was only trying to protect her. But, it made Mia weak, drove her mad in the end. I didn't want my son to go through what the former Dumont coven leader had.

But the plan was to wait until he was old enough to control it and then teach him. Not to have him experimenting on his own.

Syd, Sassafras's mind touched mine. *Gently*.

No kidding. I drew a breath and smiled at my worried

son.

"I shouldn't be surprised," I said. "My clever boy."

"I helped." Ethie clamped her lips together, eyes huge.

I laughed and kissed them both, making my daughter squeal. "Of course you did," I said. And sighed out my tension. What was done was done.

"Gabriel," I said, while Quaid ran his hands through his hair. "Can you show me, sweetie?"

His beaming smile wiped away all of his worry, turning him into a bouncing, excited ball shaking the bed. "Sure!" He turned without warning and gestured at the air beside him. Galleytrot let out a yelp and dodged out of the way as the space where he'd been divided and separated. But not like the rifts I made in the veil. It expanded upward, forming an arch, had edges, boundaries. Like a real gate. And, on the other side, a field of pale blue with a sky tinted softly green.

"Just found this one," Gabriel said with a grin. A small, furry creature resembling a rabbit, but with four front legs and six eyes, hopped over to the gate and sniffed the air. "Cool, right?"

The last thing we needed was one of those creatures on our side. Sure, it might be adorable from here, but I'd run into enough trouble with critters that seemed cute and fluffy at first glance to trust this would turn out well. "Gabriel," I said, voice shaking just slightly at how easy it was for him to do that. "Is this gate to a plane in our Universe?"

He frowned at me while the rabbit creature shrugged and hopped away. I caught the scent of salt and something crisp coming through the gateway as my son answered.

"Yes, Mom," he said. And shivered. "The other Universe feels bad, so I stay away from it."

Heart pounding, I did my best not to swallow audibly. Which meant he remembered about the other Universe. Had likely experimented with it to come to that conclusion. I waffled between feeling like I'd failed him as a mother and coven leader and pride he'd come to this amazing conclusion on his own.

"You can close it now, kiddo." Quaid's own smile was gentle, but I could feel his tension was probably about an equal to mine. Between the two of us we could have powered a city with the amount of vibratory energy we were containing.

Gabriel looked disappointed for a moment, and my heart ached for him. His sister was so often the center of attention—if only because she demanded the spotlight—I was sure he felt this was an amazing accomplishment for him. But we really needed to hash things out and doing so with an open gate hanging out in our bedroom wasn't the ideal situation. Sure, the rabbit thing may have been okay after all, but every world had predators. I'd rather not fight one off all over my fifteen hundred thread count Egyptian cotton sheets.

Our son finally nodded and gestured again. The gate closed as he slumped forward, dejected.

I had to do something. The poor sweets was crushed. "That was amazing," I said. Gabriel perked, smiled tentatively. "But I need you to promise me something."

His smile faltered and he sighed. "Don't do it anymore," he said.

"No, baby." I touched his cheek with my fingertips. "Now that I know you're experimenting, we can't close that door. You'll be making many, many more gates in the next little while." His face lit up again. "So many, you'll be sick of it by the time we're done."

His expression told me he thought I was looney. "Okay, Mom."

"But."

He hovered, intent and waiting for the "but" to be described.

"From now on," I said, "you can only do this with supervision." Ethie's mouth flew open and I glared at her, pointing an index finger. "You, little miss," I poked her belly, making her giggle, "do not count as a supervisor." I broke out into a sudden cold sweat thinking of the trouble these two could have gotten themselves into. But they were here and safe and as far as I knew nothing horrible had happened.

As far as I knew.

Dear elements.

Yet.

"Okay, Mom." Gabriel offered his hand and I shook it, Quaid repeating the gesture. "Deal."

Crisis averted. For now. I hoped.

All I could think of as our son lunged forward and hugged me was how Mom would laugh her head off when she found out. Not because of Gabriel's ability being free, no sirree. Because I'm sure she figured out long ago something I was only realizing.

I thought I only had one of me to raise. Turned out I had two.

FIVE

Sassafras leaped from the bed and waddled his way out the door, Ethie chattering at him with one hand wrapped around the end of his tail like a leash. Gabriel kissed us both and followed his sister, leaving Galleytrot behind to take up the rear.

The huge dog didn't move as the kids left, instead lifting his great head to me with a mournful expression.

"Syd," he said in his rumbling voice like a spring thunderstorm. "I'm sorry. I have no idea how they managed to sneak this around me."

"Not your fault," I said, slipping out of bed and heading for the bathroom and a badly needed shower. "Ethie is a mistress of deception." I really had to learn to watch that girl more closely. "And if she doesn't want you to know something, she'll find a way to hide it." It took me almost six months to find the baby squirrel she was nursing back to health, hidden carefully in her walk-in closet and masked with magic. She cried when I made her turn the tiny creature loose, but it still came to visit her more than a year later and I had a feeling she made sure her power would always protect it.

Determination and stubbornness wrapped in a heart of gold? I'd take it.

Galleytrot slumped from the room, head down and I knew no matter what I said he'd blame himself. We were a great bunch for guilt.

Quaid joined me in the big shower, though gritted his teeth and dodged the superheated water for a minute while I grinned at him and scrubbed, oblivious. Though, honestly, I missed the feeling of intense temperature, especially in the shower, a former hot water addict. By the time he was able to tolerate the warmth, I was done and out, snapping his bare butt with the end of my towel while he wiggled it at me.

So. Freaking. Tempting.

Instead of giving in, stomach rumbling and begging for breakfast, I brushed out my long, dark hair. No question I was a Hayle any more than Ethie. I was looking more and more like my mother every day, a faint line forming between my brows from frowning too much. I checked myself out, just in case. After all, if I had to live forever, I didn't want a body that looked the part.

While I ran one hand down the side of my face, I had a troubling thought, staring into my own blue eyes in the mirror. "Quaid."

"Yeah, babe." Soap lathered over his waist, trailing down his muscular legs on the other side of the steamy glass wall. But the worry in my heart just now didn't allow me to appreciate the view.

"You don't think Gabriel messing with his power has made things worse?" That would kill me, it really would. All this fighting Max and I were doing to eliminate the creatures of the Dark Universe. What if my son's antics, driven by the encouragement of his precocious sister, were allowing monsters to cross?

"I doubt it." His voice came muffled as he soaped his face. "You said there were no new rifts, not since Demonicon, right?"

"Not that we know of." But Max would have told me, wouldn't he? I bound my hair back into a damp ponytail, some of the tension easing as Quaid went on.

"Is Max concerned about new rifts?" He met my eyes through the glass, wiping at the condensation to see me better.

I shook my head. "No," I said, tightening my towel around me. "He seems to think we're just finding new batches of critters because they are scattered all over the Universe."

Quaid turned off the water and stepped out, taking

the towel I handed him and rubbing it firmly over his skin. "Then trust Max," he said.

I know. "But, what if—"

Quaid leaned in and kissed me, soft and lingering. He smelled delicious, like soap and chocolate and spices. "If," he said. "We deal with it. Like we always do."

He was absolutely right. I hugged him, fierce and full of love. "Okay."

"Besides," Quaid said. "Maybe it's time to find out what Gabriel's power can do. He's seven, now."

"But." I bit my lip, pressing my forehead to his smooth chest. "He's so young and innocent, Quaid."

My husband laughed softly, a deep, warm sound. "He is," he said. "He's his father's son." I looked up, saw the sadness in Quaid's face, but he waved it off. "I knew this day was coming. And I'm glad he knows, now. But Gabriel isn't just Liam, Syd. He has your strength, something Liam never had."

I wanted to protest. Liam was an oak tree, his power running deep. But I couldn't bring myself to speak. Not only because the love of my life was looking down at me, but because I knew he was right. And I was grateful for it.

Smells of breakfast lured us both downstairs. Quaid held my hand, our arms swinging between us like we were a couple of kids and when he turned his face to me just a little, I spotted the tiny smile on his lips. And caught my breath. Everything about him made me happy, filled me with joy and excitement, even after seven years. I stopped him at the bottom of the stairs and wound my arms around his neck.

My nose touched his. "I love you," I whispered over his mouth. "So much."

His lips brushed mine, a tiny spark of power jumping between us. His magic was strong, almost hot, and always made me tingle.

"Sydlynn Hayle," he whispered back. "I love you, too."

Smiling and fuzzy with all kinds of happy, I accepted his offer as he turned around and presented his back to me. Giggling, unable to contain it, I took the piggy back ride into the kitchen.

And blushed, slipping to the floor at the sight of our two visitors. Charlotte arched an eyebrow, though she was clearly amused. My former werewolf bodyguard looked away, but not before I caught the laughter in her blue eyes. Her husband, Sage, grinned openly, one hand in his jeans pocket, the other lifting to wave a welcome.

I went to them, kissed my martial arts teacher on the cheek before hugging Charlotte tight. Her werewolf magic embraced me fully as did her arms. It was only then I noticed my daughter clutching at Charlotte's leg, bouncing on her toes, Gabriel watching from a few feet away.

I released the blonde werewoman and stepped back

just in time to avoid being shoved aside by my daughter. It was clear she'd already been in Charlotte's arms, but my friend didn't hesitate to lift the girl up and carry her to the table, sitting with my daughter in her lap while Gabriel took Sage's hand and lead him to sit beside them.

"Mom," Ethie said with authority. "Auntie Charlotte and Uncle Sage came for breakfast."

Charlotte booped her nose. "And we're starving." Her last word ended in a growl as she dove forward and blew raspberries against Ethie's cheek. My daughter squealed her delight while Charlotte pulled away and met my eyes. "Have any delicious children I can eat?"

Ethie's shrieks of laughter filled the room as I turned to Shenka in time to take two plates full of pancakes. She winked and smiled at me, my sweet and caring second, and I felt a surge of gratitude she was here, taking care of all of us. I couldn't do her job.

I was just turning back with the hot pancakes steaming in my hands when the door opened and Ethie's cries changed. She leaped from Charlotte's lap, abandoning her like last week's news, with an ear splitting, "Nana!" before hurtling herself at my mother.

Mom smiled at me as she lifted my daughter into her arms, kissing the girl soundly. Ethie wriggled until Mom handed her over to Dad, grinning like a fool behind her. He bounced Ethie a few times, swinging her around and making her laugh until she was breathless. Mom came to me, a kiss for me as well, another for Quaid and finally for Shenka before she bent over Charlotte and Sage with more of the same. Gabriel shyly giggled as Mom stroked his hair and hugged him close.

I stood there in the middle of the kitchen, steaming pancakes and fresh-brewed coffee filling the room with their heavenly scents, light pouring in through the windows over the happy, chattering, loving people sharing hugs and kisses all around. In that moment, I was almost overcome with emotion, eyes burning with tears that I got to live like this, this life, with the most amazing family ever. My handsome parents doted on my kids, the retired Hayle coven and North American Witches Council Leader and former Ruler of Demonicon bought the house next door when our neighbors unexpectedly moved. Though Wilding Springs was so steeped in magic thanks to the Sidhe Gate that permeated the area with "it's all fine" power, normals still had trouble with us from time to time. And considering the light show and issues we had the night the Enforcers came for Charlotte and Sage when they were trying to prove his innocence, I wasn't surprised in the end the Harrisons finally moved.

In fact, most of the neighborhood was coven owned, now. When we first came here—could I have been sixteen, really?—the place was crowded with normals. But, over the years, we managed to buy up all the homes vacated by bewildered but clueless normals who knew something had to be wrong, but couldn't put their fingers on it.

It was so wonderful to have Mom and Dad next door, at least this time of year. The pair were still teaching at Harvard, Mom in magic theory, Dad in fire element. Summer was a blessing and the kids adored having them home full time.

Plates rattled as Shenka served more pancakes, driving me forward, out of my thoughts, to deliver mine to Mom and Dad. Within minutes we were all seated, sharing maple syrup and butter, the coffee flowing freely along with tall glasses of milk for the kids and a bowl for Sassafras, fresh ground beef for Galleytrot and hot toast to top off our pancakes.

As I sat there, I listened to them talk. The squeaking but demanding voice of my daughter, the way Charlotte handled her expertly. How my son's quiet words were a perfect counterpoint, the way Sass's purr as he licked up his bowl of milk added a soft echo under the conversation. The rumbling groan of the big hound as he settled, content, at the threshold to the kitchen door. I felt the warmth and love of my family hug me as surely as their arms.

Quaid was right. I was so used to conflict—still honed by my work with Max and the drach—the moment anyone suggested there might be a problem I freaked out. Sass's warning aside, Gabriel's experimentation, too, everything seemed quiet and peaceful. And moments like this I was happy for it, no matter it would drive me crazy with nothing to do.

It might be nice to let them know, my vampire sent.

Agreed, Shaylee sent, teary again. I really blamed her for my overly emotional state.

Gives us something to come home to, my demon sent.

Sure did.

"Thank you," I said before I knew I was going to say something out loud, despite my vampire's suggestion. Everyone fell quiet, watching me with smiles and gentle expressions. "I don't tell you enough how much I adore all of you. How much you mean to me." Damn these tears. I swiped at them and grinned. "This is how things are supposed to be, right? For a normal family?" The part of me that longed for normal was so far gone I barely remembered her. But Mom got the joke.

She laughed, raised her coffee mug, and everyone followed suit, including the kids. "To our family," she said in her rich voice, vibrating with her own emotions. "Not normal, but better for it."

I clinked mugs with everyone I could reach and whispered "Amen" in my head.

SIX

The kids ran out to play, Galleytrot plodding along behind them, but I noticed Sass remained behind, hunched over his place setting, eyes half lidded. I pushed back my plate, stomach groaning from eating far too many of Shenka's delicious pancakes and gulping way too many cups of coffee.

Dad's blue eyes meet mine, sparkling with good humor. I sometimes miss the glow of his amber gaze, the tint of red to his skin, his shining black horns, all given up for a human appearance since he abdicated the First Seat of Demonicon to spend the rest of his now mortal life with my mother. "The kids are getting so big." He said that every time he saw them and I grinned, but this time, there was an edge to mine.

"Are they ever." I sighed and shook my head before telling them all about Gabriel and Ethie's inquiry about his father. Mom's lips tightened, but she held her peace. She wanted Quaid and me to tell Gabriel long ago, but I wasn't interested in hearing her say it again.

Even her eyes widened when I shared Gabriel's experimentation with the gates.

"I thought you made sure he couldn't access that power," Mom said.

My teeth ground together, but I did my best not to react with anger. There were still some old buttons Mom and I were really good a pressing in each other and I was having too nice of a morning to let my temper ruin it.

Imagine that.

"So did I." I toyed with my fork as Mom sat back in her chair and smiled.

"It was bound to happen," she said. "The most important thing now is getting him instruction."

"Are you volunteering?" I wasn't an idiot. In fact, I was well aware of my failings. I'd make a terrible teacher, especially for my kids. I just didn't have the patience or the skill. All of the things I did, all of the lessons I learned, were done through trial by fire and I preferred my children not go through the same ordeals.

"Of course, sweetheart," she said. "I was going to suggest it when you thought the time was right." She turned to Dad and patted his hand. "In fact, we'd both like to share the job."

Relief washed over me. I had no idea I was this

worried about what I was going to do about training the two little munchkins. "You have to go back to Harvard," I said.

"I think they can do without us for a semester or two," Mom said so primly I wondered if she had this planned all along. Dad grinned at me over his coffee mug, pretty much answering my question. Maybe I should have been irritated my mother continued to meddle in my life, but I was too grateful for her offer. Besides, her meddling was often the only thing that actually went right.

When I shut up and let it.

"It's settled." Mom's smile told me she was delighted by my yes.

Quaid nodded and shrugged. "Better you than us, Miriam."

She winked at my husband, leaned forward to pat his hand. "Considering your children are very powerful magic users," she said, "and since I have experience teaching the single most stubborn witch ever born," her eyes flashed to me as I groaned and rolled my eyes, "I think we'll manage."

"Thanks, Mom," I said, laying on the sarcasm before sending her a magic hug. "Really, thanks. But I want to make sure their sorcery is woken at the same time."

Mom's head tilted to the side, the line between her brows reminding me of mine. "All right," she said. "But why?"

"No more holding back." I took Quaid's hand and he squeezed it.

"We agreed long ago," he said. "Full potential for our kids. We don't want them hobbled by outdated rules and old fears. Everything they have access to, we want them to know how to control."

Considering using sorcery meant understanding how to destroy rather than create, I needed the kids to grow up respecting all forms of power at their command and what consequences could come from misusing those powers.

"An excellent idea," Dad said. "Miriam, we could ask Ethpeal for help in that department."

I laughed out loud, shaking my head. "You both know how much I love my grandmother," I said. "But can you see her teaching Ethie?" Mom snickered and Dad grinned while Charlotte and Sage laughed openly. Even Shenka hid a giggle behind her hands, Sassafras snorting as he cleaned his paws. Gram was an amazing woman, a powerful witch and now an equally powerful sorcerer. But. There was a reason we named our daughter after her.

"Yes, I agree," Mom said. "Who did you have in mind?"

"Piers Southway." I'd thought about it long and hard. He was a good friend, a former member of the Steam Union, the branch of good sorcerers opposing the dark sect I'd fought. Though no real match for the

Brotherhood, the Steam Union weren't bloodsucking asshats who wanted to own the world. They understood the balance of power and sided with us on many occasions. Though I knew Piers parted ways with his old organization, partly due to a falling out with his mother, their leader, he was still my number one choice.

Charlotte shifts in her chair. "I haven't heard from him," she said, probably knowing I'm about to ask. "He's been spending all of his time in California lately. With the Oracle girl we met."

Right. And though I had no right to feel jealous, he and I were kind of an item once upon a time. Silly Syd. But thinking about Piers and the girl who could see the future reminded me about the past. And a pair of sorcerers I wished would just curl up and die already.

Supposedly, my old friend Rupe wasn't the bad guy he used to be. There was a time he and I were really close, when he called himself Blood and dressed like a Goth, boyfriend of poor, lost Mia. We reconnected briefly at Harvard my first year, but circumstances led him to uncover his sorcery and turn against me.

And into the arms of my enemy, Liander Belaisle. Just picturing his goateed face and pale yellow eyes gave me the shivers. While I'd beaten him long ago, stripped him of his magic and sent him scrambling—with help, mind you, and Fate on my side—I'd failed to kill his ass.

I really needed to get around to correcting that one of

these days.

"You two been to the coast lately?" Both Charlotte and Sage shook their heads. "I'm wondering if it might be time to do another search." They both knew for who, as though they'd followed my train of thought with mental wolf noses. Though, I supposed, it went without saying.

"Considering the fact Piers has been seeking Belaisle," Charlotte said in her calm and infuriatingly blasé manner, "I would think our bumbling around in his way would do little to assist. But I'm willing, if Sage is."

Her husband nodded quickly, but it was Shenka's turn to interrupt.

"Don't forget Tallah is out there," she said of her sister. The Hensley coven leader and I had our issues in the past, mostly over my supposed poaching of Shenka for my second. "There's no way Belaisle will be able to poke his nose out and not get noticed."

I disagreed, but didn't argue the point. Belaisle was notorious for his sneaky, subtle maneuvers. I wouldn't put it past him to be working on something right now that could blow up in our faces.

Syd. Mom's voice broke through my dark thoughts. *You're worrying again.*

We'd had this talk years ago, shortly after my wedding to Quaid. About me trusting the people around me, about not taking everything on myself. And I'd done well, if only because of Max and the distractions he offered.

I shrugged off her soft criticism and let it go. Time to stop letting the memory of Belaisle ruin my perfect morning.

I left the family chatting over more coffee and retreated upstairs. The loss of sleep last night was hitting me at last, no matter how much caffeine I put in my body. Quaid let me go with a gentle mental hug and I was soon curled up under the covers—fresh sheets magically applied—and closed my eyes.

I expected to sleep for a few hours, but when I finally roused the room was darkening and the clock read after seven. As I tried to turn over, I realized I was pinned by a pair of little bodies, Ethie tucked up against my front and Gabriel snoring softly behind me. Sassafras perched on my hip, eyes closed, tail tucked over his nose and a peek over the edge of the bed revealed Galleytrot stretched out next to us.

I held still, the sweet scent of my little girl in my nostrils as I tipped my face down and kissed the top of her head. Ethie murmured something in her sleep, little hands clenching a moment before she spun slightly sideways, one foot kicking me.

My jaw ached as I yawned and let out a deep exhale. I'd been burning the candle at both ends, as the saying went. Trying to help Max and be here for my family at the same time. I suppose I shouldn't have been surprised I slept the day away. As much as I admitted to myself I really did love working with the drach, using my power to its capacity, moments like this were just as precious. Just lying there, listening to the sound of my kids breathing, the soft pops and crackles of the house settling, made me wonder which I preferred.

Gabriel stirred behind me and I turned half way over, careful not to wake his sister or drop the sighing cat on his head. My son blinked sleepily at me, chin on my shoulder, his fair hair mussed around his sweet face.

"Mom," he said. "I know who my father was, now. I've met his father, haven't I?"

I wanted to choke on the answer, but nodded. "Not quite," I said. "You're talking about Fergus, aren't you?"

Gabriel's eyes sparked with green. "He's so nice," he said. "He's always happy to see me."

"Fergus was Liam's grandfather." I sighed softly, with regret. "He has to stay in the Sidhe realm, now, and can't come here." Or risk dying. Only shifting into the Sidhe realm saved him from perishing from a bullet wound. That was so long ago, and yet I remembered it like it just happened. "Your father was amazing, you know that?" I was suddenly crying, but I didn't care. He needed to know. "He was sweet and kind, like you. Had a huge heart, Gabriel. He would have loved you so much."

He nodded against my shoulder and I felt Ethie shifting next to me, her breathing leveling off, a sign she was awake.

"Mom," she whispered. "Why did you marry him and not Dad?"

Oh dear. Such a long and sad story, full of pain and death and longing. I looked up at the ceiling, knowing Sass was also listening, Galleytrot, too.

"Sometimes," I said at last, when I was able to speak again past my tight throat, "we are forced to make choices that we wish we could change. But, Liam wasn't one of them." He truly wasn't. When I was forced to choose, to marry according to coven law, though I loved Quaid and knew we were meant for each other, he wasn't willing or able. And though it hurt me to make Liam second choice, he never cared. He loved me anyway and I loved him.

"If he hadn't died," Ethie whispered, "you wouldn't have had me."

I hugged her gently. "I know," I said. "And this conversation, I think, should wait for another day."

Ethie sighed. "Until we're older."

She made me laugh. "Yes, silly," I said, kissing the top of her head. "Until we're all older."

I scooted the kids out, sending Sassafras and Galleytrot with them. But as the door closed behind them, I had a thought. And acted on impulse.

The veil parted before me, the shining green and blue of the Sidhe realm appearing on the other side of the rift. I realized then my ability to travel from plane to plane was the partial source of my son's ability, tied to Liam's Sidhe-souled control of the Gate he'd guarded. But where I was able to pass between planes using tears in the membrane and take people with me, my son's power created gateways, passages anyone could use.

The idea was mind-boggling, made me shudder. Most planes were protected from the incursion of other races thanks to the veil. Only those such as the drach and the maji had the ability to pass over, or those, like Charlotte, who have blood ties to other races. Her ability to travel to Demonicon in another form told me long ago the werewolves had demon heritage. But planes like Demonicon were protected from human interference—and vice versa—because of the veil's restrictive magic. Safeguards, I realized when my son's power came into being, that fell away when he built gates. That terrible night when he breached the way between Universes, when Ameline almost allowed Creator's Dark Brother to pass through, it took me a while to work the truth out in my mind. I'd been a little busy at the time. But when I discovered my son in his crib, happily pitching toys through portals he'd made, I understood at last the true implications of what he was able to do. Felt the shift in the magic of the veil and realized then and there if I didn't do something to shield his power, whole armies of who-knew-what could come waltzing through his bedroom door and invade Wilding Springs.

Though the last thing I wanted for Gabriel was to make him fear his power, we would have to work carefully to ensure he understood just how dangerous his ability really was. Still on that train of thought, I reached out for the familiar power of the one I sought. And the moment I called for him, the view shifted away and to the one I knew so well.

Everything I'd been thinking fell away the instant our eyes met.

"Syd," Fergus said in Liam's voice, with Liam's face and Liam's hand raised in hello.

My own hand rose even as I burst into tears.

SEVEN

Fergus didn't comment, his gentle smile watching me silently as I wept myself out of tears to shed. I sank to the edge of the bed, sniffling into my hands, before finally looking up and into his lovely face.

"Sorry," I whispered. Croaked, actually. I really had to do something about my overly emotional reactions to him. He must have been growing tired of me crying every time I saw him. But today was especially hard, considering the conversations I just had with my kids.

"Don't ever apologize to me, Syd," Fergus said, wiping at his own cheeks. "I of all people understand the necessity of fate—and the depth of your loss."

I shuddered in a breath and found I could smile at him. "Just checking in," I said. "To see how things are." A lie, but he let me succeed in my deception, shrugging Liam's—his—shoulders, running one hand through

Liam's—his, Syd, *his*—fair hair.

"All's well," Fergus said, sinking down to the grass with his legs crossed, toying with some blades as he talked. "It's been quiet for a long time, now. Even Queen Aoilainn has adjusted finally to sharing her realm and power with the Unseelie monarchs." One of the many barriers I destroyed over the years, bringing the Seelie and Unseelie courts together, no more segregation. "King Odhran and Queen Niamh have been more than gracious about the whole thing."

Good to hear. "So, nothing feels odd?" I was fishing, naturally. Any second now he'd tell me no, things were great and I should mind my own business.

But Fergus's brow furrowed, his frown Liam's frown, the same one my first husband would get when he studied a particularly difficult problem. "Not really," he said. "Anything specific I should watch for?"

I shook my head and forced a laugh. "Nothing," I said. "Just an overactive imagination." And a demon cat. And a former Enforcer husband…

I said goodbye to Fergus and closed the rift, biting at my thumbnail, knowing Quaid would hate it if he saw me. And rose from the bed, going to the bathroom to splash water on my face so no one would know I was crying. Yeah, good luck there, Hayle. I'd always been an ugly crier, my neck and face blotchy red in patches, eyes bloodshot.

Classy.

There was nothing I could do about it, not even magic helping reduce the redness. I shrugged and turned off the light, heading downstairs, hungry again. Something smelled delicious in the kitchen, but from the sounds of laughter in the back yard, dinner was happening outside tonight.

I wasn't quite ready to join them and snuck down to the basement. Now that I'd talked to Fergus, I felt a little better about Sass's worries, but there were a few more people I could check in with to reassure myself.

The moment I touched down in the cool quiet of the basement, I reached for Europe and the queen of the Wilhelm vampires. Sunny's mind connected with mine instantly and her power, cool and white, embraced me as always.

Syd. She sounded happy to hear from me, if a little distracted. *It's been weeks.*

I know, I'm sorry. I sat on the bottom step and stared out into the empty air over the pentagram etched in the concrete floor.

Not an admonishment, my darling, she sent. I felt her focus shift from whatever she was doing all the way to me. I caught a moment of her speaking with someone, a vampire who looked worried, before the image cut off. *It's as much my fault as yours it's been so long.*

Trouble? I sat up straighter, hands clenching in my lap.

She sighed in my head and another image formed, of her striding through the hall of Wilhelm castle, heading for the throne room. *You could stay that*, she sent. *Nothing to worry yourself with. Besides, I'm happy to talk to you and forget the weight of the crown for now.*

Tell me about it. I hugged her with power. *Just wanted to ask you a question.*

Anything, darling. I saw her motion, the tall, handsome man in her view smiling and coming to her side. I knew him as well as I knew myself, or at least, I used to. My Uncle Frank, once powerless and now a vampire, Prince Consort and co-ruler with Sunny, joined the conversation.

Syd. Uncle Frank's magic embraced me. *What's up, kiddo?*

I hesitated. They both felt tense, like they were dealing with something and didn't need more pressure on their shoulders. But I really needed to ask. *Sass has a worry*, I sent. *And I'm just checking around.*

If Sassafras is concerned, Sunny sent, *then we are concerned.*

Exactly, right? "Have either of you noticed anything odd? About how you're feeling?" I didn't want to lead them, but it was hard to phrase the question without coming right out and saying it.

Aside from frustration… Sunny trailed off. And paused. *As a matter of fact*, she sent, *I've been feeling rather lethargic, lately.*

Me, too, Uncle Frank sent. I caught a glimpse of him

putting his arms around her before the scene went dark. *Almost dull.*

Craptastic. And not the response I was hoping for. *Make that me three,* I sent.

How odd. Sunny's mental voice climbed a few notes. I could feel her power sweeping outward, but knew she'd find nothing.

No idea what's causing it, I sent. *So far you two feel it, but the Sidhe realm doesn't.*

You think it's something affecting our plane? Uncle Frank's power thrummed with worry.

I have no idea. I threw up my hands in the dark quiet of the basement as though they could see me. *I've dug around and found nothing. So has Sass and Shenka.*

Curious. Sunny's power stilled. *We will, of course, keep a close eye on this odd feeling. But you will alert us if anything changes?*

You guys as well, please. I hugged them both magically, loving the vampire sandwich of their power embracing me. *Miss you. See you soon?*

They let me go with murmured promises and I didn't push them. Whatever was up, Sunny would let me know the moment I needed to. If I needed to. Sometimes it was hard to remember others had their own crap to deal with that had nothing to do with me.

My next contact vibrated with power my demon recognized and answered. I received a clear vision of

King Danilo Moreau of the werenation as he sat on his throne, hearing complaints during court. I almost retreated, but Danilo caught my mind and pulled me back.

Please, he sent. *Save me from tedium.* His mind laughed. *How are you, Syd? Taking care of my kid sister?*

I ask him the same question I asked of Sunny, and Danilo seemed puzzled.

Hell, yes, he sent. *I've been bored out of my mind, but can't seem to get out of my own way. That what you mean?*

I loved the blunt openness of the new wereking. *Exactly*, I sent.

After a quick promise to each other to keep posted, I let Danilo go.

How very odd, my vampire sent. *Perhaps we should talk to Meira and see if she is affected.*

Excellent idea, my demon sent.

I was getting to that. It was hard not to grumble at them. *But Femke first.*

The leader of the European Witches Council grasped my mind with hers, hugging me close.

Syd, she sent, her particular power crisp and light, thrumming with strength. I loved Femke and was always grateful for her support and kindness when I needed someone of authority. And to be my friend.

Another repeated conversation, and a hushed sigh from Femke.

I thought it was just me. The image of her sitting back at her desk at Oxford came through sharp and clear. *Anything we should worry about, you think?*

I have no idea. I laughed. *Considering I've been known to chase shadows...*

Shadows that have turned into monsters, she sent. I felt her sit forward, more alert. *I'll poke around and see what's what.* She paused. *You know, could it just be too many years of soft living?* She drummed the top of her desk with her fingertips. *Mountains of paperwork and minor complaints are eating me alive. At times I envy you your battles with Max and the drach.* She laughed in my head. *Am I losing my edge, do you think?* There was amusement in her voice.

Could be, I sent. *And if that's all it is... Femke, I'll take it.*

Hallelujah to that, sister. Her power hugged me and she was gone.

Now can we contact Meira? My demon sounded miffed.

Fine. I grinned into the gloom, loving to tease her. And reached out to the veil, in preparation to talk to my sister.

Only to have a very different mind contact me first.

EIGHT

Sebastian. I welcomed his mind's touch with a little smile.

Sydlynn. How I loved the velvety way the vampire king's power felt against mine even as I blushed and reminded myself as I always had to when I was around him that I was happily married to the man of my dreams. And yet, there was something alluring and delicious about the DeWinter blood clan leader that heated my insides with carnal thoughts.

Didn't help we'd shared a kiss or two once upon a time. Or that I'd once considered him a candidate for my husband.

I shook off the old lust as I realized he felt far closer than he would if he were in Europe. *Where are you?*

Doing a little digging. He showed me the view from his eyes, a circular stone chamber covered in carvings. I knew the place, had almost lost my life—and my son—there. The maji chamber under the vampire mansion on the outskirts of Wilding Springs.

His power hummed affirmative. *Alison and I are testing a theory*, he sent with his usual air of mystery. I was happy to know he and my old best friend were still hanging out together, though I'd never had the courage to ask them what their arrangement entailed. The fact Alison was now a ghost with the power of a vampire, thanks to a car accident and some magical intervention, couldn't make their relationship any easier. But she'd been altered by my power as much as Sebastian had. Not only could he now walk in sunlight without being burned and had a heartbeat, she could take and maintain tangible form. And the clearing of the near-insanity which controlled her echo—the part of her that stayed behind after her soul fled at her death—made her almost seem like the old Alison again, only better.

Way better.

Maybe you'd like to fill me in? I ran my hand over the end of my ponytail, thinking I must look a fright before making him an offer. *Dinner's happening now if you want to join us.*

We would be delighted, he sent. Alison's familiar feeling passed through Sebastian's magic, also in agreement. *We shall see you presently.*

I let him go and sighed softly into the quiet air of the

basement. I would not run upstairs and brush out my hair or put on more mascara or change my clothes. So silly. Besides, I was thrilled for Alison. She earned happiness, if that was what she found, and all my old feelings for Sebastian were moot at this point, anyway.

Damned hormones.

Instead of dwelling on the imminent arrival of the vampire and his companion, I instead batted at the twitching magic of my demon as she harrumphed in my head. Grinning now, I reached into the veil and tore it open, my focus on my sister.

The gap opened easily, the soft breath of my demon grandmother washing over me as she said hello. Ahbi Sanghamitra had been part of the Demoniconian Node before, the teardrop shaped power cell holding all the planes of the demon realm together, but this time was different. When she'd died in my arms and her power inside me, she felt angry, overpowering and we waged an almost constant struggle. Her joining with the Node and leaving me only meant big problems for Meira when Dad abdicated and my sister took the First Seat. But with the fall of Demonicon and the building of the new Node— partially in thanks to Ahbi— my grandmother had mellowed quite a bit, as though all ego was lost to the making of the power cell. No matter the truth, I was just grateful she survived.

Meira and I might have been Hayles, but we had the

added strength of our demon grandmother in us for good measure.

I smiled at my sister where she sat on a divan under a giant window. The view outside of Ostrogotho, the capital city, made me nostalgic. I really had to visit again soon. Meira's own grin was fast and bright, white teeth flashing against her dark red lips, glowing amber eyes sparkling beneath thick black lashes. Her curving horns caught the light as she ducked her head, long, black curls falling loose over one shoulder, brushing the cheek of the beaming demon girl in her arms.

"Auntie Syd!" Zuzameirhaylynn squealed my name. Though only two years old, she—like most demon children—was growing at a rapid rate, with the size and intelligence of a six year old.

I waved and blew her a kiss. "Hey, Zuze. Cuteness, you got bigger since the last time I saw you."

Her tiny nose scrunched, red tinted skin pinking on the tops of her round cheeks. "Of course," she said in a tone that reminded me so much of my daughter I laughed out loud.

Meira rolled her eyes at me. "Don't say it."

We shared a knowing smile.

"Ahbi said I could come visit." Zuza bounced on her mother's lap, clapping her hands together. "Can I come now?"

"Not tonight, cuteness," I said. "But soon. I know

Ethie and Gabriel would love that."

She pouted, leaning her little head back on her mother's shoulder, but the temper tantrum I expected—thanks to my hotwired daughter's behavior—didn't come. "Okay," she said. "Soon, though, right?"

Someone stepped into the opening, sitting next to Meira a moment. Rameranselot waved at me, hands reaching for their daughter before I could respond.

"Nice to see you, Ram." Another old suitor, though one I knew would never work out. He made my sister happy, at least. I had a feeling all along he never felt for me nearly what he did for her.

"Syd." He pressed a kiss to his wife's cheek, then his daughter's. "I'll make sure Miss Busy Pants doesn't interrupt you further." I was almost sad when he swept upward, Zuza laughing in his arms, and left the gap, out of sight.

Meira's distant smile told me she watched them leave the room before focusing on me again. "Social call or end of the world, oh my swearword, we're about to die?"

I laughed, shook my head. "Ha freaking ha."

She grinned, winked, shrugged. Meira had become an amazing demon woman, the little girl I remembered from childhood long grown up, though she retained her sense of humor, at least. "So, which?"

"Not sure," I said. And asked her what it felt like I'd been asking a gazillion people all day. "Have you been feeling dull, out of it, bored lately?" And went on to explain Sassafras's worries.

Meira frowned slightly, but shook her head in return. "Nothing like that here," she said. "Want me to pop over and see if I can help?"

"It's fine." I stood up, stuck my hands in my jeans pockets. "Thanks anyway. I'm sure it's nothing."

Meira hesitated. "Just let me know, and I'm there."

"Why?" I raised one eyebrow, smirking. "Bored or something?"

She tsked at me before laughing. "Damn it," she said. "I wish something would happen." And gasped in a breath, both hands over her mouth, eyes sparkling.

It was a joke, we both knew it. But even while I grinned I tensed. Waited. Worried.

But the world didn't implode or fall apart and time kept ticking.

Meira's hands dropped and she winced. "Yeah, sorry," she said. "I'm happy with boring."

I let my sister go, turning slowly on the ball of one foot, staring at the floor as I worked it over in my mind. I hesitated on the last call I had to make, only because Erica Plower and I weren't really on good terms anymore. Not that she was my enemy or anything. Mom's former second in this very coven had taken her place as leader of the North American Witches Council. Since then, she and I had butted heads countless times over issues of law. In fact, I hadn't talked to her much in the last two years outside of official events, not since I defended Charlotte against Erica's orders to deport her and Sage back to Europe.

But, if anyone would have a bigger picture view of what was happening, it would be Erica. I might not have agreed with her way of doing business, always thought she was the worst choice possible for leader, but she was efficient, I'd give her that. And while I knew the Council only chose her because with Mom's retirement they insisted on another Hayle at the helm, it had to eat at Erica she was second best. Again.

Not my problem. I gathered my thoughts to reach out to her the same moment I felt two people cross the family wards and sighed in relief. I'd contact Erica later. I had paranormal guests to welcome.

Saved by the vampire.

NINE

I sat back and bumped shoulders with Sebastian as the long evening wound down into late night. Alison leaned in, chatting with Mom about something that made them both giggle while my husband and father played a magic game of chess, pieces floating in the air between them. Shenka, busy as usual, cleared the table though I waved her down into her seat.

"Well?" I prodded the handsome vampire with one elbow. "What were you two up to?"

He shrugged in his casual, sexy way, big shoulders pulling at the fabric of his expensive dress shirt, suit coat draped over the back of his chair. The sleeves were rolled up, the thick muscles of his forearms jumping as he leaned forward and retrieved his wineglass. The white lights strung around the table reflected in his eyes, deep, dark wells unfathomable, black hair falling over his forehead in a sultry wave.

Dear elements, he was scrumptious.

Down, girl.

"As you know," he said in his velvet voice, one big hand settling over mine in casual camaraderie that made parts of me twitch in old longing, "I've been doing everything I can to understand this change which has come over me since you brought me back from the brink."

Twice. But the first time didn't count, I guess. It was the most current that had the biggest impact. I tried to forget the wasted, dusty shell I'd found, sealed by the Brotherhood, leaving Sebastian to be drained and left for dead. My maji power was a little too enthusiastic that night, and whatever it was I did to him when I pulled him back from death gave him powers unlike any other vampire, as well as life he'd lost centuries ago when he was brought over into the undead. Since then, he'd been experimenting, not only with his own clan, but with Sunny's as well, with her blessing.

"You've been hitting a wall," I said. Sunny kindly kept me updated on each failure, though she never seemed angry or upset. Still, I was sure Sebastian blamed himself for his lack of progress.

But, from the tightness of his grin and the happiness exuding from him, I knew he had to have made a breakthrough.

"So far," he said. "But we may have stumbled on something that could make all the difference." He turned his head to look at Alison and, for the first time, I realized just how much he cared for her. No, Syd. Loved her. Admit it. The adoration flashing over his face made me sigh and swoon.

Just a little. I was allowed.

"With Alison's help," he said, oblivious to my reaction, "I may have uncovered a different means of helping all vampires evolve to their full potential."

A blessing, my vampire sent. *My people have been too long in the darkness.*

She'd spent about a thousand years trapped in a crazy magician herself, so she knew exactly what she was talking about.

"Keep me posted," I said. And winced. "By the way…"

I was really tired of talking about this. But the way Sassafras watched me from his perch on the end of the table made me speak up yet again. He had to be worried, and I wouldn't let him down or leave any stone uncracked if it meant keeping the family safe.

Sebastian paused a long moment before setting down his wine glass and gently touching Alison's shoulder. She turned toward him with a glowing smile, that same look on her face he had when he looked at her, though hers faded as she blushed a bit.

And I realized then and there neither of them had told each other how they felt. A sudden surge of irritation made me want to knock their heads together.

Leave it alone. Mom's voice cut through my frustration.

But! I glared at her. *You knew?*

It's theirs to work out, she sent, blue eyes glittering with intensity. *Do not interfere, Sydlynn Thaddea Hayle. Ever.*

I wrinkled my nose at her and crossed my arms over my chest. But I did as she asked.

Meanwhile, Sebastian and Alison shared a whispered conversation. The both turned to me the exact moment my mother's mind released mine.

"We have noticed something odd," Alison said, leaning partially around Sebastian, blonde hair brushing over his bare arm. I bit my tongue to keep from saying anything about how he looked at her, or how he seemed to inhale her scent as though in secret. "Like my curiosity was taken away or something."

Sassafras grunted. "Precisely," he said.

Mom and Dad nodded, Quaid, too. Shenka, just taking her seat again, stroked the silver Persian's fur gently, eyes worried.

"I take it this is a widespread phenomenon?" Sebastian's frown tightened soft lines around his eyes.

"But only here," I said. "I talked to Fergus and Meira and neither of them noticed anything."

"It's odd, definitely," Mom said. "But none of us have

been able to find a reason for it."

Sebastian nodded slowly. "Perhaps a concerted effort," he said. "As a group?"

Excellent idea, my vampire sent. *I expected nothing less.*

He's so smart, Shaylee sent with a girlie exhale of adoration.

Finally, someone's making sense, my demon sent.

Sigh.

Just how much of my old attachment to Sebastian was their fault?

I reached for his power before they could say anything further, the smooth, almost buttery feel of him delightful. And I knew why. He shared my magic now, it was part of him and integrating was simple because of it. Alison was the same, though colder, more distant. She might have physical form now and be something entirely new, but she was still, at heart, an echo.

Mom and Dad felt familiar, heat and bright blue warmth, followed by Shenka and the power of the family. Sassafras's magic bubbled beneath us all, touched by the power of a century and a half of Hayle witches and ancient demon magic.

Together, we reached, examined, explored everything we could. Spreading like a blanket over Wilding Springs and outward, to the border of our territory. I felt brief resistance when we came in contact with the Council magic marking the edges of our home, but it faded away quickly.

At last, we retreated as one, separating ourselves when our power returned to pool around us. I rubbed at my temples, a faint headache burning behind my eyes while the others shook off the connection.

"Sassafras," Sebastian addressed the demon cat directly, "I'm afraid there's nothing to find. But, if there is more to this than we have been able to uncover, I'm certain you'll be the first to know about it. I would appreciate contact if something were to come of this."

Sass bowed his head to the vampire king, though I could tell from his frustration he felt embarrassed by the lack of discovery.

The vampire and his companion left shortly after, with hugs and kisses all around. I embraced Alison tightly, missing her more than I ever had and, when she pulled away, there were tears in her blue eyes.

"Let's do a girl day," she whispered. "Just you and me. Soon."

I nodded, grinned. "That would be awesome."

I said goodbye, stayed in the back yard while Mom and Dad waved goodnight and drifted through the hedge and to their own home. Quaid kissed me, went inside, probably to check the kids, while I sat and stared at the twinkling white lights.

"Syd, I'm sorry." Sassafras's tail thrashed as he fretted. He hadn't moved from his spot, ears flat to the sides, whiskers curved under, head down. "I worried everyone for nothing."

It wasn't much of a reach to gather him into my arms and pull him close. Sass shivered in my embrace, his anxiety palpable.

"You never have to say you're sorry," I said. "You know the safety of this family comes first. And you of all people I trust. Even if it turned out to be nothing."

He nodded. "Still. I feel like an idiot."

His fur was soft under my lips as I pressed them to his forehead. "A million times better safe than running and screaming and panicking," I said.

He hopped down, waddling into the house with his tail down. Considering he raised me, added his power to mine when I was still inside my mom, it was no wonder I was so much like him. I wouldn't have let someone else's assurances make me feel better, either.

Poor cat.

I sighed, pushed back from the table, unplugging the lights. Looked up at the stars and the rising moon. Drew a deep, cleansing breath and let go of my stress.

And went to bed.

I woke in darkness, feeling something tweaking under my skin. Nothing like an attack or anything, but a sensation of unease. After a few minutes tossing a bit, trying to shake off the restlessness driving me from sleep,

I gave in and slipped out of bed. Quaid had no trouble staying in dreamland and I wasn't about to ruin his night.

As I thumped softly down the stairs, I kicked myself as I realized what the problem was. All that sleep earlier today must have thrown off my clock.

I didn't bother with lights, my demon's vision guiding me—along with long experience in this house—down to the main floor and around the corner to the hallway leading to the kitchen. I stood in the glow of the refrigerator, staring at the milk for about thirty seconds, feeling kind of dazed. Shaking it off only worked with a big gulp right from the carton. I grinned at it as I put it back, knowing Shenka would be pissed if she caught me.

The itchy, tingling feeling making me restless didn't fade. But when I reached out to the family, everything felt perfectly fine. The whole coven slept, for the most part, the odd couple up for personal reasons that made me blush as I skimmed over them, a couple of new moms dealing with hungry babies.

Nothing out of the ordinary. And yet, I couldn't shake the feeling something was off.

Paranoid. All the talk with Sassafras, asking the same questions over and over, obviously affected me. I finally forced myself to cross out of the quiet kitchen and back down the hall to the stairs.

I'd barely set one foot on the bottom step when something hit me in the gut, hard. I gasped for breath, clutching at the hand rail, before I realized it wasn't a physical blow.

Foreign power I'd never encountered before had just broken through the family wards.

A burst of fire blazed in the corner of my eye, jerking me around toward the back door. I barely remembered moving, feet flying over the hardwood, hands slamming against the glass and throwing it open, hurtling out into the dew-wet grass.

Fire climbed from a curled up ball of humanity, near the edge of the hedgerow leading to the park on the other side of our property. I staggered to a halt, power reflexively tightening around me, ready to attack, when the figure unbent, half sitting, half lying on the ground, her face turned up toward me.

"RUN!" Her scream pierced me to my soul, froze my magic in place before it could harm her. Flames burned her, devoured her, dark hair and eyes on fire, but she managed to stagger to her feet, eyes pure gold as she gestured toward me. "Sydlynn Hayle, if you love your family, run and don't look back!"

I stared at her, mouth gaping open, even as she rose in a gout of thermal pressure and light, into the dark night. Vast wings of flame spread out from her, sending gusts of superheated air toward me, heat even I could feel. With the anguished cry of an injured eagle, echoing so loudly my heart broke, the strange girl disappeared in a flash of brilliance and was gone.

There was no time to wonder, to go after her. Because the moment she was gone, I finally felt it. Past the tingling in my skin that woke me earlier, past the numb dullness Sassafras worried about. Between one heartbeat and the next, I understood everything in a rush of darkness that swarmed over Wilding Springs and tried to smother me.

The Brotherhood was coming for us. Were already here.

There was no thinking involved. Just action. I reached out to my family—to everyone in Wilding Springs I loved—and shifted them to the only safety my unconscious mind could come up with.

And in that precise moment, the souls of all of my loved ones in my hands, I blacked out.

TEN

My head pounded, voices whispering around me. Where was I? It felt dark, damp, smelled of mustiness and stale air. I struggled to wake, though part of me wanted to remain in the black and not emerge.

Why was I afraid?

When my eyes finally flickered open, I felt my demon groan, my vampire hiss her weariness. Shaylee remained asleep, and no amount of shaking would wake her. I left her to rest, eyelashes fluttering as I looked up.

And into Quaid's worried eyes.

He bent over me, pressing his lips against my forehead. I gasped a breath, tried to raise my hand, to touch his cheek, but it was as if someone drained all the strength from my body. My magic was there, but weary, so weary. Mom's face entered my range of vision, face pinched, but a tiny smile on her lips.

"Sweetheart," she said. And burst into tears.

They didn't last long, just a few soft sobs, a splash of moisture on my cheek. My lips opened and closed, but no sound came out. I coughed, trying to clear my throat, body aching so much I stopped immediately.

What the hell happened?

"Mom!" Ethie dove on top of me, little body trembling, but I didn't have the strength to hug her. Quaid lifted her free, leaving my mother to examine me. I managed to turn my head, to meet Gabriel's eyes where he stood next to Quaid, clinging to his father's free hand.

And over his shoulder, at the darkness, lit by a perma glow from above.

I knew this place. I'd been here a few disasters before. But, it wasn't empty like I was used to. This time it was stuffed full of people, staring at me, terrified but determined faces watching my every breath.

I turned my head slowly back, looked up at Mom. "What?" It was the best I could do.

"We're fine." Mom stroked my hair, a slow and steady motion that reminded me of when I was young, times she needed to reassure herself as much as me. "We're all here, and we're safe."

Something heavy and soft landed on my thighs. I look down to see Sassafras watching me. His eyes flared amber, ears flat back against his head.

"It was an attack," he said, and he didn't sound happy

about it. Attack. What attack? I was able to raise my arm at last, rubbing one hand over my face. I vaguely remembered a conversation we had, about feeling dull? And waking up, drinking milk. Fire—

It all came back in a rush, hitting me almost as hard as it had when it happened. I choked on the surge of fear that rose before forcing myself to draw a breath.

"Mom." I struggled to rise and she helped me, one hand on my back, the other holding my free arm. I realized then why my power felt so drained, why Shaylee was still asleep.

The cavern. Where we'd found Cesard the Firbolg magician, trapped here with the demon lord and vampire essence, both of whom possessed him. Though he was long dead and gone, the demon dealt with, the vampire integrated with me, this place remained a prison of sorts, the power of it absorbing magic, muffling elemental abilities completely.

My feet tingled as I touched down on the dirt, still bare as they were last night. Wait, was it last night? Before I could ask, still wobbly and weak, I felt the rumbling unhappiness of powerful green toned magic in the earth beneath me and had a moment of shock.

"We're all here?" I met Mom's eyes. "The Wild Hunt, too?" Gwynn ap Nudd and his Sidhe host once tried to destroy Wilding Springs and then the world. But Shaylee was his true love, reincarnated in me, and she convinced him to go back to sleep. Under the lawn in my back yard.

What were he and his host doing here?

"All of us." I looked around, spotted so many faces I knew and loved, Charlotte and Sage among them. Galleytrot lay in the dirt at Quaid's feet, panting softly, eyes flaring with red fire in time with the surging strife of the Wild. Mom's squeeze of my hand made me refocus on her. "You saved us all, Syd."

More tears, but these she was able to contain quickly.

"We don't know for certain what happened," Mom said. "Only that we all woke to a surge of your power and found ourselves here, and you unconscious."

I shook my head, hating the headache, but letting my vampire soothe it a little as I gathered my thoughts past the fear and nauseated stirring in my stomach. "There was a girl," I said. "A girl devoured by fire. She landed in the yard." I wasn't making much sense, but Charlotte came to me, crouching before me, hands holding mine.

"What did she look like?" Her intense blue eyes locked me in the moment.

"Dark hair, I think." She was on fire, for the element's sake. "Small." I shrugged.

"What did she say?" Charlotte wasn't dropping it.

"To run," I said, gasping out the word. "If I loved all of you, to run and not look back."

Charlotte half turned, looking up at Sage. "It must have been Zoe."

Who?

Sage nodded. "Zoe Helios," he said. "The Oracle girl from California."

I couldn't process that right now. "The Brotherhood attacked us."

Mom nodded. "As far as we can tell," she said. "In the day and a half since we've been here, we've managed to sneak a few people out to check into what's happening." She grimaced. "We don't know much."

"We know enough," Dad said, sitting beside her, one arm around her shoulders. I leaned back against the stone wall, the thin ledge along the edge once my bed, now keeping me from falling over by offering me a stable seat. "We know the whole family made it out and that the Brotherhood have no idea where we are."

That was a blessing. "I didn't know I could do that." I was shocked at my own ability. Even my vampire and demon seem in awe of what we'd done.

"Neither did we," Mom said with a wavering smile. "But we're very grateful you could."

Though I wouldn't want to have to do it again anytime soon. The very idea of using magic made me feel nauseated. "We're safe here, for now?"

Mom squeezed my hand. "As long as we stay out of sight and inside the cavern, that seems to be the case."

"I don't think they have any idea where to look," Quaid said. "Chances are, they assume we've gone to another plane or something. Since this cavern was only ever known to allies, the Brotherhood are in the dark. At least, for now."

It would do. But I hated the thought of the family trapped here, sitting ducks, power silenced by the magic of the cavern.

We had to get out of here.

"Did you manage to get word to Erica?" I breathed deeply, getting some of my energy back. But I knew I'd be feeling the effects of my massive power output for a while yet.

"Not yet," Mom said, her voice shaking slightly. "The few times we've tried, we felt power focus on us and had to run."

"We need to get outside of Wilding Springs," Dad said. "But even our attempts to cross the border physically are somehow tracked. Quaid and I made it as far as the edge of our territory and had to run when a small group of Brotherhood showed up."

"So we're trapped." Unacceptable.

"There's more," Mom said. She'd always been a rock to me, only stumbling a few times, and only when it wasn't her fault. She'd gone through having her power stripped, being put on trial and fought the control of the Brotherhood and made it out the other side stronger than ever. But I'd never seen her this afraid. "The power the Brotherhood is using to hold us in…"

"Mom." I pulled her toward me, out of Dad's embrace and into mine. "Tell me."

"It's the Council's power." Her words whispered into my ear, fanning my own fears. "Syd, they've somehow captured and are using our witch magic against us."

That could only mean one thing. "The Council is in trouble."

Mom nodded, wiping at tears like they were acid on her face. "I fear the worst," she said. "That our Council has fallen."

"Does that mean this is North America-wide?" I sat forward with a surge of energy fed by the anxious need to act.

"Maybe not," Dad said. "It's possible they are somehow using part of the Council power without anyone's knowledge. Think about it." His soothing voice made us all focus on him. "Sassafras's worries about being manipulated could extend further than we thought. We all searched for the reason for the dull feeling." I nodded, Mom too, while the demon cat just watched and twitched his tail. "We found nothing. If Belaisle and his sorcerers found a way to hide their activity from us, it's possible he's done the same to the Council."

"So, they could be okay," I said. "And oblivious." We could certainly use some Enforcer help right about now, though they would be little aid against the sorcerers. Unless Erica was taking a page from the European leader's book and started training her Enforcers in sorcery like Femke was.

"All I know is," Mom said, "that's the reason we couldn't find anything when we searched. The Brotherhood piggybacked their power on the Council's. And masked their movements until it was too late."

"Almost too late." Dad smiled sadly at me, leaning in to squeeze my knee. "Nice job, cupcake."

I ghosted him a smile. "How many times, Dad?" He winked. "Don't call me cupcake."

"Forever," he said.

"I'm afraid I have more bad news," Quaid said, shattering the brief moment of old humor. Wouldn't have taken much, but from the tightness of his lips and the way his brow pulled down over his chocolate eyes, I knew it had to be something big.

"Hit me," I sighed.

"I made it to an ATM," he said. "We needed money, supplies." He gestured behind him at the family, still dressed in their pajamas, some with blankets. A day and a half like this. I wished I'd risen sooner.

"And?" I held his gaze, ready for the worst.

"I have no idea how," he said, voice grim, "but the money's gone." He let that sink in. "We're broke."

ELEVEN

Okay, so not ready for the worst. "We're what?"

Quaid crouched, hugging Gabriel to him, still cradling Ethic in one arm. "All the accounts were cleaned out, babe." He looked about ready to cry himself, jaw jumping, voice thick. "The Hayle family fortune is gone."

I spluttered at him. "That's impossible," I said. Our money was old, really old, and vast. I'd lost track of how much we were worth, where it was all diversified and hidden.

"I hit an internet café," Quaid said. "I checked every single account I could think of. Stocks, investments, all of it." He swallowed hard. "Gone."

I didn't care about the money. But that meant I couldn't provide for my family.

"What have you been doing for supplies?" Desperation washed over me, crushed me like the

84

weariness never did. My world was spiraling downward and I felt like there was nothing I could do to stop it. This was worse than anything I'd been through before. Every other time I'd been in trouble, I'd kept the family out of it as best I could. But this…

This was intensely personal.

"You must have been hacked." Sage's soft voice broke through to me, but I just stared at him with nothing to say. "From what Charlie told me, the Brotherhood are known to use modern tactics to their advantage, right?" I nodded, and so did his wife, my mother, all of us. "Can you generate more money?" He waggled his fingers in the air with a grimace. "You know, with magic?"

Of course I could. "It will take time," I said at the exact moment Mom spoke the same words. "Time we don't have," I finished for us both and met Quaid's eyes. "I take it supplies—food and water and clothing—are the priority?"

His jaw jumped. "And blankets. Yes." He looked back over his shoulder. "A few of us have been raiding coven houses, but it's getting risky." I realized then I hadn't seen Shenka yet and tensed, though I was sure she was fine because Mom said everyone made it. I finally spotted her sitting with Esther and Estelle Lawrence, the old twins, helping them cover themselves with a quilt. "The Brotherhood sorcerers are everywhere, Syd." He sounded offended, as in, "How dare they be in our town?" Like he wanted to wage a one-man war on them, and I was with him all the way.

"No one's been caught yet," Mom said, "but it's only a matter of time if we keep going this way. Our safety up to now has been based on them not knowing where we are." She sagged a little. "We were waiting for you to wake so we could decide what to do."

"A few of the family have mentioned turning ourselves in," Dad said, so softly it was clear he didn't want anyone to hear. "But the majority are waiting for us to rally and kick some ass."

If only. I felt like a day-old kitten left out in the rain to die. But, I did have some hope to offer. "There's a cash stash in the house," I said. Waved off Quaid when he frowned at me. "In the basement. Set it up ages ago, back before you and I were married." I almost forgot about it. I put it down there, buried under a magicked chunk of concrete, right behind the mummified remains of Batsheva Moromond. Quaid's former adopted mother, witch-turned-vampire queen and all around evil bitch stayed down there after her defeat and draining, gathering mold and dust. And marking the spot where my secret cache of emergency funds were hidden.

"I'll get it." Quaid handed Ethie over to Mom, standing after a quick hug for Gabriel. But I shook my head and forced myself to stand. My muscles protested at first, but as I stretched out, the deep and persistent ache finally eased.

"Too big a risk for just money," I said. "At least until we know what's going on. We need solid information. The family is safe enough for now."

"I'm coming with you." Mom's mouth opened, a clear protest on her face, but I squashed it with a scowl. For the first time since I'd woken, anger—real and burning anger—jerked to life inside me, making Shaylee stir at last.

"You have no idea where I'm going," I said. "And I'm the only one who can use the veil in this family."

"Not true." Charlotte stood to face me, grim and threatening. "There's three of us, in case you've forgotten."

Right. Four if we counted Dad. She'd developed that ability, along with Sage, when the pair of them accessed their full power by accepting wolf form. "Have you tried riding it out of Wilding Springs?"

She nodded, irritation in her eyes. "Twice," she said. "Blocked both times."

Probably because they could only ride our veil, use our plane's membrane to travel, though it was likely Charlotte and Sage could reach Demonicon if they tried. I, on the other hand, had access to all of them. Surely the Brotherhood didn't have a corner market on the entire Universe. If Meira's and Fergus's lack of issue was any indication, it was a safe bet I'd have better luck than Sage and Charlotte.

"I'm joining you." I was hardly surprised by her insistent tone, her flat stare.

"Of course you are." I hugged her and she hugged me tightly back after a moment of shock. "I wouldn't have it any other way."

The family stirred when I stood and now that I was mobile, I knew I had one further responsibility to deal with before I went anywhere. It only took a short time to make the rounds, Shenka joining me with a tragic and fearful look on her face. I'd never seen her so shaken, though she handled the family as carefully and kindly as ever.

By the time I released the last of them from a gentle hug and turned to Shenka, I knew there was something much deeper troubling her than our present predicament.

"Tallah." She managed that one word before throwing her arms around me. I hugged her tight and wrapped her in what magic I had access to, vampire and demon both.

"We don't know what's going on yet," I whispered to my shaking second. "Until we do, we can't assume the worst." Shenka leaned away, wiping her nose, nodding. "I know it's cruel, but I need you to be strong for the family."

She gripped my hands in hers. "Always," she said.

"Just… find out what happened to my sister?"

"I'm not coming back without news." And maybe a Brotherhood sorcerer's head or two.

Mom joined us, Charlotte with her, Quaid hanging back though he didn't look happy about it. "I know exactly where you're going, by the way. We need answers."

"Harvard." I nodded sharply. "On it." And took her hand. As I reached for the veil, Mom on one side and Charlotte on the other, my rage built, sizzling in my gut. No one attacked my family. No one.

Someone was going to die today.

The veil welcomed me as it always did, my demon magic easily cutting a way through the rubbery membrane. But I wasn't going to Demonicon. At least, not yet. I immediately felt the resistance that must have stopped Charlotte and Sage as I stepped into the gap and tried to push my way through.

Okay then. Plan B.

Instead of riding the veil itself, I pulled us out of it, into the vast network beyond. I was so used to sailing through it on Max's back, the weightless feeling caught me like a shock. I could feel Mom and Charlotte hanging onto me and adjusted my focus as I turned us around, supported and suspended as my full maji power surged back to life now I was out from under the influence of the cavern's control. I was still weak, but with some reserves remaining, thankfully. I didn't have time to figure out how much, nor did I want to. Knowing might scare me.

We're safe, it's fine. I hoped reassuring them would ease their tight grips on my hands.

Just take us to Harvard, sweetheart, Mom's mental voice cut through to me. *And stop playing with the Universe.*

It made me laugh, easing the terrible, devouring fury living inside me. *Yes, Mother*, I sent before plunging us toward the edge of our veil again, and through it.

I'd never done anything like this before, usually leaving it up to Max to guide our way through the veil network. And so, I was privately relieved to step out the other side and into the dark and silent office of the Council Leader.

Didn't kill us. Bonus.

Mom released my hand, stalking toward the empty desk. She spun on me as Charlotte sniffed around the room, growling softly under her breath.

"She's not here." Way to state the obvious, Mom. But I could understand her anxiety.

"That doesn't mean something's happened to her." I felt around me, the thrum of the Council magic present. "Don't jump to conclusions."

Charlotte spun around. "This way," she said, command in her voice.

This way, you betcha.

I followed the werewoman, Mom at my side, through the office door and into the main sitting room. This place always gave me the creeps, and tonight was no exception. All those staring portraits of former Council Leaders, Mom's nearest the door even seeming to glare at me with contempt.

"I hate that damned thing," she muttered on the way by.

Guess I wasn't the only one.

The whole of Massachusetts Hall felt dead and empty. It was still summer, but there were usually people around, regardless. But there was not a trace of late term students or Enforcers or anyone.

So weird.

By the time the creaking old elevator delivered us to the bottom floor, I was seriously creeped out. The green expanse of Harvard Yard stretched out from the bottom of the stairs at the base of the red brick building, giant trees shading the lawn. It felt like late afternoon, though the sun was hidden behind a giant bank of angry looking clouds, a roll of thunder making me jump as we touched down on the walkway.

University Hall stood across from us, the statue of John Harvard beckoning us onward. If we were going to find anyone associated with the Council, it should be there. Hidden from normals who attended Harvard and called this their workplace, the long, white-stoned hall was home to the main council chamber.

If Erica wasn't there, then I would worry.

Not true, as it turned out. While we strode with—in my case, anyway—false confidence under the trees and to the front entry, I found my anxiety level rising. Erica and I might not have been getting along lately, but she was like a second mother to me once, had helped Mom raise me. If anything happened to her and I could have done something to change it…

I'd never forgive myself.

A silver Persian and his embedded sense of guilt. I blamed Sassafras.

My questing threads of power sneaking out before me encountered only barriers. Shields upon walls upon wards. But they were all Council magic, at least. Did that mean they had somehow fortified themselves inside, were working, even as I strode toward them, on a solution? I hoped so. And maybe I could help.

Or, this was a trap and I was walking into a Brotherhood snare. Either way, I was going in.

The idea there might be a light at the end of this particular tunnel that had nothing to do with me burning at the stake drove my feet faster. Mom and Charlotte kept pace easily, obviously as eager as I was to get answers.

The big doors at the entry swung open easily, the halls eerily silent. I stepped through the false wall at the end of the hall and felt a wave of relief wash over me at the sight of six Enforcers standing guard at the doors to the council chamber.

One glance at Mom told me I should reserve my relaxing of worry for later. And, as we approached the silent, black-robed witches, I started to believe she was right.

They barely acknowledged us, staring anywhere but in our direction. I chose to ignore them in turn, though I kept careful watch with magic to make sure they didn't turn on us as we walked by.

Nope. Nada. Zippo reaction.

Enforcer statues? As long as they stayed out of my way.

By the time I hit the doors to the council chamber with power, flinging them wide, I was pissed all over again, anger giving my waning energy a boost. That irritable feeling grew into temper as I stomped my way, barefoot and in my sleep shorts and t-shirt, into the middle of the room. The Council sat in a semicircle, elevated above me in their usual places, though the Hayle seat remained empty. I'd failed to fill it after Erica took over, and now I wished I hadn't.

They watched my approach, some with open fear, others hiding it better, though I wasn't paying attention to them. My gaze was locked firmly on Erica. Only the wash of their anxiety came through, heavy under the thrumming power of the Council.

I guess I should have been nervous when Erica glared at me like I'd intruded on something important. But I couldn't bring myself to worry about what petty crap she was dealing with right now. Because here was proof only my coven had been attacked. And the rest of the freaking continent?

Business as usual.

Oh, hell no.

"Listen up." My words snapped out of me, cracking whips of magic with them. "The Hayle coven is in trouble. We've been openly attacked by the Brotherhood."

No gasps of shock. No worry or concern.

Just crickets.

A terrible fear warmed up my insides, feeding the rage that threatened to explode out of me as Erica jabbed an index finger in my direction and spoke.

"Sydlynn Hayle," she said. "We've been looking for you." Her blonde bob swung as she sat back. "You're under arrest."

I felt the Enforcers closing in about a second before I slammed up shields to protect Mom and Charlotte. My mother was faster than me with her question.

"On what charge?" Her voice vibrated with anger. "This had better be good, Erica."

The council leader didn't bend, not even under her former coven leader's displeasure.

"You and your entire coven are charged with resisting the new order." Erica's hands dropped to the surface of her desk. "When our allies arrived in Wilding Springs to present the announcement of our association, you fled and have resisted all efforts to locate you." Hell, yeah, I did. She was cracked if she thought I'd do otherwise. But, she was counting on this, and so was Belaisle. They knew I'd never go quietly. So, my family was to be an example, was it? We'd see about that.

Erica went on as though she had no clue my mind was whirling. "Because of your failure to present yourself, you will turn over your family to this council and submit to trial."

"What new order?" I spit the words at her. "What are you talking about?" But I think I already knew, that fear in my gut searing around the edges of my rage.

Made flesh as a medium-height man in a pinstriped suit, his chin dark with a goatee, pale yellow eyes locked on me, sauntered forward from the side entrance with a smirk on his face.

"There is a new power controlling your coven now," Liander Belaisle said, nodding up at Erica who held perfectly still, rigid even. "Thanks to the brilliance and foresight of your Council Leader, we have combined our magicks to make a stronger, more enduring force." His smirk deepened. "For the good of all."

TWELVE

I choked on the surge of absolute consuming fury trying to launch itself from my lips and smother his smug ass with fire. But I managed to hold back, partly because of the added pressure of sorcery that layered over my shields, adding to the magic of the Enforcers surrounding us. A ring of sorcerers joined Liander Belaisle. I struggled to make it past the hate in my heart and understand what was happening here.

The leader of the Brotherhood. I defeated him eight years ago, stripped his power and won the battle foretold by the Fate twins. I won, damn it. And though he escaped, he was powerless, broken.

I'd been too complacent, it seemed. Let life take over, Max's need draw me away when I should have spent every waking moment pursing this man and destroying him utterly.

What had I done? More to the point, what had Erica?

"You will surrender," she said, voice like stone.

"Like hell I will." I held my place, Mom's mind connecting with mine.

We need to get out of here. She sounded calm, reasonable, considering our position. And I took great support from that. Mom was back and we could handle anything together.

"There will, of course, be some growing pains." Belaisle's smirk never faltered. He leaned casually against the base of the Council dais, the old, polished wood panels glowing softly in the light. "But I assure you, when the integration is all over there will be a new dawn for all magic users."

It's all of us. Mom's crisp announcement wasn't a surprise. *She's thrown the entire continent to the wolves.*

But why? She had to have been coerced. I was so familiar with his tactics, thanks to Mom and what she endured. He tried for several years to break her and failed. But Erica was weaker than my mother. If I could free her, this could be over in a moment.

Are we sure it's just North America? Charlotte's cold calculation made me pause. *We need to check in with Femke.*

Panic rose, stormed my resolve, almost won. But I had two frighteningly strong women at my side, and three furious alter egos who refused to let me fall.

"This is your last warning," Erica said, power behind

her words, crackling along the edges of my shields. "Give over the Hayle coven and turn yourself in. Allow your family to survive, to be assimilated, and we shall consider your good judgment during your trial."

I lunged into her mind, not allowing her a moment to resist me. I was far more powerful than her, tired or not. Still, no matter how exhausted I felt, there was no missing the fact she was free and clear, her own agent, without a trace of coercion in her magic.

"Erica," I breathed as Mom gasped softly beside me. "What have you done?"

I felt Mom scour the Council too, while Erica answered me. They were sad, but compliant, and I realized as Erica spoke again they had all done this by choice, on purpose, knowing what they were getting into. What they were dragging all the witches of this continent into.

"I have created balance where once there was none," Erica said. "Too long have witches stood outside and allowed other races leeway in our territory. Combining our magic with the Brotherhood will allow us to assert true dominion and uphold the law while providing a peaceful world for all paranormals to live in."

Did she really believe that? Did she even have a vision of what that would look like? Or was this all a pipe dream wrapped in a steaming pile of crap?

"Protection for all paranormals," Erica said. "Equality

in power." Whatever that meant. Considering the Brotherhood were thieves and parasites… "And a formal truce and peace between the sorcerers and witches who have been at odds for centuries." The lovely Brotherhood burned innocent women in the Dark Ages as witches, hunted us down, and tried to put the fear of God into normals. They succeeded. So why should we work with them now?

She's lying to herself, I sent to Mom. No answer. But, then again, I wasn't really expecting one, stating the obvious like that.

"Sydlynn," Belaisle said with a chiding drawl. "You should be happy about this. You're getting what you wanted." He took a stride toward me, arms outstretched, as though embracing all of us. "The Brotherhood and witches, working together. Soon, we'll include vampires and werewolves, too. And even the Sidhe who live among us." He winked. "The odd lost demon." My skin crawled at the thought. "Strengthening our position among the normals as a whole, as the Brotherhood have always done. Taking advantage of their naiveté, placing ourselves in positions of control. So magic users of all kinds will never have to fear normals again." The council was nodding in time with his words. They feared persecution, and I guess I didn't blame them. But the fact it was the Brotherhood who began all the hate toward our kind was rather ironic and chillingly disturbing. "All coming together in perfect harmony." He paused for effect. "We will rule this territory and, in doing so, protect ourselves from normals forever. For the common good, of course."

And not for power, right, Belaisle? Sure. Not buying it. "For your good," I snarled before I could stop myself. I knew he was baiting me, and kicked myself for responding to him, but I just couldn't help it.

"For everyone," Erica said, voice booming over mine, silencing everyone until the room felt like a haunted tomb, the soft in and out of breathing frozen as the council held their collective breath. "That was the point of this." If she was trying to convince me, she was doing a terrible job. But, for the first time since I'd known Erica, she didn't seem to care what I thought, what Mom thought. There was no urging to believe her in her voice or her magic, only conviction and icy cold resolve. "No more fighting. No more deception. This coalition will be my legacy to all witches, and all paranormals." She nodded once, a sharp gesture. "Peace, at last."

I laughed, bitter and crackling, another impulse reaction. But I didn't care at this point. Not in the face of such blatant lies and misconceptions.

"You," I said, pointing at her as she once pointed at me when this debacle of a meeting began, "are so full of crap, I'm surprised your eyes aren't brown." She didn't answer, though some of the council members gasped at me. Let them, the nasty old biddies. "If you think Liander

Belaisle," let him stew over the fact I was talking about him like he wasn't even here, "has anyone but his own best interest at heart, you have completely cracked your nut."

Erica's stony face greeted me with silence.

I couldn't just let this go. I had to get through to them. But Mom was faster than me.

"Tell me," she said, voice cold and clear. "What will happen to those who disagree with this new order?" She met the eyes of those on the council who would willingly do so. Not many, that was. She finally settled on Erica. "Have any of the covens been consulted on this matter?" The council's guilty silence made my blood run cold, though it made sense. No way the collective witches of this territory would agree to such a plan. They might have been a pain in the ass, but even they weren't that foolish. Mom's grim expression even made me feel guilty, and I hadn't done anything. "Which means this is an arbitrary decision of the council." If things hadn't been so damned broken and dark right then, I would have grinned. She was the master of disapproval and guilt. Her vibrant voice rang with indignation. "Might I ask what punishment you have arrived on for those witches who might choose not to comply?"

Was Mom onto something? How could they do this without talking to all of us first? Maybe there was a way out of the law and back into sanity.

Erica looked suddenly grim, but it was Belaisle who answered.

"An unfortunate set of circumstances," he said, still grinning. "But, naturally, such opposition will have to be dealt with immediately." He looked up at Erica. "Am I correct, Council Leader?"

She nodded, brusque. "For the good of all." She paused, almost hesitant. "The price of peace."

My two-baby-wide ass.

Mom's next question made me freeze in place.

"Are witches being executed, Erica?" It was suddenly as though only the two of them were in the room as I stood, shaken and cold, waiting for her reply. Surely not. She would never go that far.

Would she?

The council stirred, uneasy, even upset. And we had our answer as Erica spoke.

"Only those who oppose the new alliance with violence." I wondered if she really believed that. She had to in order to sleep at night.

I, on the other hand, knew better.

"You have been demanding change, Coven Leader Hayle," she went on. "And the council has delivered."

"Without the input or approval of the covens," I snapped back.

"Your approval wasn't necessary." She held up a sheet of parchment, glittering with blue magic. "The council has full autonomy. Doesn't it, Miriam?" Mom flinched next to me, worried eyes meeting mine as I turned to look at her. "One of your laws, I think."

Syd. Mom's fear hit me like a blow. *She's right. Oh, dear elements. I think Belaisle has been setting this up for years.*

Just like him to make Mom do something while under his influence that could possibly give him an advantage down the road. "Whatever twisted logic you're calling on to justify this," I said, "never in a million years would anyone in their right mind get into bed with Belaisle and his Brotherhood. We have far too much sense for that. Sense, it seems, you're lacking, Council Leader Plower."

That got through to her. Erica's nostrils flared. "You will surrender," she said, gesturing and the Enforcers closed in tighter, joined by the sorcerers of the Brotherhood. I could feel the noose jerking around my neck and knew we had very little time if we were going to escape. "And there will be order!"

Syd, Mom sent in a sharp jab. *We have one option. I suggest we take it.*

That being? My shields strained. I was still so weak from saving the family.

Her next words make me gasp all over again. But I met her eyes and saw the determination there.

And trusted her, like I always had.

"You have no authority over me or mine," I said, voice ringing in the silence. "From this moment forward,

I declare the Hayle coven autonomous."

That got their attention. I didn't know Erica could sit up any straighter, but she managed it, as did the rest of the council while Belaisle's smirk of confidence faltered.

Gotcha, you asshat.

"You can't do that." Erica's voice vibrated with fury.

"But she can," Mom said, her own tone reasonable and almost sweet. "The law is clear. Unless you've changed it recently?"

What does this mean? Charlotte was nervous, I could tell, but she held it together, as always.

It means, Mom sent to both of us, tired but almost gleeful, *we should be safe enough. For now.*

"The laws have not been changed." Lauren Noble of the Hensley coven almost sounded relieved as the others nodded. I wondered again about Tallah and why her representative didn't say a word to her or anyone else. "Any coven leader has the right to sever her ties to her council at any time, and is therefore, forevermore, no longer under the control or purview of said council."

I had no idea.

It's an old law, Mom sent. *From when the council was first created. A back door to appease the coven leaders, just in case they decided to bail. I remember finding it, wondering why anyone would want to leave.*

I guess we just found a reason.

"This choice will make you and your family outcast,

Sydlynn Hayle." There was the soft begging sound I expected to hear earlier. Was Erica cracking? "You would be without territory or support, your power severed from the magic of the Council. This is a huge choice to make that could mean the end of your coven. You're making a big mistake."

"On the contrary," I said. "It means their survival. I want out. Now." She hesitated. "It's not like I had any support in the past." I couldn't help the jab. I just couldn't. "So this will be no different."

Her jaw tightened again and I knew we'd won.

Or, maybe not so fast.

"This is preposterous." Belaisle's fury was written all over his face. I feared he'd thought of everything, but maybe he wasn't as far ahead of me as he thought. "Arrest her!"

But the power of the council was already acting, on Erica's prompting. I felt it embrace me, even through my shielding, and worried a moment about what this would do to the coven. After all, our magic was part of the Council power, and had been for a very long time. But I shoved aside my worry as the magic of the council softly, sadly released me.

Not before it let me feel its pain at what had been done to it. I couldn't help. I was out of options and had to think of my family first. Sighing its blue flames, the Council magic cut ties with me and let me go.

One thing was for certain as I swayed slightly at its loss. I needed to get in touch with the other major coven leaders and find out if things were as grim as I now feared they'd become.

It was odd, at first, not feeling the magic of the council. But as I drew a breath and settled into the feeling of being alone, I realized, now more than ever, we didn't need the council. The heartbeat of the coven thudded strongly inside me, as warm and powerful as ever. And I grinned, knowing Erica would understand without me having to say a word.

The Enforcers backed away, but the sorcerers didn't move.

"Take her," Belaisle snapped.

The combined power of the council and his sorcery crackled between his people and my little group. I had no idea how much control Erica had over Belaisle, but I was surprised she could do even that much. I certainly didn't expect her control to last.

"We must let them go." Deep regret colored her words. Her grave and judging gaze fell on me. "Understand this, Sydlynn Hayle. You are no longer a member of the North American Witches organization. Therefore, you are no longer welcome in our territory."

Not shocking, Mom sent. *Saw this coming.*

"That being said," Erica went on, "if any of your outcast family are discovered in this territory, beginning at dawn tomorrow, you will be captured and executed without further warning. Do you hear me?"

I nodded, power gathered tight around me, ready to tear the veil. But I couldn't resist one last stare down with Erica, one I was determined to win.

She didn't flinch. And I was finally forced to let it go.

"I hope you can learn to live with what you've done," I said. And jerked a hole in the veil. Belaisle roared, his power smashing through the council barrier, but he was too late.

I saluted him with my middle finger as Mom, Charlotte and I leaped into the veil and out of his reach.

THIRTEEN

I didn't take us far, dropping us out on campus. I shivered despite my lack of sensitivity to temperature and met Mom's eyes.

"Now we know," I said.

"There is more to uncover." She wrung her hands a moment before stilling them at her sides. "I have people to find and talk to. But this is dangerous, Sydlynn."

"As long as we avoid the Brotherhood," I said. "We have until dawn, remember?" I turned to Charlotte. "Go with Mom and watch her back."

"And who will watch yours?" Charlotte's no-nonsense glare pinned me and I almost laughed.

"I have three whole other people in my head, in case you'd forgotten," I said, tapping my temple with one finger. "We'll be fine." I looked around me, at the quiet, wondering where the tourists were, why this placed seemed so empty. The Brotherhood must have cleared the campus to keep normals out of the way. "Just stay in constant contact. I'll come for you if you run into trouble."

Charlotte's heavy stare didn't falter as Mom took her hand and led her away, the blonde werewoman watching me over her shoulder as my mother disappeared back into Massachusetts Hall. I had another destination in mind, the towering front entry of Widener Library just around the corner.

Why did I feel like I was skulking?

Because we are skulking, my vampire sent.

Stupid, if you ask me, my demon sent. *Let's just start picking off the Brotherhood one idiot at a time and see how Belaisle likes it.*

Tempting, I sent in return, my bare feet slapping on the stone steps. For the first time since I woke in the cavern, I felt self-conscious about my lack of attire. But for no reason, it turned out. Even the library, dim and quiet, was as empty as the rest of the campus seemed to be.

I stood inside the big glass doors, looking across the lobby toward the stacks, shivering and hugging myself though I wasn't cold. This was seriously weirding me out.

Agreed, Shaylee sent. *Where is everyone?*

I believe you are right, my vampire sent. *The Brotherhood must have cleared the place.*

To which my demon hissed a long, slow curse. *You*

don't think Belaisle would have the balls to hurt normals, do you?

I wouldn't put it past him, I sent while my vampire murmured agreement and Shaylee sighed sadly.

We can't worry about them. Damn it. Belaisle knew how to make me feel torn in multiple pieces. Saving others was so ingrained in me, I had to act. But every distraction to the contrary of my original goal just weighed on me heavier and heavier.

I shook off my conflicted emotions. Family first.

My alter egos hugged me with power, in full agreement.

After we know they are safe we deal with the Brotherhood. My vampire's gentle words were anything but.

I paused by the maintenance door on the far left of the lobby, hand trembling slightly as I reached for the thin shield hiding Coven Hall from the normals. It had been years since I was here, since graduation, but it felt as familiar as if it was only yesterday when the way parted and I stepped through.

Maybe I should have been more careful, but I honestly didn't consider the fact there could be Brotherhood here. They weren't witches. It wasn't until I passed through into the dark central hub I drew a sharp breath and looked quickly around, the thought occurring to me I could be walking into a trap.

But no, nothing. Just silence and a long hallway ahead, the round room I found myself in bracketed by multi-colored doors. How odd. I knew these doors. They were the same ones I used for classes in my fourth year.

The system must not reset for each individual, my vampire sent. *There's no need, I suppose.*

I nodded absently, turning in a slow circle. My first day, I handed off my course list to the sparkling pink sprite who managed the courses of all students. She and the magic of this place, made sure I only had access to the doors I needed. Convenient, but always made me feel a bit like a little kid being herded.

Where was she? I reached out with power, trying to trigger her appearance, but the bright eyed and cheerful rotund sprite never showed.

Whatever holds the rest of the denizens of the campus away, my demon sent, *must have affected her, as well.*

Made sense. I sighed, sagged forward, hands shaking before me.

I was hoping for some answers, I sent to the hitchhikers in my head.

No time to falter now, Sydlynn. My vampire's tone held confidence, encouragement. *We will uncover what we need to remove Belaisle and his sorcerers from their place of power.*

I wished I shared her optimism. Everything seemed so hopeless at this point. I'd not only torn my coven free from our council and made us outcast, I'd put prices on our heads.

The soft swish of fabric spun me around, mouth

opening to greet the pink sprite. Only to freeze in place, lips agape at the sight of Council member Willa Rhodes hurrying toward me.

"Sydlynn," she gasped, panting slightly, her black robe swirling around her feet, small, wrinkled hands fluttering before her. "Thank goodness you're still here." She glanced back over her shoulder as though fearful she'd been followed. "I knew you wouldn't just leave us to our fate."

She was an old lady. The sister of the Rhodes coven leader. Probably should have retired ages ago. But despite her advanced years, it was hard not to scowl at her, the need to plant a fist in something soft and squishy of hers almost overwhelming. "Tell me why I shouldn't."

Willa's face crumpled as she grasped for my hand. "This wasn't supposed to happen." A soft wail echoed in the back of her voice, desperation pulling her lips down into furrowed wrinkles. She looked just like her sister, Violet. And though I liked both of them, they were always sticklers for the law. Which mean whatever ridiculous rules were being upheld, she would support them to the bitter end. And yet, here she stood, almost weeping as her tiny body quivered inside the black velvet of her gown.

I led her to one of the benches between two doors and pulled her down beside me. Willa gulped some air, tiny bow lips pinching into furrows as she gathered herself. "Tell me what really happened."

Her unhappy expression wasn't encouraging. "Erica is correct," she said. "It's all on the up and up. We agreed as a council when she brought the proposal to us."

"What does your sister think of this?" I wanted to shake Willa. "Did Violet agree?"

Misery woke in Willa's eyes, moisture gathering to the tipping point on her lower lids. "It was decided our action would be best served if we ratified the laws without the interference of the covens." She shook her hands at me, tears trickling through the lines under her eyes. "I know, I know! Foolish, arrogant. I have no idea why we thought this was a good idea." I opened my mouth to comment, but she patted my hand. "And before you ask, no, I assure you. There was no coercion involved. We were led by the hand like tiny children. Convinced by a slick-tongued charlatan and his pack of bully sorcerers, into thinking we could change the world." She fell still a moment, heaving a deep sigh. Her thin shoulders barely filled out the breadth of her robe. "We'd all been through so much, Sydlynn. Faced our own failings and lost our leader." Like this was Mom's fault for retiring. "All of us," she looked up and met my eyes again, hers pale and watery, "to the last council member, only wanted to make a difference finally. Instead of standing by and watching history happen."

Considering Liander Belaisle is a crafty and convincing man, my vampire sent, *I suppose I can understand how they fell for his ruse.*

So can I. I wanted to weep myself at the screwed up mess this had become when I wasn't looking. When I thought I'd done my part and just left them to work it out. I should have known better.

"This is not what I agreed to," Willa said, insistent, intense, as though she feared I wouldn't believe her. "I am sickened and horrified by the heavy handed finale of our plan. It was supposed to be a triumph, Sydlynn. A council reveal to all covens. But Belaisle and his sorcerers made certain events turned in their favor. By the time we understood just what we'd done, it was far too late."

"You could have warned them." The accusation clipped from my lips.

She shrank down again, nodding. "There was no time," she said. "The Brotherhood acted before we knew they were putting anything in motion." She paused. "Though I worry Erica was duplicitous."

I'd deal with Erica later. And she would not enjoy the experience.

"Listen to me." Willa grasped my hands again, hers cold, the thin, wrinkled skin almost powdery, nails digging into my flesh, caterpillar eyebrows bobbing up and down over her watery eyes. "No matter what you think of us, we need your help." Her lips thinned as the lower one trembled. "Erica has lost control, despite the show she put on for you. And because of her loss, witches are dying." She choked on a single sob as she spoke those words, driving fear through me, blades of anxiety. "As far as I know, thanks to your quick thinking—and you must tell me someday how you managed it—the Hayle coven is the only remaining family still intact."

"You're correct." I looked up, startled, to find Mom and Charlotte watching us. My mother crossed to Willa, sat on her other side, hugging her gently as the old woman wept on her shoulder. Charlotte came to stand next to me, grim and furious, eyes snapping with power.

"Not good, I take it." I met Mom's eyes while she rubbed Willa's back. "What happened to the other covens?" I didn't think it was possible for goosebumps to grow that large on my skin. I was not going to like this one bit, but had no choice but to listen as Willa spoke.

The old woman's nose ran, whole body trembling. "Every one of them was hit at the same time," she whispered the admission. "Belaisle's idea. Behind our backs. Erica was supposed to call a meeting of coven leaders. Instead..." Willa wiped at her shaking lips with one hand. "From what we've managed to uncover, the majority of families put up a fight. And lost."

Belaisle was a dead man. "And there's nothing you can do about it?" I turned to Mom as Willa shook her head. "What the hell kind of law did Erica sign?"

"A heavily biased one," Mom said. "If Erica had read

the drafted law more carefully, perhaps things would be different. We would have options." She shook her head as Willa leaned away, snuffling, fishing in her robe a moment before retrieving a lace handkerchief. "But Belaisle was clever in some of the clauses he included."

Willa blew her nose softly. "None of us caught just how much power we'd given up until it was too late."

Mom's face blanched, bright points of pink on her cheekbones, the rest of her face ghostly pale. "You knew?"

"After." Willa's dull voice silenced all of us and held for a long moment. "Just before the attacks began."

I opened my mouth to ask Mom what she was talking about, what the law had granted Belaisle he could simply walk into witch territories and attack without provocation, but she was already talking.

"I won't ask how you could let this happen." Mom's disappointment almost seemed to affect the old woman like a blow. My mother had been a respected Council Leader for many years, despite the attempts of the Brotherhood to control her.

"Mom," I said. "What?"

She looked away, jaw tight. "I spoke to Phillip," she said. Who? Oh, right. Erica's red-headed flirt of a secretary. "He's devastated. Agreed to sneak me a copy of the new law."

I turned my head toward her, knowing I wasn't going

to like a word Mom said from here on in.

"Thanks to Erica's incompetence," she said, though in my mind I had already convicted her old second of treason against all witches on purpose, "the Brotherhood now have permission to police all infractions against the new order."

I stared at her, trying to process what she said. "What about the Enforcers?" Willa made it clear the security arm of the Council was now as powerless as the rest of us.

No. Not us. Them. We weren't part of the family any more.

The old woman shrank from me when I asked the question while Mom went on. "The document gives the Brotherhood carte blanche to enforce the law, against all witches." Mom's hands tighten on mine, whole body trembling and stiff. "That damned fool," she whispered, looking away from me. "She's turned our home into a police state, and the Brotherhood are in charge."

Heart thudding, I could only stare at Willa's crumpled face. No time for threats, accusations or anything else, though, as much as my demon was screeching for a target. I'd melt down and punch the bag at Sage's dojo until it died a horrible death once this was over. There was a time I would have allowed my temper to rule me. But I had a whole population of witches to worry about.

Maybe my coven was autonomous now, but I wouldn't abandon innocents to Belaisle.

"It's time to fight," I said. "And we could use some inside help."

I might as well have poked the old witch with a cattle prod. Willa leaped to her feet and backed away, eyes huge, terror on her face. "I can't! They'll find out." Again she looked over her shoulder, anxiety a living thing surging inside her magic.

"Not even for your sister?" I had ammo and I wasn't afraid to use it against her.

Way to torture a broken, little old lady, Syd.

"Not even for Violet." It looked like admitting it finally destroyed Willa's soul. Her face closed off, eyes dead, shaking stilled. A shell of a witch stood before me, her heart shattered at last. "It's every witch for themselves now, don't you see that? Anyone who speaks up disappears." She half-turned away, paused. "Even Enforcers." Was she talking about Pender Tremere, the Enforcer Leader? I hadn't seen a hint of him and that made me worry. "If you can help us, Sydlynn, please. Have pity. But if you can't..." She turned her back on me. "Save your family and leave us to burn."

FOURTEEN

I sat there for what felt like forever after Willa left, staring at Mom as though doing so might change what we'd learned. "Tell me again what the hell happened?"

My mother's mournful expression didn't alter, though her set jaw told me she was about as happy at this turn of events as I was.

"I don't know what Erica was thinking," Mom said. "But we're in serious trouble, Syd. All witches."

My knees popped as I surged to my feet, anger fired and ready to fly. "We're going back in there," I snarled at Mom, "and we're wringing necks until there's some sense in that damned room."

She stood as quickly, hand on my arm, holding me back with her grip and her steady gaze. "We can't," she said, ever so softly. "It's the law."

I snorted. Like that ever stopped me before. "We're

not part of the Council anymore."

"Even more reason to steer clear," Mom said. "Any infraction against them means we're encroaching on territory. We could be burned just for talking about it."

"What about the werewolves, vampires?" Were they the next targets?

Mom's mute unhappiness answered me all too well.

"Syd," she said at last, her worry and fear and hurt in her eyes, "Willa might have been right about one thing." She swallowed, almost looked away, blinking a few times as moisture rose to glitter from the blue of her gaze. "There are times when we simply must put ourselves first."

Mom did not just say that.

And yet...

Damn it.

"The family." They were my responsibility. I had to do everything I could to protect them, even more now. "You're right, Mom. I know. It's just... how can we walk away?"

Mom's face creased in a frown, deep line between her eyes reminding me she was getting older. "It's a hard choice," she said, voice stronger, full of decisiveness and other such powerful emotions I couldn't muster just yet. "But, in the end, it's no choice at all. Syd." Her grip on my arm tightened. "You're so used to saving everyone, to being the salvation of the Universe, you forget sometimes about the little things." I could tell it wasn't an accusation. Just the truth. "But there are fights even you can't win."

"Maybe," I growled. "Not right away. But I won't let the Brotherhood ruin everything, Mom. Or kill witches on a whim."

She nodded, let me go, touched my cheek with the same hand, her fingers steady. "Nor will I," she said, and I pitied Erica the next time Mom met her face-to-face. She'd been Council Leader herself, once, after all. Surely this must feel like the greatest betrayal of all. Or a reminder of Mom's time in the thrall of the sorcerer's sect. Not sure which was worse. "But we must ensure the family is safe first."

I drew a deep breath. "What about the other covens?" I couldn't just let them fend for themselves, could I? The steady, knowing look on Mom's face forced me to be realistic.

And sigh, chest aching. I couldn't save them all, maji or not. At least, not without help. And running off half-cocked wasn't my style anymore. I used to be highly temperamental, once upon a time. Okay, stop giggling. Seriously, I'd mellowed somewhat with experience and time. But nothing could cool the need I felt to act, to seize control of the situation and make it right.

"You can expend all of your energy running around the continent trying to save everyone," Charlotte said. "Or you can focus on the source of the illness and excise it."

Big picture. Got it.

"Family first," I said as I followed Mom toward the exit, grim faced Charlotte on my heels. "Then we come back and kick some ass."

The veil embraced me as always, whatever barrier Belaisle had tried to use to contain me now broken. I hoped that meant Charlotte and Sage would be able to ride again. Having three of us who could travel this way could be an advantage. Just as soon as I figured out if we actually had a plan or not.

Details, details.

The cavern's cool semi-darkness greeted us, murmurs of anxious witches watching our return. The smothering effect of the wards quieted my elemental power, but when I pushed against it, I realized just how frail the wards really were. One firm shove and my maji magic could break the shielding at any time. Interesting, but a discovery to be investigated later.

Mom was already talking with Dad and Quaid, Shenka tucked in close to them with Sassafras at her feet. Sage hung back, eyes locked on Charlotte and I wasn't surprised she went right to his side and hugged him.

Quaid pulled me against him as Mom repeated what she'd told me, filling in our little group on what was happening. Shenka's trembling hands covered her mouth, eyes brimming with tears.

"I have to help Tallah." The words gasped out of her as though she didn't intend to speak out loud. But I nodded to her, reaching out to take her hand as she dropped both of them to her sides.

"Family," I said, all that I needed to say.

"We'll go with you." Sage nodded as Charlotte made the offer, and I wondered if they'd made this plan before now. Shenka shook her head, eyes locking with mine.

"I can't leave the coven." Her hands wrung before her, so torn up by her need I left Quaid to embrace her.

"Go get Tallah," I said, the family magic hugging her, too. "Bring her and her coven here. We'll all fight this together." It put the family at risk, my offer. There was a chance any excessive coming and going would alert Belaisle to our location. But I couldn't abandon Tallah and her family. I loved Shenka too much. Besides, if the Brotherhood leader did show his ugly face anywhere near me, it would give me the opportunity to make sure he never, ever did so again.

Shenka sobbed softly, nodded. "Syd, are you sure?"

"I've never been so sure." I pushed her gently toward Charlotte who caught her and pulled her close. *Keep her safe.*

As if she were you. Charlotte's free hand locked with Sage's as she turned and opened a cut in the veil. I felt inside it, relief rising.

You should be okay, I sent.

I assumed as much. Charlotte's blue eyes sparkled, though her face remained as stoic as ever. *We will see you soon. Be prepared for refugees.*

It hurt to watch them go, my pajama clad second, the two werewolves I loved. But I knew they had to. And this was the only means I had to help other covens.

I turned away before the slice sealed shut, focusing on Mom and Dad and Quaid, Sassafras now perched on my husband's big hands, watching me with intense amber eyes.

"What are we going to tell the coven?" Quaid kept his voice down, dark eyes hooded and serious.

"Nothing, for now," I said. No one protested. "No panic, at least, no further panic. Agreed?" They all nodded. "At least until we have a plan to share. A way to make this right."

"If we can." Sassafras's ears drooped. "How could Erica have done such a thing?"

Mom's anger returned in a flare of blue fire that cascaded from her hand as she fisted it before her, falling in sparks to her feet. "It doesn't matter anymore," Mom said. "Our only job, at this moment, is finding a safe refuge for the family." She looked around, one eyebrow raised. "While a good temporary shelter, this won't do us for much longer."

Where was safe? Impossible to tell. "What about one of the other territories?" I knew Femke would likely help out.

"If they aren't compromised," Dad said, regret in his voice at the speaking of such a mind blowing idea. "How do we know the other leaders haven't signed similar agreements?"

I stared at him as I'd stared at Mom, certain I didn't understand the words that just left his mouth. Not Femke.

I couldn't believe that.

And yet.

"We need allies," I said. "Someone outside this mess." I already knew who I was going to call. "Then money. Then a safe haven to hide the family. Agreed?"

More nods.

"Give me a second." I stepped away from them, mind reaching through the veil, searching for one individual in particular. If I had the backing of the drach, I could at least worry less the Brotherhood would find and harm the family. I knew Max would offer his support.

Hoped he would. I'd been down this road with him before, hadn't I? When I needed him most? Fate forced him to hold me back, to keep me from my dying husband, Liam, when Ameline Benoit killed him before my eyes. There was a time I thought I'd never forgive Max for what he'd done, though I came to understand he had no choice, as I'd had no choice.

And even though the two of us had been allies and

friends for many years now, I still harbored a tiny seed of fear he might, one day, be forced to turn his back on me again.

I wasn't sure if I had it in me to forgive him the second time.

But when I reached for Max, I found nothing. The veil felt empty, the spaces between planes quiet and solemn. There were times inside I thought I knew what it was like to go to church, to feel as humans with religious convictions felt, the sacred silence of a place where everything and anything was possible. I searched for several minutes, pushing my limits and the blanket of shielding trying to block my power, until I finally gave up and retreated.

No Max. Where could he be? One way to find out. My demon chuffed softly as I tugged at the veil, focused once more on my sister.

Her reaction this time, as I waved at her wearily through the slice in the membrane between planes, was a shriek and tears as she threw herself toward me, tall, strong demon body and huge, platform boots giving her a good foot over me. She crushed me against her chest, holding me so tight I gasped for air.

She released me, lunged for Mom, then Dad. It was odd to see her stand next to him, taller than he was now he had mortal form and had given up his demon power. Meira snatched Sassafras from Quaid, bending to kiss my husband's cheek before turning toward me again.

"What the bloody freaking hell happened?" She shook, long, curly hair trembling around her, the hem of her silver gauze skirt rattling. Her thick, black nails dug into Sass's fur as she clung to him, cheeks wet and shining with her tears. "I've been trying to reach you for two days!"

I shook my head, impatient suddenly, tired of talking and wanting to act. "Long story," I snapped without meaning to. "Where is Mabel?" The drach woman had given up traveling with Max, mostly, spending the majority of her time with Meira in Ostrogotho. Our great-great-never-mind-counting grandmother rarely left my sister's side.

Meira's eyes flew wide. "She's gone," she said. "Almost two days ago. Vanished without a word." Her shaking stopped, face stony. "What happened to the drach?"

"I have no idea," I said. "But I need them. We need them." I gestured around me, caught Meira's frown, gasp of surprise, growing anger.

"Long story or not," she snarled back, "you'd better start talking."

Mom took over, thank goodness. Neither Meira nor I were angry with each other. But she had the temper of a demon and we were both afraid. That always brought out the worst—and the best—in me. Thing was, if I wanted the best, I needed a target and a clear field of sight.

And I had neither right now.

Meira growled some curses when Mom finished. "Give me half a day," she said, "and I'll have every demon with an effigy on your plane ready and waiting to come and do some damage to the Brotherhood."

"You know that won't work." I bit my tongue, sighed out my anger. "Sorry, Meems, but it's true."

She sagged, Sassafras's soft purring the only sound in the quiet. I recognized then the whole coven was watching, listening. With hope? Maybe. I had to tell them something, after all.

"We've been working on sorcery control," she said. "I'm sure we can make a difference if you'll let us."

"What we really need," Mom said, interrupting with her typical Miriam Hayle calm and poise, "is a safe place for the family, out of the control of the Brotherhood."

We all stared at each other, our minds clearly turning over as we desperately tried to come up with something. But the only places I could think of were either potentially under threat, or off plane and inaccessible to the family. Without demon blood, for example, the coven couldn't cross to Demonicon. Without Sidhe souls, they couldn't go to the realm. And most of the other planes were the same. If I could have shared my maji power with them, my drach blood, I would have. Just to get them out of here.

"Keep me posted." Meira turned toward the gap in the veil, the suns setting over her capital city. "I'll start assembling my people, just in case you need us."

Mom hugged her, Dad, too, Quaid taking Sassafras back from her. I squeezed her hard, not wanting to let go.

Sorry to be a crabapple, she sent.

Same here. Thanks for the offer. We just might take it.

Meira blinked back more tears. *I can't just leave you here.* Her desperate anguish broke my heart.

Go home, I sent. *We'll work this out.*

She left at last, the gap sealing behind her. And I turned, to find the whole coven had risen as a body, come to stand in a semi-circle around us, from the oldest to the tiniest babe, eyes locked on me with hope shattered.

"There was no escape that way," I said. It was hard not to touch their magic as I always did, forced to rely on words and not the pressure of the coven's power. "But I promise you, all of you, we will be okay." Their pinched faces eased slightly. They trusted me still. But for how long? There was a time they didn't believe in me at all. Hopefully I'd given them enough proof of my commitment to them they wouldn't fall apart before I figured this out. "If it takes every ounce of power I have, I will keep you safe."

Their tentative smiles, hesitant nods, eased my mind. But not my heart.

I had to do something. And fast.

FIFTEEN

I took a step toward Quaid, ready to go back to the house and fetch the cache of money, when the ground under my feet began to shake. Galleytrot's howl jerked me to a halt at the same instant. I stared as he began to glow with faint green magic, eyes flaring with red fire. Ethie and Gabriel lurched awake where he'd lain beside them, eyes wide and staring. I rushed toward them, Quaid and my parents on my heels, as the great hound began to grow.

"Syd!" His huge voice like a spring thunderstorm boomed through the cavern. "The Wild Hunt is waking."

Damn it, now? Perfect freaking timing.

I gathered Ethie into my arms, Quaid releasing my silver Persian to hoist Gabriel as Mom and Dad hovered next to us. Sassafras scampered to me to sit on my feet, tail thrashing.

"Do something." He looked up at me, amber eyes sparking with magic.

I gritted my teeth, reaching deep beneath me to touch the Wild Hunt. "I can't," I said, hating it was true as Shaylee struggled to soothe and calm the trapped spirit of her love and his enchanted hunters. "The move was too much, the smothering of power broke the tether. They're rising."

Galleytrot howled again, the black hound reaching massive height, shoulders arching up toward the perma light.

I promised them, Gwynn and his people. I said they could sleep, safe and protected, in my back yard. And I failed them. There was no way I was going to let them tear this place apart, my family unprotected. Or, once risen, leave the Wild Hunt vulnerable to possible use and control under the Brotherhood. Belaisle would be invincible with all that magic at his control.

There had to be another way.

One, Shaylee sent, hesitant. *If they will agree.*

And it was she who reached for the veil this time, who opened the way. To the Sidhe realm.

The scene before me gave me hope and a further dash of anxiety. The worry was born from the dead, flat look on the queen of the Seelie's face. Aoilainn still blamed me for the loss of her daughter, though it was she who had her put to death on false pretenses. But my surge of maybe this might work rose from the way Odhran, king of the Unseelie and Aoilainn's counterpart, met my eyes with his.

"Sydlynn Hayle," he said in his deep voice, the waves of the ocean crashing against a rocky shoreline, dark brow heavy over his eyes. "You have need?"

How did he know? "Here's the deal," I said, abandoning any and all attempt to be formal. That would take time, the flowery, double talk of the Sidhe just too much for me to handle right now. "The Brotherhood control the North American territory—and maybe the whole plane. I had to move our family to save them. And the Wild Hunt is rising." Both monarchs blinked at me. "Too fast for you?"

Odhran's scowl wasn't aimed at me. "How can we assist?"

Aoilainn glanced sideways at him, but didn't make the same offer. Screw her. Shaylee's mom was a bitch and always would be.

Agreed, Shaylee sighed in my head. *But we need her if this is to work. Allow me.* I felt her gently nudge me aside and let her do so, though I cast a quick glance at Galleytrot, who had stopped growing and stood, panting, over the cowering coven.

"Mother," Shaylee said, "dear Odhran. The time of the Wild Hunt must end."

She said *what*? That was possible?

Aoilainn's brow quirked, a tiny frown in her perfection. The ground beneath me heaved at the same moment, making me stumble. We had minutes, if that. She must have seen it. And yet, the Seelie queen simply shrugged.

"They were created to cleanse that plane," she said, cool and precise. "When the time of the humans was done and we could again reclaim our original home."

Odhran nodded slowly, though he seemed far more concerned. "Aoilainn is correct," he said.

They couldn't be serious. "Listen up," I snapped, shoving Shaylee aside. "Your little plan to take back this plane is how freaking old now?" Neither commented. "Does it really look like we're going away any time soon?" I snapped my fingers at them. "Either disband the Wild Hunt or I send them through after you."

I'd never threatened Odhran before, and didn't really want to. We'd been allies pretty much since the first time he tried to intimidate me. But, damn it, my family was locked in this cavern with the Wild Hunt about to rise and I would not expose them by making them leave.

Would. Not.

"Don't push us, Sydlynn," Aoilainn said.

Oh no, she did *not*. "I'll push you so hard your whole realm falls to pieces around you." Okay, so I snapped. Sue me. "I've saved your sorry Sidhe asses how many times now? Deal with your mess. Or I'll deal with you.

Permanently."

Syd. Temper.

Even Odhran didn't like that so much. "While we owe you, it's true," he said, leaning back in his throne as their stupid magic tried to destroy the floor under me and Galleytrot stomped one step closer, "you have not earned the right to order us in our own realm."

Shut. Up. I could feel the vein in my forehead throbbing, the need to leap through and show the two of them just what I thought of their arrogance so powerful I was shaking. Or was that the damned floor again? Hard to tell.

Galleytrot saved me the trouble. He bent his now massive, boulder sized head and glared through the tiny gap at the pair of Sidhe monarchs.

"Bring us home," he rumbled, the pressure of his voice blowing Aoilainn's hair back, rattling the dishes on the elaborate table where they sat, tearing one of the gauze curtains behind the queen almost in half. "Now."

Odhran opened his mouth to speak just as a tall, Goth-like Sidhe stormed into view. She spun to face me, expression furious, spiked black hair vibrating. Though when Queen Niamh of the Unseelie spoke, I knew it wasn't me she was angry with.

"Sydlynn Hayle," she said, dark rimmed eyes as black as Galleytrot's, "ignore these fools. Send the Wild Hunt home. They were our problem when they were first created and we will take responsibility for them once again."

They were what? "I thought the Wild Hunt was created to cleanse this plane?" That was what I was taught, what the pair of frowning but slightly guilty looking monarchs behind me had just said. Don't tell me I'd been lied to all this time.

I would not be happy.

Even Galleytrot seemed confused. "I know not what you mean, great queen of the Unseelie," he boomed.

She sighed, cocked one hip, fist resting on the shining, skin tight leather hugging her tall, lean body. Niamh gestured with the other, a dark sprite who reminded me more of a rock star than a Sidhe queen.

"You wouldn't," she said. "Great hound, you were added to the Wild Hunt a century after Gwynn ap Nudd went mad and we were forced to remove him and his supporters from our realm."

Went mad? Shaylee gasped in my head. "Over my death." She spoke through me, but Niamh must have known it was the former Sidhe princess. Killed by her people over the supposed blood magic attack on her sister, Cydia. A lie, a jealous untruth on Shaylee's wedding day that ended her life.

"They made the story all pretty, over time," she said, glaring over her shoulder at her fellow monarchs. Her husband looked decidedly uncomfortable. "Convinced themselves it was their design originally. But I was there when they worked together for the first time in the history of the Sidhe." Her tone softened, face, too. "Shaylee, when you died, Gwynn blamed himself. His grief was so powerful he gathered a group of fellow Sidhe, Seelie and Unseelie, and created the Wild Hunt himself as a punishment for the Sidhe for destroying his true love."

Well, how do you like them apples?

"Send them home, Syd," Niamh said. "It's time."

Good thing she thought so. Because Gwynn ap Nudd chose that exact moment to surface.

The floor cracked at last, sending shards flying everywhere. I did my best, my demon assisting, to shield the family as a giant hole opened in the floor. Galleytrot turned, a mournful howl rising from him when a huge black horse, eyes flaming red like the hound's, burst from the ground. The tall, blond Sidhe on his back rode forward, the Wild surging after him, though the space could not contain them. A handful of hounds, like Galleytrot but of much smaller stature, loped out of the ground to stand at their master's feet.

I breathed a soft sigh of relief at the muffled feeling of the Wild Hunt. Even they were being controlled by the power of the wards, though the moment it began to rain, a soft, miserable drizzle over all of us, I knew Gwynn wouldn't allow such controls to keep him and his people contained for long.

"Shaylee." His voice sounded hollow, as though coming from a great distance, face blank and cold.

"My lord," Shaylee said. "My love."

His eyes shifted to Galleytrot. "We were meant to rest," he said. "Has the time come so soon?"

"No, my lord," the big hound said. "We are to be freed at last."

Gwynn's whole body twitched, the hounds at his feet whining softly as his black steed stomped one fore hoof. "Explain."

I drew a breath, let Shaylee take over. "Your time here has come to an end," she said, slowly approaching him, forcing my body into calm though I fought her a few times and my demon snarled her worry. "Your hurt and pain have gone on long enough, my love. Surely you are ready to return home?"

Gwynn's expression finally altered. I could see now the line of riders waiting in the hole behind him, the Wild Hunt ready to rise and destroy at his calling. But even some of those looked suddenly hopeful, where once only darkness held their terrible beauty in thrall.

"How is this possible?" His face crumpled. "You are gone and I have nothing."

"You have your life," she said. "A life everlasting. And your punishment has gone on long enough." She pushed us forward again, to press one hand to his thigh, the hounds sniffing around us, shivering flank of his horse next to our cheek. The scent of a summer thunderstorm and the zinging touch of coming lightning almost broke her hold, but she clung to him and I clung to her, hoping she knew what she was doing. "Darling Gwynn," she said. "Your rest is ended. Life must begin again."

"I would remain with you." Hope blossomed in his eyes and the entire power structure of the Wild Hunt sighed, what little made it through the wards. The rain stopped, a faint mist rising as the temperature warmed to a summer's afternoon.

"You must go to the realm," she said with gentleness I would never have been able to muster. "And I must abide here."

At first I was sure he was going to flip out and go on a stormy spree of destruction. But he finally sighed, looked up and past Galleytrot. To Niamh and Aoilainn and Odhran. He saluted, his horse snorting. "My queen," he said, voice full of sorrow. "I would come home again."

And that was that, right? I turned, stared Aoilainn down. She could ruin everything, with one selfish word. But her face twisted in sorrow of her own as she bowed her head.

"Return, Gwynn ap Nudd," she said. "Reminder of what I have lost. And be welcome."

I stepped back as Gwynn's horse pranced past me, to

one side. The coven remained tucked against the walls, staring as, one by one, the riders of the Wild Hunt, their faces now glowing with joy where once they'd held only the desire to destroy, passed through the gap in the veil.

The hounds followed, panting, heads down, leaving, at last, only Gwynn behind. Galleytrot shrank in size as the procession passed him, until he was again just the big dog I knew so well. My heart tore as I realized setting free the Wild Hunt meant he would most likely be going with them.

What would I tell the kids? I crossed to Quaid and my children, Ethie's arms wrapping around my neck, weeping. They'd lost their home and what stability they knew. Their little hearts would shatter to lose Galleytrot now.

"He's leaving, isn't he?" She buried her little face in my shoulder before bravely looking up, watching as Gwynn dismounted from his horse and approached Galleytrot.

The big Sidhe fell to one knee before the hound, gold armor clanking on the stone as he did. Oversized, the pair of them, a knight of old and his faithful dog. My throat tightened and I kissed Ethie's forehead, ready to say goodbye to my friend.

"Galleytrot." Gwynn's hand settled on the hound's shoulder. "I've missed you in my sleep, faithful one."

"And I you, my master," the big dog said. "But I've

had comfort with these witches," he nodded toward me, "and their children."

Gwynn glanced sideways at me, eyes widening at the sight of Gabriel clinging to Quaid. "A Gateway?"

That shook me. "How did you know?"

Gwynn sighed, stood, one hand on Galleytrot's head. "Keep him safe," he said, sorrow in his tone. "He will be the savior—or the downfall—of all." The big Sidhe saluted my son. "Think well of me, from time to time, Lord of the Gateway. Gwynn ap Nudd will always be at your service."

Gabriel saluted back, bowed his head, face grave.

Gwynn paused one more moment, eyes locked on mine. "Farewell, Shaylee," he said. "I will wait for you. But you are right." He looked down at his gauntleted hands. "I've been too long in despair." He strode for the edge of the veil, Galleytrot at his heels, head hanging low, not looking at us.

I cuddled Ethie close, not wanting her to watch, only to see my son wriggle from Quaid's arms and run for the hound. He grasped Galleytrot around the neck, looking up at Gwynn who towered over Gabriel like a statue.

"Please, sir," my son said in his sweet voice. "Can't he stay?"

Gwynn's face broke into a smile, shocking me. "Galleytrot," he said, a hint of happiness in his voice. "Is this what you wish as well?"

The big dog shuddered slightly, sank to his haunches. "You know I was once a terrible man," he said. "With a heart as black as any you'd encountered." Gwynn nodded. "But this life you've given me, as a hound, has served its purpose. Even more so since my time spent with the Hayles." The big dog turned to look down into Gabriel's eyes. "I've grown to love this family," he said, massive voice quiet for once. "And though if you needed me I would go with you, I would ask instead you grant my boon to guard them as I guarded you, my lord."

Gwynn nodded, a real smile on his face. "Then," he said, "like I, dear hound, you are free."

Without another word, Gwynn crossed over the veil and stepped into his realm for the first time in millennia.

Niamh nodded to me. "Be well, Sydlynn Hayle," she said. And sealed the way between us.

Silence met the closing of the veil, and for a long moment no one said anything or moved, as a boy and his dog hugged in the fading mist, the only sound the soft panting of the hound and the quiet weeping of my son.

SIXTEEN

I left my children in my parent's capable hands, with a good scratching for Galleytrot and a quick hug.

Thank you. I sent it directly to him, worried he might not hear me.

No, his big mind reached mine even through the wards. *Thank you, Syd. For the first time in my life, I have a home. And I didn't want to give it up.*

More tears, damn it. I wiped at them and took my husband's hand. "Let's go home ourselves," I said.

The veil welcomed me, and I it, the shivery membrane hugging me tight as Quaid and I traveled the short distance to our house in Wilding Springs. I stepped out into the basement and immediately shuddered.

Empty. All of it quiet and dark and lifeless. The family magic was gone.

It took me a moment to remind myself all that power

was safe with the coven, back in the cavern. That this house that had been our home was just a shell, now. A place of wood and concrete, filled with stuff but without life. Is this what normal's houses felt like? Of course it was. I'd been in enough I knew that was true. Still, I shivered. How could they stand it?

Because they didn't know any different.

Quaid's power reached for mine and from the way his face visibly eased from tension I knew he was embracing his magic's return as much as I was. Shaylee was quiet, and I hardly blamed her, the other two egos comforting her as I wrapped us in shields and headed for the north corner.

And froze at the mess before me. The Brotherhood—or someone—had been here, torn apart boxes and scattered china still packed after years. Shard of glass threatened my feet before Quaid caught my arm, pulled me back.

We circled around, found a few boxes, also ripped wide, but bearing old clothes we'd meant to send to charity. It felt good to slide into a pair of jeans, to slip on a fresh t-shirt and scuff my feet into a rather wretched—but still comfortable—pair of discarded sneakers.

My toes were immediately happy with this change of events.

I would have used magic to clear away the destruction under normal circumstances. Instead, Quaid and I, he now also dressed in a shirt I remembered from before we were married and jeans with a giant hole in one knee, had to pick our way through the slivers and chunks of broken china. Bits rang as my feet shoved them aside, searching the dark with my demon's eyesight, rendering the space almost lit like daylight despite the growing night outside the basement windows.

We worked in silence, pulling free broken hunks of furniture, Quaid heaving an old rug out of my way. It felt so still here, so oppressive, I didn't want to break the quiet with words and I suppose he felt the same way.

By the time we reached the back corner, I realized two things. One, the cement block protecting the cache hadn't been discovered. So a big phew moment. At least, until understanding number two hit me like a freight train doing a hundred miles an hour on fire.

The marker for X marks the spot had vanished.

Batsheva Moromond's mummy was gone.

I think Quaid must have made the realization the same moment I did, because he stared at the spot with his mouth open. I reached out and tapped his chin, his teeth clicking together as I sighed and shrugged.

My fault. I should have put the old bitch out in the sun when I had the chance instead of leaving her down here, gathering mold. She'd tried to kill me multiple times, it seemed only fair to make her suffer. And now, she was out of my control again, likely in the hands of the

Brotherhood.

Not good. Not good at all.

Whatever. I'd deal with her later. For now, I bent over the concrete floor and fished around for what we really came for.

This took a little subtlety. I had to use magic to unseal the hidey hole, just a breath of it, carefully shielded. Quaid kept watch over his shoulder, though I felt him moving away from me, possibly searching for anything valuable he could take to the family. More blankets, old clothes, pillows. Our lives now revolved around the barest creature comforts, so I hardly blamed him.

Pale blue flames flared around a square of floor before lifting gently into the air and settling beside the hole with barely a rattle. I breathed a sigh of relief before reaching in a liberating the large black, square can inside. I'd left the key in the lock, not even thinking someone would stumble on it. And good thing they hadn't. There was maybe only five thousand dollars and a small sheaf of personal bonds, but it should be enough to keep us going for a while.

I stuffed the wad of bills into my jeans, the bonds sliding under my t-shirt and into my waistband at the back. Maybe I should have resealed the hole, but whoever had been here came up empty already and there wasn't anything left to take.

The stairs creaked behind me. I turned, watched

Quaid going up, though he didn't look any more upset or worried than normal, so I followed him. Ran into him at the top of the steps, looking around his wide shoulder at the destruction in the kitchen. More broken dishes, the table on its side, cracked down the middle, chairs shattered into kindling. We'd spent so many hours at that table, since I was sixteen years old. Memories flashed through my head, eating cookies with Mom, helping Meira with her homework. Talking to Alison for the first time. Planning the salvation of the Universe with all my friends waiting and ready to help. My life revolved around this house.

And the Brotherhood tried to destroy it.

At least the walls were still standing, even if the cupboards were ripped from the studs, the front door glass shattered. Quaid moved to the hall, me trailing behind him, one of my fingers hooked in his back pocket. The living room was a flurry of stuffing, the sofa and chairs all shredded, giant holes in the walls. As if Belaisle took our escape out on our things when he couldn't have us. My sneakers squeaked on the first step as we climbed to the second floor. I winced at the state of Ethie's bedroom, though I went inside anyway, her pink chandelier—mine, once—in a shattered mess in the middle of her torn mattress. The contents of her closet were strewn on the floor, some of her things wrecked, but I managed to find one of her little backpacks and fill it with clothing for her.

I met Quaid in the hall. He was just leaving Gabriel's room, a bag of his own in his hands. Great minds. Yeah, right.

We paused outside our bedroom, looking in, and for the first time I let out a little cry of hurt. This was Mom's room before I became coven leader. It still vaguely smelled like her, lilacs lingering. But we'd made it our own when we got married. I loved this room, the feel of it, the way Quaid's and my power mingled here.

Empty now, like the rest of the house. Our beautiful four poster he'd made with his own hands and magic was crushed and broken on the carpet, the mattress tossed against the far wall. Both end tables were upside down, drawers emptied out. I ignored the little things, just stuff. But the sight of the antique dressing table Quaid had given me for my birthday four years ago shattered, the mirror in shards scattered as far as the bathroom tile, for some reason finally broke me.

I turned with a sob and clung to my husband. His arms pulled me tight to his wide chest, voice soft as he whispered words I didn't hear into my hair. This was our home. Where we lived and loved and had our family. Where I grew up finally, after trying my hardest not to.

I thought it would always be home. Fooled myself, really.

Time to let it go.

I finally pulled back from him, sniffling, wiping at my running nose. He bent and handed me a tissue from a box lying crumpled at our feet and I blew aggressively into it.

"It's not just here," he said, voice cracking. "The whole town feels lost. Doesn't it?"

I hadn't reached out yet, didn't have the courage. But now, I had to. And met head on what he meant.

Wilding Springs had been built by a Gatekeeper, a Sidhe soul carrying family, the O'Danes, that power buried in the very fabric of the town, protecting it. Keeping it safe from harm and expansion, and from the locals noticing anything was amiss.

When I closed the Gate after Liam's death, I worried Wilding Springs would change. But it didn't. Likely due to the fact the Wild Hunt lived under our house, and the power of the coven's magic—and my maji wards— continued where the Gate's energy left off.

I'd taken the family magic with me when I stripped everyone from town to safety. Including the Wild. Leaving Wilding Springs alone and unshielded. Normal. With a gaping hole where magic used to be.

It was almost enough to crack my shell again, but I held on. Maybe our home wasn't anymore. But I wouldn't let the people of this town down. I'd find a way to come back, to salvage what I could. To take back Wilding Springs.

The thought filled my heart suddenly, drove me to a moment of excitement. To hope.

"We'll be back." I looked up into Quaid's eyes, saw his surprise, then his determination.

"Damned right we will," he said. "This is home, Syd. And they can't take that from us."

"We could run," I said, one hand on his chest. "We could find a place to start again. And leave the council idiots to their mess."

He nodded. "But."

That made me laugh, despite the new tears that tracked down my cheeks. "Since when have we ever backed down from a fight?" I sighed, stepped away from him, slinging Ethie's bag over my shoulder. "We stand our ground. And we take our territory back."

Quaid hugged me from behind. "I have an idea," he said. I turned toward him. "I still have some friends in the Enforcers." I wondered at times if he missed being one of them. He'd left, thanks to some stupid law keeping us apart. And though I knew he loved me, it was the one thing the two of us didn't talk about. "I can't believe they are all in on this. Which means there's probably some kind of resistance movement in the works."

I didn't have the heart to tell him he was probably wrong. And, what did I know?

Witches. I knew witches. And didn't trust them to do the right thing, ever.

Still, if that was what he wanted. "Let's go back," I said. "Then we'll figure out what to do next."

I led this time, stopping to go back, to search the drawers of the bathroom vanity where I found, tucked carefully into an old sock, the slumbering crystal I'd given so much power to it had developed a soul, held all of my magic on the Stronghold plane while Demetrius asked me to sacrifice everything to save the Universe, only to have my magic returned through this very crystal. It shivered as I prodded it gently, embraced me with excitement.

They hadn't found it. And now, it was safe with me. I smiled at Quaid, real hope in this one discovery and he held out his hand to me with a grim one of his own.

I was half way down the stairs, fingers stroking the angles of the crystal, when I froze in place at the sight of a black tunnel appearing just inside the living room. I hissed at Quaid, reaching for the veil, only to freeze in place and gape as a tall, handsome man with flowing blond hair in a gray coat stepped out. The lovely woman beside him looked familiar, but I was already hurtling myself down the stairs and into Piers Southway's arms.

He hugged me tight, thin dress shirt soft under my cheek. "Nice to see I haven't lost my touch," he said, winking as I pulled away.

I laughed, Quaid, too, despite Piers's usual innuendo that typically raised a frown from my husband.

We all felt it the same instant, the pressure of

approaching power. The Brotherhood must have sensed Piers's appearance and were coming to investigate. I jerked open the veil as a wave of darkness crashed into the house. With one hand holding Piers and the other pushing Quaid, I dragged us all into the gap and sealed it behind me just before the sorcery hit.

Let Belaisle suck on that failure like a popsicle from hell.

SEVENTEEN

We stepped out in the cavern and Piers immediately gasped, staggering forward and into me.

"What the bloody hell just happened?" He stared at me with huge gray eyes, lips thin from stress. I had no idea the cavern also suppressed sorcery.

Good to know.

"Sorry about that," I said, releasing his hand as Mom and Dad came forward with the kids. I handed off Ethie's bag before turning to face the sorcerer and his guest. "Only way to keep the family safe." I punched his shoulder, feeling a wash of relief he was okay. "I take it you know what's happening?"

He shook his head, a rough gesture for polished Piers, the young woman beside him distressed. I took a closer look at her as he spoke, the brief flames in her brown eyes making me frown.

Where had I seen her before?

"Sydlynn Hayle," Piers said, ignoring my question in favor of his British politeness. "May I introduce Zoe Helios."

I gasped out loud as the wheels in my head clicked together and I finally realized from where I knew her. She raised one hand to say hello, presumably, but I was already in front of her, arms around her, squeezing her tight as I breathlessly whispered in her ear. "Fire girl."

It was her. From the back yard. The young woman on fire who saved our skins.

She hugged me back, tentative at first, then with more pressure. "Sorry about running off like that," she said. "I was in the middle of something." Her nose wrinkled as she smiled. "But I promised Iepa I'd save you." She looked around as I gaped again at the mention of the maji woman who Fate had sent to mentor and guide me. I hadn't seen her in years. Zoe knew her? "I'm happy to see I made it in time. I wasn't sure I had."

"You were a little busy burning up and everything." I grinned at her and she grinned back. "Nice to see you're okay, too."

A tiny frown pulled at her brows. "I am," she said. "Though, for whatever reason, I've lost my ability to see the future." Her hand sneaked into Piers's. His fingers wound around hers and he pulled her tight to his side as she went on. "I woke, perfectly fine, but the fire…" Her distress made me sad for her. "I can't call the flames. Or my foresight."

It had to be the Brotherhood. "I'm sorry," I said. "But maybe when we get this mess sorted out, I can help." I met Piers's eyes. "Where's Tallah?" And Shenka. And Charlotte and Sage…

"No idea," he said. "I found Zoe at the beach where we met in secret from her family. Only her mother and I were there when she rose from the coals." He sounded stunned by that fact. "By the time we made it back to Hensley house, everyone was gone." Guilt colored his words. "We searched for her and her family, but…"

I squeezed his hand, sympathy aching inside me. "It's not your fault," I said. "I'm just glad you made it out okay." I turned to Zoe. "You're mother?"

"Safe," she said. And nothing more.

Okay, then.

Piers's frown deepened. "Okay," he said. "Now your turn. Tell me. What the hell?"

It was down and dirty, my explanation, but Piers got the gist quickly enough, hissing his fury at the turn of events, while Zoe's free hand rose and covered her mouth.

"Liander is pure evil," she said. "He drained the maji, Gaia, used her power to his own advantage while controlling and manipulating my people." She paused a moment, distress powerful. "He used us against you, Syd.

I'm so sorry."

Well, that explained a lot. The cheating ass. But, I'd been without the benefit of seeing the future all along and still kicked his scrawny butt. No reason I couldn't do it again.

So there, worry. Take a freaking hike already. I had work to do.

"We've been trying to reach you," Piers said. "But I've been hitting roadblocks like mad." His arm tightened around Zoe, as though to unconsciously protect her from something. "I'm pinned down here, no access to Europe or any of the other territories. I can make short distance tunnels, but I run into walls and have to step out again. Usually in the middle of nowhere."

"Belaisle's control of the Council power is keeping you out," I said. "Has to be. Though, as a sorcerer, I wonder how he knows the difference?"

Piers sighed. "I spent some time in his not so tender mercies. It's possible he tagged my power somehow." I wanted to ask, but left it alone. We'd have a drink when this was over and talk about it.

Or not. But the drink? Hell, yeah.

"I didn't think we'd make it here," he said. "But I found a crack and shimmied through it."

"Probably left on purpose." Quaid ran one hand through his dark hair. "Enforcer tactics, lure you in and trap you." He shrugged. "It's what I would have done."

"And it would have worked," Piers said. "If you hadn't been there to open the veil and pull us out."

Zoe shivered. "There's more to tell you," she said, fear on her face. "I've seen things, Syd. I've been seeing visions of you for my entire life." She swallowed visibly, her distress a living thing as she clung to Piers, though I doubted she was weak, just tired and stressed. "There was a time I thought you the enemy. That I was told you were the Dark One."

Typical Brotherhood. "I take it you came to see the error of your ways?"

"I did," she said. "Thanks to Piers and Charlotte. They made me question everything." She stepped away from Piers at last, came to me, gripped my hands in hers. The flames were back in her eyes and I wondered if her power was as lost as she thought. "When I finally understood I was being manipulated, I pushed my visions, tested them for truth. And what I saw…" She bit her lower lip. "Fire, Syd," she said. "Burning witches, whole families of them. And cities in flame."

I choked on any kind of reply. I had no idea what to say to that.

"We need to act," Quaid said. "I'm going to contact my Enforcer friends."

I turned and nodded to him while Piers cleared his throat.

"Have you spoken to anyone outside this territory?"

Was he worried about his family? The Steam Union followed the leadership of his mother, Eva Southway. And while I wasn't the blonde ice queen's biggest fan, nor she mine, I could understand why he would be afraid for her. After all, the Steam Union accepted a great number of ex-Brotherhood members after Belaisle's defeat. I always worried their defection might be a ruse, a way to plant themselves in the Steam Union. But Eva wasn't listening to my counsel and it was her choice to handle things the way she did.

Still, Piers was right. I had to get outside North America and see what was going on. If the whole world had gone insane, or if it was just us. And I knew the perfect person to contact first.

"Your trip is going to have to wait," I said to Quaid. "I'm going to Europe. It's time to talk to Femke."

Quaid wasn't happy with me leaving him behind, especially when Piers insisted on joining me.

"I need to know what's happening with the Steam Union," he said. "Just the two of us, in and out. Yes?"

Honestly, I could use the backup. And though Quaid was already opening his mouth to protest, Zoe stepping away and hugging herself, resigned look on her face, I took the sorcerer up on his offer.

"Mom," I said, turning and gesturing her forward. "Take care of Zoe. We'll be right back." The last was aimed at Quaid. His scowl said we'd talk about this later.

Okay then.

This is risky, I sent to Piers as we stepped into the veil, his hand in mine. *For all we know, Femke is compromised.*

Only one way to find out, he sent, his usual cheerful cheekiness dulled by worry.

Right-o.

My target destination appeared before me as I cut my way out the other side of the veil, traveling through it without solidifying where I was going until the last moment. Paranoid much? You betcha. Especially now, with so much at stake.

The tall, stunning blonde behind the desk gasped and ran for me, arms wrapping around my neck, her pale blue eyes full of worry as Femke almost cracked a rib in her need to squeeze me.

"Syd!" She let me go in a rush, making me wobble, off balance as she lunged for my sorcerer friend. "Piers." From his wince she hugged him just as hard before spinning back on me. Her lean body quivered with emotion, face almost hollow with worry. "I'm so glad you're all right. We feared the worst."

Did Femke know already? "We're fine," I said. "Though from the looks of things, we're the only ones."

Her brow furrowed, her blue eyes darting back and forth between us. "Something is horribly wrong," she said. "That's all we know." She scrubbed at her face with both slim, long fingered hands. "Approximately two days ago, we were abruptly cut off from the North American territory and there has been no communication in or out since." Her lips thinned as she hunched her shoulders, sinking to sit on the end of her big desk. Warm overhead lights cast a pale yellow glow over her washed out face. The sky outside was dark, full night here four hours ahead at her headquarters in Oxford. "And worse," she said, looking up at Piers, real grief in her eyes, "we've had no contact from the Steam Union despite our attempts to reach your mother."

I feared as much. "We have a lot to tell you," I said. "And only a little time." A great sense of urgency kept me from sitting in one of the comfortable chairs in her office. Instead, I took to my favorite stress time passion, pacing.

Piers sank into a wing back as I proceeded to throw the whole mess into Femke's lap. She gasped once, cheeks even paler than before, but heard me the whole way through before saying anything, as she always did.

"The dull feeling," she whispered. Coughed and cleared her throat, voice cracking. "You were right."

"Sassafras was." I nodded, suddenly tired. I'd pushed myself to my limits and kept going, at least when it came to my magic. I had no idea how long it would take before I crashed. My invincible nature seemed to sustain me no matter how hard I shoved and kicked and scratched my way to the end. I only hoped that was still the case, even after all the energy I expended.

"The Brotherhood own North America," I said at last, coming to a halt before her. "We have to find a way to make sure that ownership is as short and painful for them as possible."

Femke lurched to her feet, circling her desk. "I'll summon the other world leaders," she said, voice shaking slightly, but with fierceness in every word, every gesture. "We'll deal with this, Syd. I promise you."

I glanced down at Piers, only then noticing he had chewed one nail to the quick and was working on the next, squinting into the distance, mind elsewhere. I set one hand on his shoulder, catching his attention. "Do you want to try to find your mother?"

He stood immediately, shaking his head, but not speaking.

Femke's worried expression told me she wished he'd said yes. Maybe I should have pushed him harder, but, like Mom said, the family came first.

"Syd," Femke returned around her desk and came to my side. "You know the Hayle coven has a refuge here. We are happy to help in any way we can."

I smiled at her, but the word "refuge" led to "refugee" in my head and I just couldn't bend my pride enough to let that sit well. Not my coven. And besides, I'd already made my decision about taking back our home. I'd find them a safe place, somewhere neutral, where we were in control and not at the mercy of other witches.

Did I say paranoid? Yup yup.

"Thanks," I said. "But I have it handled."

She hugged me again, embraced Piers one last time before stepping back. "It shouldn't take long to assemble the leaders," she said. "Give me until morning and, by the elements, I'll have them here or I'll have their asses."

I saluted her, managing a grin. "No doubt," I said. "Stay safe."

She shivered, hugged herself. "You too, my dear friend."

Piers's hand squeezed mine as we stepped back into the veil.

Where now? His mind was in a frenzy behind the thin veneer of calm he allowed me to feel. But he couldn't hide from me.

You're sure about your mother? I didn't want to deal with her, but maybe we should check in.

I'm sure, he sent.

Okay, I sent. *Then there's a few other stops I want to make. People to see. If you change your mind—*

I won't. His refusal to talk about it made my mind up for me.

With a resigned sigh, I pulled us through the veil in search of vampires.

EIGHTEEN

I touched down on black carpet to the startled greeting of the Wilhelm blood clan monarchs. Sunny ran toward me, huge skirts rustling, Uncle Frank close behind her. I let the pair of them sandwich me in a hug and sank into the cool perfection of the vampires.

After a moment, they released me, greeting Piers with a kind kiss to the cheek from Sunny and a handshake from my uncle. Before I even opened my mouth, I saw the stress on their faces and hated they were worried.

"We're fine," I said. "The family, too."

Sunny looked surprised, then anxious. She and Uncle Frank exchanged a glance that told me I'd just made a massive assumption and now had other issues to worry about.

"What happened?" The three of us spoke at the exact same time, the exact words and tone. How well we knew each other.

"You first," I said, tired of telling my story while Piers hung back, clearly lost in his own worries. "What's going on?" Only then did I feel the discomfort in the air, the tension from the other court vampires watching us. Chambrelle Strait, Sunny's human servant and daytime representative, joined us with a nod to me, her thick, red hair in a tight knot at the base of her neck. I always felt a little intimidated by her size, tall and broad shouldered, and wondered if she knew how to throw her weight around.

"Some internal strife, I'm afraid," Sunny said. And then sighed as I wrinkled my nose at her.

"Seriously?" She was not getting away with the company line. Not with me.

"It's Piotr," Sunny said, voice dropping as she closed the circle for our ears only.

"Wilhelm?" The slimy bastard had betrayed me, betrayed her, over and over again in his misplaced continuing loyalty to his long-dead queen, Yvette. What was he up to now?

"Ever since Sebastian's attempts to help us evolve began, Piotr has been the most vocal against such a change." Sunny's beautiful face tightened, pale blonde hair in curls, shivering against her shoulders as she shook her head. "He's been more and more abusive and I finally decided to remove him from the family."

"About time," I muttered, though I knew better. Wasn't my business.

"No I told you so's, please," she said. "I had my reasons. Piotr and I... we've known each other for a very long time."

I didn't know that. "So, what did he do?"

"Two nights ago," I sensed a theme, here, "he and a group of my vampires defected. Abandoned the blood line. Cut ties and left the castle."

"Problem solved," I said.

Chambrelle's pale green eyes told me otherwise as Sunny let out a disgusted sigh.

"Not quite, Syd," the human woman said, as temper rose on her queen's face. "Such a breach in the family is... troublesome."

Sunny cut her off with a sharp gesture. "And challenges my authority as queen."

I felt for her, I really did. But it seemed petty, compared to what I was dealing with. "I hate to add fuel to the already blazing fire," I said. "But you're not going to like what I have to tell you, either."

Sunny and Uncle Frank stared at me in silent, frozen shock, not breathing or moving a muscle as I spoke while Chambrelle shook her head in disbelief. At least she moved. The two vampires creeped me out, honestly. When they were acting "normal" they pretended to be just like the living. But when they were surprised, vampires tended to stop faking life and fell into that statue-perfect mode that gave me the solid heebie jeebies.

Chambrelle saved me from shuddering and embarrassing them by speaking up.

"The Hayle coven must come here at once," she said. "The Wilhelm family will host you."

Sunny nodded, breaking the spell of her statue-like stillness while Uncle Frank sighed. "Yes, a brilliant idea," she said.

But I was already shaking my head. "Thanks," I said. "I really appreciate it. But you have your own troubles, and Wilding Springs is mine, damn it." My demon howled her agreement. "And I'm going to get it back."

Sunny hugged me again. "What can we do?"

I shrugged when she let me go. "I don't know," I said. "I honestly don't. I just wanted to see you, to tell you we were okay. And suggest you steer clear of North America for a while."

Uncle Frank kissed my forehead. "Thanks for the warning," he said. "Take care of yourself, kiddo."

"You, too." I stepped back. "Going to check in with Sebastian. I'll be back, probably tomorrow morning before the meeting of the world leaders."

They waved together, looking forlorn and about as lost as I felt as I pulled my companion into the veil with me.

But when we stepped out on the other side, into the

cold darkness of Castle DeWinter, I realized we had one more issue on our hands.

"Where is everyone?" Piers shivered, hand releasing mine to dive into the pockets of his longcoat.

I reached out with my power, searching the entire castle. As empty as my house back in Wilding Springs. "I have no idea." Okay, this was uber weird. *Sunny*, I sent.

I'm here. I could feel her moving through the castle. *What's wrong now?*

Did you know Sebastian and his vampires vacated their place? Why would they do that? It made no sense.

They what? Her forward motion jerked to a halt.

I showed her the empty throne room, let her feel the vacancy. *No clue?*

Not even a guess, she sent. Paused. *He's been quiet lately. But I assumed he was busy.* Her mind fretted against mine. *I'll have my people search for him. But Syd...* she paused again before rushing on. *The castle hosts a base of power, much like your family magic under your home. Do you feel it?*

I scanned, reached. Nothing. *Nope.*

Then something is wrong, she sent, now firm and queenly. *If he's stripped his home of its magic, he's running from something.*

Great. Just what I needed. *Can I help?* I really didn't need this, but Sebastian was important to me.

Go, she sent. *I'll handle it. And update you in the morning.*

She cut me off before I could say anything further, so I let it go.

"Okay," I said, holding out my hand to Piers. "One last stop. You ready?"

He nodded. "Could anything else go wrong, you think?"

I kicked his leg, gently. "Do not," I said, "say that out loud." And thought of the conversation I had with Meira. Felt a little guilty over it. She wished something would happen.

Doozyville, sister.

This time, when I emerged from the veil, it was onto a lush, green lawn in front of a giant palace. The two wereguards standing at the huge doors looked startled to see me, but bowed as I strode past, through the elaborate portal and into the inside of a Faberge egg. The werewolf palace always reminded me of old Russian royalty, the Ukrainian home of the werenation based on the tastes of the old Czars. I strode down the purple carpet toward the throne room, ignoring the wereguards who got out of my way.

I'd earned a little respect around here in the past.

Piers was as familiar with the place as I was and the two of us made a beeline toward the back of the vast foyer. The doors to the throne room were wide open, welcoming, lights blazing from crystal chandeliers overhead, casting a yellow glow over the giant werewolf in human form sitting on the throne. An equally large, if older, were sat next to him, their conversation broken as

Piers and I approached at a solid clip.

Danilo stood to greet me, his grandfather, Oleksander, the previous wereking, smiling as he joined his grandson. But that smile faded as I drew close and I could only blame his loss of good humor on the expression that had to be all over my face.

Danilo's frown pulled his heavy brows down across his dark green eyes. He looked nothing like his younger sister, Charlotte, but the unstoppable passion of her soul was mirrored in him.

A slim, older woman with my werefriend's blonde hair and blue eyes slipped around some wereguards and came to join us. I nodded to Charlotte's mother, Olena, before facing off with the wereking.

No niceties this time. And the telling had become smooth, practiced almost. So much so, I barely halted through their intakes of furied breath, their werewolfish exclamations of sorrow and rage.

By the time I was done, Danilo had partially turned into his wereform, fading back from a pronounced muzzle and clawed hands to human again before coming to me and grasping my shoulders in his massive hands.

"I will leave for Oxford immediately," he said, voice booming with conviction. "We will fight together, Sydlynn Hayle. And we will be victorious." Such a werewolf.

The wereguards lining the carpet all shouted a word

in Ukrainian I didn't understand. But I got the message. So loud and clear I teared up for the umpteenth time and firmly decided to do something magical about my waterworks first chance I got.

"Thank you," I said.

"No," he said, releasing me, massive shoulders swelling as he threw them back, tanned skin darkening his already angry expression, his heavy beard making him look ferocious, more bear than wolf. "Thank you. Our werenation owes you much. And, because of you, we've learned we are better served fighting together, using the strengths of those around us, than trying to do so alone."

Well, sheesh. Make a girl blush and everything.

Stupid tears.

Another few minutes of hugging and promises of help and Piers and I were retreating back out to the lawn. While I knew Danilo probably wouldn't care if I traveled from inside the palace under the circumstances, the rule was outside. After that little talk, I wasn't about to disrespect him or the werenation.

Piers took my hand voluntarily this time as our feet slipped over the soft grass, wet with dew. The air was cooler here, though it was still summer, and I breathed out a puff of pale mist as he spoke.

"Smart werewolf," he said. He seemed to have pulled himself together again, though his eyes were haunted. "We do need to work together." Was he thinking of his mother? Likely.

"Last chance," I said as I reached for Sunny. *We just left the werewolves*, I sent.

I assumed, she sent. *Is Danilo going to Oxford?*

That surprised me. *Are you?*

Of course, she sent. *Already on my way. Sebastian has managed to alter me enough I don't have to sleep at sunrise. So, as long as the room is free of sunlight, I will attend.*

Sunny. I could hug her. *You have your own troubles.*

If this Brotherhood infection spreads, she sent, *my troubles won't matter one bit. I'll see you at Femke's.* And then, she was gone.

Piers stared down at me, eyes intent. "Do you think talking to Mum would make a difference?"

He was asking me? "I don't know," I said.

"Neither do I." He squeezed my hand. "Let's go save your family."

I nodded, reached for the veil. Just as a black tunnel burst open right in front of me and a woman hurtled through and attacked me.

NINETEEN

I almost panicked, except I knew her face, her dark hair, the blue of her eyes. My grandmother, Ethpeal Hayle, looked like Mom, only a little older, though she'd aged from fear and weariness. I caught just a glimpse of her making it through before she grabbed me and wouldn't let me go.

Love attack. My favorite.

My heart wept as she rocked me, lips on my cheek, heart pounding against me. "Girl," she whispered in my ear. "Oh, girl."

"Gram." I'd spent a great part of my life with her witch power inside me, then several years leading the coven with her at my side. She'd sacrificed everything for the Hayle coven long before I was born and her mind shortly after my birth to a battle that stranded her power in my body. Freeing her from her insanity was one of the finest moments of my existence, after seventeen years lost and wandering in her broken mind. She was a sister of my soul and one of the few people who really understood me and the choices I'd been forced to make.

Feeling her tremble against me, the grasping of her hands on my back as though to reassure herself I existed still, made me weak kneed with guilt.

"Damn you." She leaned away, beautiful face far younger than the one she used to wear. I still missed the soft, white hair that had a life of its own, her wrinkled skin and faded blue eyes. The flower covered dressing gowns she used to wear, her favorite fuzzy socks. Most of all, I missed the connection of our magic, her witch power gone to protect the Universe from Ameline Benoit after that evil creature stole the majority of Gram's magic away to feed her rise to maji. Though Gram survived, her sorcery, long suppressed, awakened by her true love and husband, Demetrius Strong, it wasn't the same anymore. I loved her still. But my heart missed her every single day.

"Sydlynn." Speak of the devil, he came to me and hugged me when Gram finally let me go. "We were so afraid for you." His white cap of curls were the only indication of his age, sweet, cherub face kind and creased in worry. Crystal blue eyes held more innocence than ever. He, too, had been lost to insanity, tortured and turned from the Steam Union to the Brotherhood by Liander Belaisle, transformed back to the sorcerer Gram loved when he helped me defeat Belaisle in the final battle the Fates predicted. I'd gone from being repelled by him when he was the leader of the Chosen of the Light, to hating him for stealing my demon from me. To pitying the shell of a creature he became and, finally, loving him for all he endured and survived, only to save my grandmother from death.

I hugged him, too. "Where have you two been?" Not an accusation, not at all. Just worried wondering. After all, they were connected to the Steam Union. To the silent Eva Southway.

From the tension in Piers, he was as anxious for their answer as I was.

"It's not good," Gram said directly to my tall sorcerer friend. "I'm sorry, Piers. The Steam Union fell apart two days ago."

My jaw tightened. "Their timing is impeccable."

Both older sorcerers whipped their heads around and focused on me.

"We've been trying to reach you," Gram said, one shaking hand on my arm, though the former Enforcer and coven leader she was shone behind her blue eyes. "Is everyone all right?"

"Our family is," I said. "But I'm afraid the rest of the continent isn't so lucky."

When I was done repeating my story again, Gram's fists were tight at her sides, tears in Demetrius's eyes.

"I should have killed him when I had the chance," he said.

"We both should have," I said. "This isn't your fault, Demetrius."

He shrugged. "I had so many chances, Syd. Lost opportunities." The old sorcerer sighed. "But guilt won't save anyone now."

Great philosophy, that.

"My mother." Piers's words choked off as he drew a shaking breath. "My sister and father?"

Gram squeezed his arm, face compassionate but stern. "I don't know," she said. "We were away, felt the recoil in the Steam Union's sorcery. When we arrived at headquarters in Nottingham, the damage had been done."

"I'm guessing the former Brotherhood members who joined ranks with our people turned on us?" Piers's casual question was anything but. If he didn't let out his rage soon, he'd burst from it.

Demetrius nodded sadly. "We tried to warn her," he said. Stopped himself. "Guilt, again."

Gram kissed his cheek. "It's our birthright, I think sometimes."

Tell me about it.

"No news could be good news," I said, more for Piers's benefit. "Eva's clever and powerful. If you couldn't find her, it's possible she escaped."

Gram didn't argue, but she didn't agree with me

either. Bless her for not adding to my friend's worry. "We've kept our distance," Gram said. "Since you left, Piers." He bobbed his head. "She's become harsh, almost impossible to talk to."

"I know," he said, a single tear tracking down his cheek. He wiped at the moisture with a trembling hand before stuffing his fists into his coat pockets, shoulders hunched and rigid. I wished I could help him somehow. "It's part of the reason I left. And she never gave me a good enough excuse to come back."

"You, my boy," Gram said, linking her arm through his, "are not to blame for your mother's decisions. Or for standing up for what you believe in."

He didn't say anything, but the horrible tension in him eased a little.

"We could search for her." I had no idea where to start. If the Brotherhood had her, she'd be well shielded. And, knowing Eva, if she was safe somewhere, I'd never find her anyway.

Piers shook his head, leaned in to kiss Gram on the cheek. "Mum can take care of herself," he said.

"You're going back to Wilding Springs?" Gram and Demetrius almost looked eager.

I nodded. "I take it you'd like to join us." Nothing would make me happier.

Gram's grin had nothing to do with humor. "Figured it was time to pay Liander Belaisle a little visit," she said.

"By way of Erica's guts."

I laughed. I couldn't help it.

Gram was the best.

The moment we stepped through the veil and into the cavern, Gram went right to Mom, hugged her. I have no idea what the pair said to each other, but gave them space to say it. My kids, on the other hand, swarmed their great-grandmother, Ethie pawing at her namesake until Gram lifted the girl into her arms.

I took a few minutes to make the rounds, happy to see Quaid had put the cache of money to good use. Blankets and food and water had been distributed, fresh clothing as well. A few tents were set up, giving families privacy, a toilet facility cobbled together. It would do for now, but not for long. And how Quaid managed to drag a porta-potty in here with no one noticing was beyond me.

By the time I returned to the small knot of my immediate family, Gram was sitting with Ethie in her lap, Sassafras perched beside her. Demetrius sprawled on the ground at her feet, Piers a few feet further along the bench with Zoe in his arms.

Something clicked in my head and I kicked myself for missing it. The way they looked at each other, how he held her like that. Another of my suitors had finally found love. The one I never thought would settle for anyone.

Good for them, finding each other in this mess. I hoped we survived for them to see it through.

Quaid delivered a bottle of water to my grandmother who pulled him down for a kiss.

"Feel like taking a ride?" He glanced sideways at me. "My turn."

Right, his Enforcer friends.

"Where you thinking?" Gram winked at Ethie who winked back with child-like exaggeration.

"The Stronghold," Quaid said. "I want to track down Leader Tremere and see if there is anyone fighting back."

Gram nodded immediately, standing and setting Ethie back down in her place. She brushed dust from her long skirt and held out her hand to him. He took it like a gallant suitor, kissing the back while she grinned.

"Good choice," she said, staring right at me.

Why was I blushing, exactly?

They disappeared down the exit tunnel, heading for outside so Gram could carry them somewhere they could access the Stronghold. I fretted, knowing most of the access points were at Harvard. Instead of sharing my concern with those around me, I retreated myself, heading after them, toward the surface, just needing a minute alone now my present tasks were done.

You're never alone, my vampire sent, her mental voice soft.

Never, my demon sent.

We are here for you, Sydlynn, Shaylee sent. *As always.*

Thank you. I stopped at the entry, the way mostly

covered by a giant rock, magicked for ease of removal. The darkness called me and I couldn't resist, slipping out the thin crack and out into the grassy clearing on the other side.

Shields firmly in place, I sat with my back against the rock, knees up, staring at the stars overhead. Did they even know what was happening? Did anyone out there care? A weight like the entire world settled on me, pushing me down to slump, weak and frail under the pressure of the past two days.

He took advantage of me being away, I sent to my alter egos. *Liander.* I'd finally found time to wallow. Old habits were hard to break.

This was my fault.

I'm not even going to comment, my vampire sent, decidedly snippy.

Real piece of work, isn't she? My demon's mental voice burned and sizzled. *After all this time, still beating herself up over things out of her control. I thought we raised her better than that.*

Clearly not, Shaylee sent, sniffing in irritation. *We've failed utterly. What a disappointment.*

The chuckle that escaped me was answered by three other voices, all in my head.

Okay, I get the point. I hugged them together inside me. *Just figured a little poor me for old time's sake might make you nostalgic.*

My demon snorted. *If it got us somewhere, I'd be all for it.*

Agreed, my vampire sent. And sighed. *Options?*

We go to Harvard and challenge the council. My demon's temper burned hotter than mine.

I believe we've already agreed even we are not strong enough to take on all those witches and sorcerers. Shaylee shifted inside me. It had to be odd for her, I thought out of the blue. Of all of my egos, she'd lived a life before this one, had her own body. How strange it must have been for her to share mine.

"I thought I'd find you here." Sassafras's furry head nudged me until I stretched my legs out in front of me. He hoisted his fat cat body into my lap, looking up into my eyes. "Beating yourself up, are you?"

"Actually," I said with false arrogance, "I was figuring out how to save the Universe. Feel like chiming in?"

His tail thrashed. "Now that you mention it." Sass lowered himself, curling up on my thighs, head on his paws. "I'm open to suggestions."

"Sass," I said, hand stroking his fur in a slow motion. "Why do things always get to this hopeless stage before we seem to be able to do something about it?"

"Nothing is ever hopeless," he said. "You should know that by now."

"I guess so."

"Besides," he said, looking up at me, "you thrive on being the underdog. And don't tell me you don't."

That made me laugh all over again, partly because it was true. Was I really that much of a lone wolf, a free agent acting on whim and impulse, trusting my intuition and the incredible power I possessed to save me?

Oh dear.

SYDLYNN!

I jerked upright, Sassafras hissing at me, fur standing on end.

"Did you—"

He fell silent as the voice screaming my name reached me again.

HELP US!

I didn't think. Didn't pause or wait to act. Someone needed me. And the underdog in me couldn't say no. I was on my feet, Sass bundled against my chest, dodging into the tunnel before tearing at the veil to hide the power surge, long before my mind whispered to me to be careful.

TWENTY

You do realize this is most likely a trap. Sassafras's mental voice was calm, regardless of the panic I felt.

I know, I sent, sliding through the veil so fast I felt the pressure of suction against me just as the other end opened and I hurtled through. *But what choice do we have?*

My sneakers squeaked on marble tile as I landed in chaos.

It would appear, Sass sent as I ducked under a wave of blackness hurtling toward me, *none*.

I didn't have time to respond. My maji shields protected both of us from the oncoming wash of sorcery, deflecting most of it, absorbing the rest, giving me a boost as the dark flower beneath me blossomed and opened wide, the presence of other power like it waking my sorcery and making it hungry.

Sass hissed as I stumbled over something soft,

landing hard on my butt on the smooth, white floor. I caught my breath, taking in the sweeping staircases, one on either side of a large foyer, the old, dark stained wooden walls, the feeling of age in this place. Witches loved their old houses full of pretense. All the while chaos rippled around me.

I looked down, into vacant eyes, and bit back the shriek of fright that wanted to escape. The old woman whose body tripped me died with her hands outstretched, a terrified expression locked on her wrinkled face.

No time to mourn as a dozen or so black robed sorcerers swept toward me, driving back a thin line of witches, shouting and screaming tearing the air, numbing my hearing until I could barely distinguish individual voices. I recognized their leader as she turned her head, desperate eyes locked on me.

I lurched to my feet, Sass leaping free, my power gathered, ready to strike.

At the exact moment a spike of black drove itself through the center of Violet Rhodes' chest and sent her flying backward to crash to the marble floor.

I stared at her, stupid and shocked, while her witches gathered around her. The sight of the silver Persian scampering toward them drove me to move at last, my shining rainbow shields encompassing the handful of witches who huddled, shivering and terrified, around their fallen leader.

I wondered what Willa would think of sacrificing her sister and coven now.

My knees ached as I fell to them beside Violet, pulling her into my lap.

We have to get them out of here, Sassafras sent.

I reached for the veil, felt my power stutter and struggle. Damn it! Why did I have to reach my limit now, when I needed it most?

My throat tightened, the scent of smoke wafting toward me, the sound of screaming in the distance joined by the crackle of what had to be an approaching fire. They'd set the coven house ablaze, the bastards. I looked up and into the arrogant face of a young sorcerer I'd never seen before. But there was no doubt who he worked for.

"The master was right," he said. "You are weak and pathetic. Allowing your need to serve others to lead you right to us."

"How do you know I don't have you where I want you, kid?" I grinned at him, pushed against my shields. The row of sorcerers—all young, from what I could tell—backed off a half pace, faces flickering with fear.

I guess I still had it.

Their leader snapped his fingers and the group returned to their old position, though I could still feel their fear. And allowed my dark flower to bloom outward, past my shields to tuck under the feet of the

Brotherhood. It only took a second, but by the time the young sorcerer realized what I'd done, it was too late for them.

I'd never used my sorcery for this purpose before, partly because it freaked me out, made me feel unclean. But I knew how, sure did, thanks to Ameline and Belaisle. I'd seen it done a bunch of times, felt the exit of my own power through sorcery.

Desperate times, desperate measures. And though I worried I'd hate myself later, they'd left me no choice. With a gleeful burble, my sorcery latched onto the gathered Brotherhood, their power wide open as they tried to crush my shields, and drained them in one swift draw of energy.

They collapsed as a group, a choreographed ballet of falling young men, with barely a sigh as eyes rolled back into handsome faces, bodies appearing boneless and graceful as they fell to the white floor. Their leader held on the longest, a half heartbeat or so, enough his stare of shame made me sad.

Belaisle sent them, lambs to the slaughter, as much as he'd killed this family.

My sorcery burped softly, swelled with power, yearning and reaching for more—

Enough. My vampire cut it off. *Focus, Sydlynn.*

Like she had to tell me.

"Are there more of you who might have made it to

safety?" I looked around at the witches who now stared at me with desperate hope and horrible, broken despair.

"No," one said, so softly I almost didn't hear her past the thunderclap of someone's power echoing outside. "They surprised us two days ago, hit us before we could react. We've held out this long, thanks to Violet." Her voice shuddered speaking her fallen leader's name. "But we just couldn't combat them. They herded the rest of the family outside only a few moments ago." Her lower lip trembled, whole body shaking.

She's going into shock, Sass sent, leaping into her lap, purring and pushing his demon magic into the woman to keep her stable.

"What's outside?" I felt hollow, suddenly, as though someone had scooped me out with a giant spoon leaving only a terrible fear behind. The witch lifted her arm, pointed behind me. I turned, looked out the open door to the front yard.

And the stakes, at least a hundred of them, all ablaze, lighting up the sky. I wasn't seeing this, didn't catch the last few wriggling forms before they fell still, hear their dying screams echoing through the night and past the front door, punching through my horror with the keening of their final wails. No, I refused to smell the oily taint of crisping flesh carried in on the hot breeze pushed forward by the flames, washing me in death. My mind simply would not allow me to comprehend the stillness as the last of the bodies sagged into the giant blaze, all backlit by the raging fires.

Nor did I see the row of black robed Enforcers, hovering in the sky above, doing nothing to stop the large band of sorcerers watching the blaze.

I didn't. Couldn't have. Because if I really did, I'd lose my damned mind.

"Sydlynn." The whisper of my name whipped my head around. I looked down, the light from the bonfires casting a glow over the thin, wrinkled hand that rose, only to fall back to Violet's concaved chest. She bore no wound, but I could feel her life slipping away. I pushed energy into her, but the sorcerers had done their work well. Her soul was adrift, leaving her, unable to return to her stripped body even as her old eyes met mine.

"I beg you," she said, so softly I had to bend to hear her, drops of moisture pattering on her cheek as tears overwhelmed me. "Care for my family. And may the elements save us all."

I didn't get to respond, to swear to her with a fierce commitment that would have shattered bone and bent steel that I would never, ever let anything happen to her people again. The moment she finished speaking, Violet's soul finally sighed and left her at last, leaving the body a tiny, old woman I once adored lying in my aching arms.

They wept with me, the seven witches who were all that remained of the once mighty Rhodes coven, their heads bent, hands touching her fallen form in reverence and loss as the remains of their family burned just outside. She was a great leader, had protected and guided her family for many years. And though she was a stickler for the law, Violet had always been kind to me and stood up for me at times when no one else would.

So tragic her unspeakable loss would be one more footnote after this war was over. Make no mistake, we were at war. And our own people were letting it happen.

The pressure of power approaching behind me finally broke my sorrow and turned me around. Anger poured through my veins, my demon roaring, flames erupting around me as I released Violet's body to her people and stood, glaring my fury at the Brotherhood, but more so at the small number of Enforcers who joined them in the foyer.

My rage was aimed at them, the supposed protectors of our people. How many years had I been in awe of the Enforcers? Only to discover they were as weak as the rest of the witches who threw us to the wolves.

I had no idea which of them was leader, but I didn't care. As my demon's power flared, my black blossom begging to feed again, my vampire's cold rage rippling white around me, I let Shaylee loose instead.

The entire floor heaved, sending the Brotherhood to their knees while the Enforcers hovered, blue power holding them steady.

"I have never been so ashamed," I snarled, low and rumbling with as much power as I could pour into my voice, "as I am of you right now, at this moment."

"We have our orders." A tall, blond Enforcer, with a face I think I recognized, spoke up. But there was no conviction in his tone and I could tell from the quiver in his lips he was fighting his own battle with this.

I chopped one hand through the air, another rumble from Shaylee shattering the glass of the large plate windows just behind them. They started that time, shields flaring to repel the shards, though the Brotherhood, still recovering, weren't quite so fast. Hot air rushed into the foyer, bathing us all in sparks from the raging fires, the scent of charred meat and death feeding my fury.

"Arrest her!" One of the sorcerers jabbed a finger at me.

And I smiled at him. It wasn't a nice smile, not with my demon doing the smiling. "Come and get me."

None of them moved, though they swayed, as if considering their options.

Sydlynn. Sassafras's mind cut through my rage. *We have to go now. This fight must wait for another time. We have witches to protect. And an oath to fulfill.*

Damn him. Damn us all.

"Cowards," I snapped at the Enforcers. "When the Brotherhood are done murdering entire covens, who do you think they will turn on next?"

It was clear they'd thought of that, their nervousness showing as I punched a hole through the veil, using the power I'd stolen from the fallen Brotherhood to do the job. My knees wobbled, but I managed, crouching to grasp Violet's body with one hand. The sorcerers finally decided to risk it, a wall of black heading for us while the Enforcers continued to stand there, to watch.

To do nothing. I'd remember their faces. And I'd make sure if the Brotherhood didn't get them, they'd have their due handed to them if I had to deliver it myself.

With my small group of refugees right behind me, I dragged their dead leader's body through the veil and headed for home.

TWENTY-ONE

We burst through the other side, my power taking a second hit as the magic wards of the cavern pushed down against me. Not that I cared. My heart was far heavier, the gasps and cries of fear from my waiting coven only making things worse.

Mom was first to reach me, hands taking Violet's empty shell from my grasp. Dad joined her, lifting the feather light remains and carrying the fallen coven leader to the shelf by the wall, laying her out on the natural bench protrusion and covering her gently with a blanket.

"Syd." Mom wept, though her face remained calm and poised. "What happened?"

"Your daughter," Sassafras said while the handful of Violet's people collapsed into a sobbing heap, "just declared war on the Brotherhood and the North American Witches Council." He didn't sound accusatory.

Just pissed off.

I knew the feeling.

Mom looked over at the remains of the Rhodes coven. "Where are the others?" She met my eyes, her blue ones huge, full of need. "Where is the rest of the Rhodes family?" She waited for me to tell her what she wanted to hear, not the truth. But I knew better. Mom was strong enough to handle it.

"This *is* the Rhodes family," I said, weariness bowing my shoulders, though the fire of anger still burned hot and bright within. "What's left of them."

Mom shook her head, dark hair shifting around her shoulders, lips quivering. "Syd," she whispered. "There are almost two hundred witches in that family."

"Were," I said, dull and listless. "The rest are gone, Mom. Staked and burned by the Brotherhood. While the Enforcers watched and did nothing." The last word I spit out, biting my tongue to keep from screaming.

The only thing that saved me was the generosity of my coven. They came forward, offering blankets and comfort, leading the shivering, stunned Rhodes witches away with them, giving them water and shoulders to cry on. More mouths to feed. How practical in this moment of despair. And yet, I was proud of my family for embracing the terror stricken newcomers without question or resentment.

This coven. This was what witches were supposed to

be.

Mom hugged me close, and we both shook, the last few minutes etched forever in my memory. "Mom," I said, choking on my words. "It was horrible." Such a simple statement. But I was unable to describe to her what I'd seen, only now truly absorbing the truth. Relived the image of twisting bodies falling still in the flames, knowing there was nothing I could do for them.

She leaned away, gently wiped tears from my face before repeating her gesture on her own cheeks. "The world has gone mad," she whispered.

Motion distracted me, the tunnel mouth in my peripheral vision. I turned and watched Gram enter, Quaid at her side, a tall, older witch I recognized instantly striding behind them. And gargled a cry that drowned in my sudden need to stop them from coming closer. To halt the old Enforcer leader who followed my husband and grandmother, to protect Varity Rhodes from seeing what she was about to see.

I was far too late, my feet moving, dragging me toward her, to Dad and the prone, silent form of the fallen coven leader. Varity staggered as one of her family reached her, wailing the truth of their loss. The old witch turned, eyes shining with tears, hands clutching at Gram who jerked to a stunned halt before turning to find me running toward her.

Gram let Varity go as the old witch stumbled the final

few steps and fell to her knees at Violet's side. A few of the Rhodes family joined her, holding hands, rocking together and weeping. Dad left them, joining Gram and me, Demetrius and Quaid, Piers and Zoe. Sassafras wound his way between our legs to stand in the middle of our little group.

My grandmother's pale face seemed older again, though she hadn't changed since I last saw her. "Syd," she said. "Tell us."

I wished I could show them. And realized maybe I could. We linked hands and I pushed, as hard as I could, reaching for my demon who burned through to them, her need to do something tying into the wards protecting the cavern. I focused on the crystal in my pocket, begging it to help me, and my sorcery rose, seeking power.

I couldn't risk destroying the shielding protecting this cavern. But if I could channel through them...

I felt them connect to me, my family, in a swirling, ever evolving mass of protections that held this place in some kind of stasis. So, not a smothering of power, but a holding still, like time didn't know this place existed, at least where the elements of magic were concerned. This, I could use.

A small victory, considering what I was about to show the ones I loved the most.

They held it together, all of them, while Sassafras's purr, now powered in our little bubble, soothed them as much as he was able. Even when they watched the stakes burn, even when I relived Violet dying in my arms. They remained strong, for me, for each other.

When it was over, I let them go, the bubble collapsing and pushing us back out into muffled space. But I knew how to access it, now. And would again if necessary.

Gram finally broke our long silence by clearing her throat. "Violet was a fine leader," she said. "I'm not surprised she fought to the bitter end."

Neither was I. "How many more covens have we lost?" I met my grandmother's eyes. "And can we save the ones who have held on before it's too late?"

Gram shook her head, still holding Demetrius's hand. "Girl," she said. But that was all.

There was nothing to say.

"We found Varity at the Stronghold entry at the chapel in Harvard," Quaid said, changing the subject, bless him. None of us looked her way. She deserved the right to her time of mourning. "But there's no sign of Pender." The Enforcer leader had always followed orders. But I wondered if maybe Erica pushed him too far this time. Which meant either he was in trouble, or he fled. I hoped it was the latter. He'd been through so much since taking leadership.

"The oddest part," Gram said, "when we tried to cross into the Stronghold, Varity couldn't come with is." She frowned, glanced at Quaid. "But neither of us has a problem."

My husband nodded to her. "There was an odd feeling when we entered," he said. "Like it was testing us for something." Quaid's hands slipped into his back pockets, head down, dark eyes on the floor as he thought through what he was saying. "At first, I thought it was going to send me back. Is that strange to say?" He looked up again, met our eyes in turn, still frowning. "Almost like it sensed something in me it didn't like."

My jaw tightened as I made some connections. "You were an Enforcer," I said.

He nodded. "But I gave up the power a long time ago."

"Could traces of it still exist in you?" What was the Stronghold doing?

Quaid shrugged. "Anything is possible, babe."

"What are you thinking?" Mom was tucked in beside Dad, his arms around her. But her focus was on me.

"I don't know," I said. "Who else was there?"

"That's the thing," Gram said. "No one. From what we could tell, the whole place is empty."

Someone stumbled into me. I turned and caught Varity, her tall, lean body shivering from stress. But her grim expression won over the tears tracking down her cheeks, eyes snapping with rage.

"Two days ago," she said. "I was standing in the main hall at the Stronghold. And two seconds later I landed in a heap in Harvard Yard." She gestured wide, almost hitting Gram who caught her hand and held it. "All of us, at once. Every Enforcer in the place, scattered like dice around the campus." Her head bent, iron gray hair coming loose from its tight bun, sweeping over her damp cheeks. "We'd just received our orders," she choked out. "Pender told us what our Council had done. There were Brotherhood with him, he told us to fight and was taken." Damn it. Worst case scenario, then. "I was about to show the Brotherhood what real Enforcers thought of their orders when everything went sideways." She sagged against Gram who held her carefully. "And not one of us has been able to get inside since."

"Brotherhood included?" A sneaking suspicion woke inside me.

Varity nodded, head bobbing on her thin neck. "They were furious," she said with a weary chuckle that turned into a soft sob. "Started killing Enforcers until they fell in line. I hid, like a coward." She wiped at her nose with the sleeve of her torn black robe.

"Don't be an idiot," Gram snapped at her, patting her back with one hand while she held Varity up with the other. "You were smart."

"So no resistance, I take it." I met Quaid's eyes.

"Not that we know of," he said, face troubled. I know he respected the order of witches still, but they didn't deserve his loyalty.

"Not true." Varity staggered again, as though drunk, though I assumed it was shock. She needed to sit down. Gram must have had the same thought and guided her away toward the back wall, twenty feet or so from where the remains of her home coven mourned, and pressed her down into the natural bench. The old woman laid her shaking hands on her skinny knees, the black robe making her look ghastly in the low light. "There are a few of us, the numbers growing slowly, who have managed to evade the Brotherhood." She shook her head. "Under my command, the fools. Like I know what I'm doing."

"I can't think of anyone better to lead them, Master Rhodes," Quaid said, leaning in to squeeze her hand.

She patted his cheek with a thin smile. "Always a sweet boy," she said, voice distant. Her gaze sharpened again, fell on me. "Some of my recruits have gone missing, others who contacted me, too. I fear the worst." Her eyes tightened around the edges. "But I'll never quit."

My kind of ally. Even as I tried to formulate some comforting thing to say, I had an idea in my mind that wouldn't leave me be and I had to explore it.

"Get some rest," I said, stepping back from them all. "I need to check on something."

Quaid straightened, offering his hand. "Not alone, you're not."

I stepped in and kissed him, hands sliding into his

hair. He hugged me, but let me go when I backed away.

"I'll be fine," I said. "And this I need to do alone."

"Where are you going?" Sassafras had hopped up into Varity's lap, her hands absently stroking his fur, something I'd always found soothing and hoped it gave her comfort.

"Where the Brotherhood can't," I said. "The Stronghold."

TWENTY-TWO

I was tired, so tired, as I entered the veil and slid along the rubbery membrane toward the Stronghold plane. But I couldn't stop. There wasn't time to lag, get some sleep, not for me. Even more now I was determined to stop Erica and Belaisle from depopulating North America's witch compliment if it meant killing my mother's oldest friend myself.

I stepped out into the cool quiet of the Stronghold a moment later, hand reaching for the wall as all the strength ran out of me. Panting for fresh air, I leaned heavily into the stone, forehead pressed to the rock wall, begging my body and energy to hold out just a little longer.

I'd been so powerful for so long, this feeling of being drained to the edge was new and frightening. It had to have come from moving my family en masse. There was nothing about it that felt like foreign interference, so I only had my own body's weakness to blame.

We'll manage, my vampire sent, sounding weary herself. *We always do.*

We just need to stop putting out so much energy for a little while, Shaylee sent. *See if we can recover.*

My demon grunted angrily. *I'm not tired*, she sent, while I felt her own strength flagging. *Leave it to me.*

The family magic coiled inside me, as drained as the rest of us, my maji power tying them together the only thing keeping us moving.

That, and the black blossom of insatiable hunger that never seemed to feel weary.

Okay, then.

I straightened at last, even as a soft voice rumbled through my mind.

Light One, the Stronghold sent. *I've been waiting for you.*

I reached out to him as best I could, beginning a slow walk down the hall. I'd been here before, this particular corridor leading all the way to the central tower. Memories of releasing Ameline, of being imprisoned here myself, flickered through my head. *I'm happy you're okay*, I sent.

Nothing can harm me. No arrogance, only belief in utter truth. *At least, not now I'm free. I will forever be in your debt, Light One, for releasing me from my millennia of stasis.*

A large, open window beckoned and I paused, leaning

over the wide lintel, breathing in a deep lung full of fresh air. There was a time this plane was dead and empty, in limbo as it had been since the Universe was created. Waiting for me, for Fate, and the battle I fought against Liander Belaisle.

Now, lush green spread out from the base of the giant castle, trees and flowers in the meadow below. Birds like I'd never seen swooped and sang, a wide, fast running river dumping into a distant ocean twinkling in the sunlight.

Good to hear it, I sent. *Though, I understand you've evicted your last tenants.*

The Stronghold's anger rippled through me, not aimed at me, but making me feel shaky none the less.

There was a time, he sent, *I had no control over who walked my halls. But my freedom has granted me the power to act on my own behalf much more decisively.* I could almost see him nodding his head. If he had one.

And the Enforcers are now off your list? I turned a corner, coming to a halt in the large, main room of the Stronghold. Or, at least, the one the Enforcers used in the past. I knew from my aerial view—thanks to a flyover on Max—the Stronghold was massive, stretched out for miles. Who knew what lived and lurked in the halls of this place?

They are no longer welcome here. His flat tone felt like stone grinding over stone. *They carry the taint of the sorcerers who sought to use me for their purpose, the taint of the one you defeated to free me.*

Belaisle. I sank to a bench along the curved wall of the hall and leaned back against the stone, sighing. *Makes sense to me*, I sent. *Do you have any idea what's happening on my plane?*

I do not, the Stronghold sent. *Beyond what I gleaned from observing the fallen ones.* He must have meant the Enforcers. *Should I be concerned?*

I told him everything, allowed him to skim through my thoughts and see. When I was done, the Stronghold sighed, a sound like the earth shifting on its plates.

I'm sorry about the loss of your lesser kind, he sent, referring to the witches, I presumed. *But I am immobile and unable to assist.*

You already have, I sent, savoring the quiet moment, the solitude with only the ancient mind of the vast Stronghold to keep me company. My eyes tried to drift shut, forcing me to stand and pace so I wouldn't fall asleep. *You can keep the Brotherhood out of here, then?*

I can, the Stronghold sent. *They will never be permitted on my plane again.*

And other sorcerers? I let him feel Piers, the first person I thought of. Funny, I still immediately placed Gram as a witch despite her transformation.

The Stronghold was silent a moment. *I allow such here*, he sent. *They have their own personal magic and are not like the evil ones. But if they attempt anything the Brotherhood did, I will act.*

Understood, I sent. *There are Enforcers who do not agree with the laws that have been written, who are fighting against the hold of the Brotherhood. Are they permitted?*

No. That was abrupt and I guessed I could hardly blame him. *I'm sorry, but their taint would remain. They would need to sever their connection entirely, if that is even possible.*

My husband was here, with Ethpeal Hayle. You remember her?

I do. Again he paused. *She is different now. One of the sorcerers you spoke of. I allowed her to explore. With the man you married.*

But you almost repelled him.

He had the feel of the Enforcers, the Stronghold sent. *But he had severed himself and so I permitted his presence.*

Confirming my first guess. *You mentioned personal magic*, I sent. *What did you mean by that? How are the Steam Union different?*

They have taken the time to develop their own power, the Stronghold sent. *The Brotherhood are mere parasites, helpless and without magic except that they steal from the Universe.*

Well, now. I hadn't heard that before. Interesting. Maybe there was a way to use it against them. Then I shrugged. They would always have access to something they could strip for power. So I was probably wrong. Still. Nice to know.

The fundamental difference, the Stronghold sent, going on. *The Brotherhood are takers. The sorcerer who was a witch is of another ilk. They are earners and would not steal from me.*

And yet, I'd taken, hadn't I? From the Brotherhood themselves. The Stronghold had seen that, when I shared what happened. *How am I still welcome?*

You took from those who are evil, he sent, as though that was all right. *Removed power they didn't have the right to hold, not for your own gain, but to stop them from hurting others. And you are the Light One.* Couldn't argue with that kind of logic. *I will always welcome you. As I welcome all who come in peace.*

That was the opening I needed, the last bit of my weary mind's wanderings.

There is one thing you can do to help, I sent.

For you, Light One, he sent, *anything. Except allowing the Brotherhood here.*

Amen to that, I sent. *My family are in need of a place to hide.*

A rush of joy washed over me, making me smile as he answered.

Your people are welcome here, he sent. Was that loneliness and longing in him? He'd obviously grown accustomed to people roaming his halls. The silence had to be frustrating. *I will care for them and keep them safe for as long as you need.*

I stopped pacing and hugged myself. First major problem solved.

Now, how to take on two vast powers who were determined to control—and, in the case of the Brotherhood, destroy—my race.

Piece of cake.

TWENTY-THREE

I stood off to the side, arms crossed, back braced against the wall as the mirror in the main chamber of the Stronghold shimmered and my coven made their tentative way through. Quaid helped the Lawrence twins, Estelle on one arm, Esther tottering on the other, his eyes searching for me the moment he passed through the portal. I waved but held back, letting Mom and Dad take over, just needing to stay out of it and catch my breath.

There was no surprise when the Stronghold led me to a small, museum like room filled with old documents and artifacts in glass cases, showing me where the archivist left his mirror shard, along with a small case full of more. The keys to the main portal were sanded smooth around the edges and coated in silver, almost pieces of art that cast back the reflection of my tired face, the bloodshot look of my blue eyes.

It took only a moment to ride the veil to the cavern, to tell Mom and Dad and the others what I had planned. The coven seemed almost eager to move on and, as they looked around in wonder at their new home, I caught a few tentative smiles and the first breath of optimism.

Your family is strong. The Stronghold's voice in my head ground gravel across rock. *I am honored to have them in my halls.*

A tiny lump of gratitude formed in my throat, threatening tears. *Thank you*, I sent in barely a whisper. *This means a lot.*

I owe you everything, the Stronghold sent with a slow and ponderous hug of his massive energy. *This small thing I consider only a down payment on my debt.*

You don't owe me a thing, I sent. *I'd rather call you a friend than someone who feels they have to help.*

He paused a long moment, silent, the cool touch of stone behind me warming slightly. Temperatures didn't bother me, but I could still sense the subtle variations.

I have never had a... friend. His gigantic mind seemed to shift sideways, to grind around the idea. *I would like that very much, Light One.*

Then call me Syd, I sent, finally pushing off from the wall, patting the rock with one hand.

Syd. He sounded almost shy, tentative.

My kids ran toward me, a few of the coven children joining them, cheeks pink and faces smiling. Was this a game to them? I hoped it came across that way. Ethie didn't even pause as she tore past me.

"Going exploring!"

I groaned and rolled my eyes at her, Gabriel stopping to hug me quick and hard.

"I'll watch her, Mom," he said. But his hazel eyes sparked with green and the grin on his face was far too enthusiastic for my liking.

"Be careful!" I watched them run off without the energy to stop them, though I knew I should. Galleytrot shook his tail at me as he galloped after them.

Fear not for your offspring. The Stronghold's mind felt amused. *I will ensure their safety and steer them away from places it's best they don't go.*

An entire giant castle as a babysitter and a former hound of the Wild Hunt trailing along? I'd take it.

The coven came to a halt, the Rhodes witches held carefully in their midst, all eyes turning to me. The main room was full of bodies held in limbo, waiting for me to speak.

I cleared my throat, hoped I wasn't too tired. The last thing I wanted to do was freak them out all over again. "This is the Stronghold," I said, deciding to keep it simple. "It has intelligence, like Sassafras and Galleytrot." Not quite, but it would do. Everyone looked around, whispered a moment. Some of them even waved up at the ceiling as if the Stronghold could see them.

I can, he sent, more good humor in his tone. *Greetings, people of Syd.* I grinned, ducked my head. *Be welcome in my halls. Know I will keep you safe from harm and that anything you need I will provide for you. Your difficult journey is over for now. Rest and be at ease.*

A murmur ran through the coven, and I felt them physically relax, their power now restored with the leaving of the cavern a welcome feeling as their magic, linked so closely to mine, rode through me like a breath of clean air. The family magic circulated among them, evenly distributed. Without a place to embed itself, I figured it was safer if everyone carried a piece, just in case.

Quaid. I met his eyes across the hall. *You know this place the best.* He nodded. *Can you get everyone situated in quarters? And see if there's anything to eat. I'm sure the family would love a hot meal.*

You're planning something without me. His dark eyes flashed with anger, even from that distance.

Shenka is gone. I let him feel the desperation in my heart. *I need someone to take care of the family. Someone they love and look up to and trust. That's you, my darling.*

Your mother could do it.

Don't argue with her, Quaid. Sassafras's voice cut through like a whip. I ground my teeth at the intrusion. *The family comes first.*

Quaid didn't respond, but when he turned and addressed the family, I knew he'd accepted what I asked, even if he wasn't happy about it.

Dad, I sent. *Can you help Quaid, please? I don't want him to feel like I've cut him out. I really need the family comfortable.*

My father's chuckle warmed me up. *I've been with a Hayle witch long enough—and fathered two more—to know when to stand back and get out of the way. I'll take care of Quaid.*

I smiled at my father as he crossed to my husband and clapped him on the shoulder. Heads down together, they spoke a moment while Mom came to my side, Piers and Zoe joining her. When Quaid looked up again, he nodded to Dad and the pair began divvying up family, assigning groups. I sank to the bench again, Sassafras leaping up into my arms.

"I'd rather you stayed out of my marriage," I said. "We agreed to that a long time ago."

"You agreed." Sass sniffed. "Besides, this wasn't about your marriage, Syd. It's about the coven and what we're going to do to protect them."

"They're safe enough now." Gram sank down next to me, Demetrius joining us. I missed Shenka and Charlotte, Sage. Wondered how they were and if I should go looking for Tallah now that my family was taken care of. "This place won't allow enemies in, I take it?"

That is correct, Ethpeal Hayle, the Stronghold sent, making Gram shiver. There was a time when I first heard his voice I had the same reaction, so I grinned at my grandmother.

"You get used to it." I patted the bench on the other side, inviting Mom to join me. She did, as Varity Rhodes made her long legged but ponderous way to us. She'd been old when I first met her, but so vigorous and full of life I rarely considered her age. Now she was drawn, pale, shaking with a near palsy as she stroked a stray hair from the corner of her mouth. But when she spoke, her voice was as steady and gravel filled as ever.

"Now what?" I knew she had to want revenge. Frankly, so did I. "I take it you have a plan, Sydlynn."

Not yet, but I was working on it. "Mom," I said. "Since we can't fight the entire council and the Brotherhood, there has to be a less physical way to end this."

She hesitated before nodding. "I've been thinking about it," she said. "We would have to have the council declared defunct and disbanded. That would nullify all laws created by this particular iteration of the council."

That sounded perfect. "How would we do that?"

"You would need the support of every other world council leader," Mom said. "Unanimous vote."

Since the meeting of the council leaders was pending in the morning—was it morning yet? I'd lost track of time—then maybe there was hope after all.

"Syd." She took my hands in hers, her power hugging me gently as her blue eyes, eyes I shared with her, locked on mine with serious intensity. "Consider what you're going to ask of them. To declare another council rogue and broken. What do you think they will say?"

"What can they say?" And yet, even as I spoke, worry gnawed at me, frustration, too. I knew better than to feel much optimism. Witches were notorious for refusing to act, weren't they? But. "This is different, Mom," I said, going for reasonable. Who was I really trying to convince here? "Every witch could be in danger. If Belaisle succeeds, what are the odds he'll stop at North America?"

She sighed. "I know that," she said. "And you do. But as a former council leader, I can tell you this won't be easy. You'll have to convince them of imminent threat to their specific territories. And I have no idea how you're going to do that."

"I'll just have to find a way." Bullying them came to mind, while my demon snorted and offered a few burning piles of wood topped with empty stakes for emphasis.

There is no other way, my vampire sent. *We must try.*

I refused to relent under the pressure of my anxiety. If only I had Max and the drach, I could throw some serious weight around. Where the hell was he? *Stronghold*, I sent. *Can you sense the drach anywhere?*

He was silent a long time. *No, I can't*, he sent, sounding puzzled. *And I usually can feel them, even if they are far away.*

Great, now I had to worry about Max instead of being pissed at him.

The portal shuddered and I leaped to my feet. The coven was already through, all my people here and safe. Who was coming? And though I was assured of our safety, fight mode kicked in and I was running for the shimmering pool of the mirror just as a pair of familiar faces passed through, a small knot of witches trailing behind them.

I closed the distance and threw my arms around Lula Kennecott, kissing her cheek before hugging her twin brother, Phon. The Council healers looked like they'd been dragged through hell and back, soot covering their clothing, cheeks dark with the stuff. The stench of smoke and Lula's singed ponytail made me panic, checking her over for hurt which she stopped by grasping my face between her hands and making me meet her hazel eyes.

"We're okay," she said, voice shaking. "I promise."

I nodded and she let me go, stepping aside to allow the other witches with her to slink through the portal. There were about a dozen, faces I didn't know, and I nodded to them and offered them welcome through my power as the young woman who guided them past her finally turned to face me.

"Karyn," she said, voice rough and deep, probably from the smoke clinging to her. "Barrett coven." She looked around at the misery in her people's eyes. "What few of us remain."

Quaid appeared at the entry to one of the halls,

frowning as he approached. I gestured to Karyn. "More refugees," I said. "Can you find them a place?"

He nodded, guiding them away, though Karyn stayed behind, hands clutching her coat closed around her throat, tattered remains of what looked like party hair and makeup a mess, cocktail dress tattered at the hem and one stiletto missing a heel. "They were all I could save," she choked out, bending over as her grief took over. I hugged her, comforted her with power as she pulled herself together. "They came out of nowhere. With Enforcers." She pushed back her dangling bangs, blonde hair darkened by ashes, mascara raccooned under her hazel eyes. "You're Sydlynn Hayle," she said. "I recognize you."

"I'm sorry," I said. "Have we met?"

She shook her head, managing a little smile as tears made tracks through the grime on her face. "No," she said. "But my coven leader spoke highly of you."

I wished I could recall the Barrett leader's name. "Where is she?" Like I had to ask. I did it as gently as I could, but the expected answer followed.

"Dead," Karyn said. Sobbed, really. "Like the rest of our family." Again she hunched over, hands covering her face. "Danielle and our second, Mimi, both sacrificed themselves to make sure the last of us escaped." She dropped her hands, panting air. "I watched them burn as we ran away."

There wasn't much I could say to that.

"Perhaps it would be best if you got some rest." Lula met my eyes over the young woman's bent head. "Phon, be a dear?"

Her brother led the girl away, following my dad as he reappeared and showed them where to go. I turned to Lula, grasping her hands as she sighed out a shuddering breath.

"How did you find us?"

"Guesswork," she said. I guided her toward Mom and the others, sat her on the bench. She stretched her feet out, the soles of her shoes almost burned away and I wondered how many she'd saved from the flames.

And how many she'd lost.

"We'd only just arrived ourselves," I said.

Lula shrugged. "When we found out the Enforcers no longer had access to the Stronghold, I wondered if that meant we would be safe here. I didn't know if you'd have the same thought, but from the talks we had about the battle against the Brotherhood and the fact the Stronghold has its own intelligence, I had to take the chance."

You, too, are welcome here, the Stronghold sent to her.

Lula sat up very straight, eyes huge. "Well," she said. "That's something, isn't it?"

I grinned weakly at her. "You have no idea."

"I also ran into Charlotte and Sage," she said. "Briefly. They were searching for Tallah."

"Was Shenka with them?" Panic rose in my chest.

"Not at the time," she said. "But Charlotte told me she was safe, that they'd split up to avoid the Brotherhood and the Enforcers."

"When?" It felt like forever since they left, but it hadn't even been twelve hours.

"Just a few hours ago," Lula said. "Listen," she leaned toward me, "whether the Brotherhood likes it or not, their attempt at containment is starting to fail. I can only imagine the amount of power it's taking them to keep the entire continent on lockdown. But because some of the walls around territories are falling, people are hearing about you. About the fact you stood up to them, Syd." Her hazel eyes shine with pride. "You may not know it, but you've given everyone hope."

Nice to know I was good for something.

"That being said," she went on, "you might want to prep for more arrivals." I stared at her in shock. "I sent word back through when we arrived to some witches who volunteered to remain behind, in secret. They know you're here now. And they'll be coming, looking for someone to protect them."

TWENTY-FOUR

Phon joined us a few minutes later while I pondered what his sister just said. He sat next to her, lifting Sassafras into his lap. The healer twins weren't affiliated with any covens, keeping themselves outside the family system, working directly for the Council, but I couldn't help thinking of them as mine.

"Did you have any idea this was happening?" If anyone had, it would be them.

But they shook their heads in unison, fraternal twins as identical as they could get being opposite genders.

"Not a whiff, Syd." Lula's face crumpled while Phon slipped his arm around her shoulders. "No, that's not true." She sighed away her tears. "The odd weird instance. But nothing that made us think Erica was going to betray everything to the enemy."

"We're going to go back out there and save as many

as we can." Phon's face darkened with determination, as though he expected me to argue with him.

"That," I said with the first hint of excitement I'd had in a while, "is an excellent idea."

They both stared at me. "Really?" Unison again. They were so adorable.

"It's dangerous," Gram said, but I knew from the narrowing of her eyes she was ready to join them.

"I can't go," I said. "I have to try to figure out how to put a stop to this." Still killing me. "But you lot can." Piers and Zoe both nodded, my sorcerer friend's unhappy eagerness making me sad for him all over again. "The more witches we save, the more witches we have to rebuild when this is over." I couldn't stand against the entire Council alone, all the Brotherhood. But damn it, I could do something, even if that meant rescuing a few here and there from the flames. "We need to assemble volunteer teams," I said. "Distribute mirror shards so they can bring the ones they find here."

"We've heard many are leaving their homes on foot, in car caravans," Lula said. "Coming to Harvard to talk to the Council. Or, to seek you." She broke down again, head on her brother's shoulder. "Syd, I've never seen such devastation. Whole families devoured by fire, left to smolder where their caravans were captured. It's disgusting and I've never hated anyone as much as I do the Brotherhood for destroying our people." Phon rubbed her shoulder, cheek pressed to the top of her head.

"We'll fall apart later," I said, knowing my own collapse was closer than I thought if I didn't get a chance to rest. But I refused to quit just yet.

She nodded, sighed. "A shower would be great," she said. "Before we go back out there."

Lula and Phon left us, heading for the hallway where Quaid and Dad herded the rest of the coven and refugees.

I didn't have time to think the plan through any further, the pond-like rippling of the mirror spinning me around to watch for who was arriving. When Shenka's dark head passed through, I let out a whoop of relief and pushed my body to run again.

Pulled up short at the sight of the woman floating behind her on a platform of blue magic, a small group of ten or so witches trailing behind with empty looks on their faces. Shenka's crumpled into tears, but she held herself rigid as I bent and looked down on Tallah. Her ashen skin and shallow breathing worried me instantly, but at least she was alive.

"She's hurt," Shenka said. The sound of footsteps coming toward me made me glance up, the sight of Lula and Phon returning making me feel a whole lot better. I stepped aside as the pair bent over Tallah, their combined power sliding around her.

"We'll take care of her, Shenka." Lula smiled gently at my second who then collapsed against me and sobbed as though being told her sister would be all right meant she could finally fall apart.

I met Charlotte's blue eyes over my second's shoulder. She looked tired but fine, Sage, too.

"You have no idea how happy I am to see you guys." No crying. Later with the tears and the crumbling into a weeping pile of messiness.

Shenka pulled away as the twins began to float her sister toward the corridor where the family had disappeared, the tiny group of witches trailing along behind. Shenka watched Tallah go with a frozen expression.

"It took longer than I thought to find her." Shenka sniffed, wiping her nose on her sleeve, eyes glassy. Shell shocked? Probably. She turned to meet my eyes. "We spread the word as best we could, that you were fighting for everyone."

"Shenka," I said as gently as I could. "Where is the rest of the Hensley family?"

I needn't have asked, was foolish to, considering the slight posse that had arrived with Tallah.

My second's face showed me her horror a moment before falling back into her daze. "Gone," she whispered.

I figured as much. And yet, it was so hard to accept. Seventy-five witches, minus their leader and the frail crew who made it through. Yet another tragedy in a long list of charges I would lay at Erica's feet.

Shenka shook herself, grasped my hand. "I told everyone who would listen," she said. "That help was coming." She stopped, face twisting in grief. "Is help coming, Syd?"

I hugged her tight. "Like there was any doubt," I said.

Quaid joined us, leading Shenka away. She tried to resist, but I waved her off.

"Please," I said. "Go get something to eat. Check on your sister."

"I'm your second." She stopped moving, Quaid's hand on her arm. "I'll look in on the family."

"The family," my husband said as he planted a gentle kiss on her forehead, "is just fine. And will more than likely want to look in on you." His mind touched mine as he led her away. *You were right*, he sent. *I'm sorry, babe.*

Love you. I let him go, turning to hug Charlotte while she make my ribs creak in protest with the power of her embrace.

She and Sage joined me when I returned to Mom and the others for the second time. I filled the werewolves in on what we'd been through since they left and Charlotte nodded.

"We've heard some whispers," she said. "We arrived in California, but the house was trashed, everyone gone. We searched everywhere, crossing as best we could across territories. Syd." Her blue eyes flare with magic, her wolf in her gaze. "There's a lot of dead witches out there."

I swallowed and nodded. "Go on."

"The normals are starting to notice." She stuck her hands in the pockets of her leather jacket, leaning sideways against Sage.

"There's only so many fires you can explain away," he said. "We were almost grabbed for questioning when the cops showed at a mass burning."

On the one hand, I was proud of the witches for standing up to the Brotherhood. On the other... this was a time cowardice would have served them well, for once.

"The Brotherhood aren't accepting surrender," Charlotte said, as though reading my mind. I frowned at her, thinking of Erica and her assurances only those who stood against the new law would be harmed. "It's wholesale slaughter out there."

We had to act. Even if that meant putting our own people in the direct line of fire.

I told Charlotte of Lula and Phon's idea, to send small parties out and rescue who they could. She and Sage instantly volunteered. As I knew they would. Together, Sassafras sashaying his furry way ahead of us, tail waving like a flag, we followed the tunnel to the interior of the Stronghold, to a giant cafeteria where the family gathered, cooking together, almost happy.

Silence fell when they saw me appear, everyone

turning to watch, to wait and listen. Their fear was gone, the strength of the Hayle coven embracing me as I spoke.

"We are safe," I said. "But there are those who could use our help." Not one soul rejected the idea. In fact, a surge of relief and courage hit me like a blow. They needed to act as much as I did. "We need volunteers to go and infiltrate territories," I said. So many hands shot up, I had to chew the inside of my cheek to keep from bursting into tears. "Please," I said, waving their hands down. "This is dangerous. Very dangerous. You'll be on your own with the Brotherhood and the Enforcers everywhere. Trying to do something that might only lead to your capture at best. Your death at worst." Total silence. Total trust. "We are alone, but we are strong. And there is no one else."

Again, almost every hand in the room shot up and I had to turn away, pressing my face into Quaid's waiting chest, his arms around me.

What had I done? I just got them to a safe place and now I was going to send them out into danger again?

TWENTY-FIVE

I wasn't surprised when Gram and Demetrius volunteered to go, and Piers and Varity did the same. When Quaid put his name in, I just sighed and nodded. Four more teams of witches I trusted formed groups of five, leaving through the mirror with shards in their possession.

I kissed my husband with aching worry, but let him go be a hero, knowing how hard it had to be for him I was usually the one in that role. Besides, these were his friends standing by and allowing witches to die. Enforcers he once considered himself a part. It had to hurt.

I hesitated to ask Lula and Phon to remain, but they had already decided to stay.

"We're better utilized here," she said, hands hovering over a burn on an older Rhodes witch's arm. "And we know it." She watched the woman leave, hands beginning to shake once we were alone. "Syd, the Brotherhood are crushing bones. Scattering the remains. Witch magic lost forever." Her face tightened with horror, the expression of one who had seen far too much.

But I knew better as I nodded and walked away. That power wasn't lost. If the Stronghold was to be believed, I knew exactly where the witch magic was going. Right into Liander Belaisle's possession.

I'm sure Zoe would have preferred to go with Piers, but her lack of magic made her vulnerable. She shivered next to me as he left, waving at her, a small group of witches surrounding him.

"He'll be okay," I said.

"You're an Oracle now, are you?" Her brown eyes twinkled despite her worry.

"Trust me," I said, arm around her shoulders, turning her away. "If anyone will come through a mess and not even muss his perfect blond hair, it's Piers Southway."

She giggled and nodded. "He's so vain about that hair."

Nice to smile, to feel a little normal again. If only for a moment. Zoe stopped me, turned me to face her, expression fading to serious. "There is a lot you don't know about me or my people," she said. "It's time I filled you in."

We found a quiet corner of the cafeteria and, over a shared plate of stew and fresh bread that smelled like heaven had found us at last, Zoe told me her history.

"Our people were always Oracles," she said. "The Helios family is descended from the Delphic order in Greece." I wracked my brain for that history lesson I knew I'd taken in high school and nodded for her to go on. "Our Goddess—or, who we thought was our Goddess," her face twisted with pain a moment, "was Gaia. I only recently discovered she wasn't who I thought at all. She was maji."

There was a revelation and a half. "Did she create you?" After all, the maji had tried something like that before. Iepa had made the vampire essence herself.

"No," Zoe said. "At least, Iepa told me she hadn't. But Gaia took it upon herself to nurture our family when she discovered our ability. The only problem was, my grandmother." She shook her head. "I'm sorry, I know this must be confusing. The woman I thought was my grandmother." Sounded like she'd lived a lot of lies in her short two decades. "Sibyl, it turns out, was one of the last Delphic Oracles. She made a pact with the Brotherhood, gave up Gaia to them." She did what? My heart skipped a beat, ears ringing with sudden anger and shock. "They've been drawing power from her ever since."

Using the almost infinite magic of a maji to fuel their foul order. "No wonder he was not only steps ahead of me," I snarled. "He had tons of magic to counter me, too."

Zoe's face fell. "Not exactly," she said. "By the time I became aware of this—in fact, just before I came to you to warn you—I discovered Gaia's magic had run out and that Liander was looking for a new source to power him and his people."

Bastard. "You told Iepa this?"

"She figured it out," Zoe said.

"So he's drawing on all these witches to replace Gaia's energy." Typical parasite.

"I fear his goal is much more diabolical," she said. "Iepa is worried Liander's ultimate goal was never to kill you, but to capture you." I frowned. It took a moment in my tired state to put the pieces together. But when I did, Zoe nodded as I gaped at her. "He wants to replace Gaia with you."

It made total sense. Where was he going to get his hands on another maji? They had vanished from the regular planes, keeping themselves aloof and apart. It was very likely if Ameline had won, he'd have just tried the exact same tactics on her—capture and control. He didn't care about the witches. He just needed the power to tide him over until he managed to pin me down.

"I need to talk to Iepa." I swept to my feet, leaving Zoe to stare up at me with doe brown eyes.

"She told me to save you." Her hand clenched around her spoon, food forgotten. "Please, don't throw yourself into danger when I'm not in a position any longer to help."

I sank down again, reaching for her hand. She was young, I forgot how young from the way she talked, her self-assurance. But she couldn't have been more than eighteen or twenty. Scared and vulnerable without her power. I'd been there.

"You'll get your magic back," I said. "I'll help you. But, for now, you have to trust me. I've been through a few scrapes before. I can handle this."

She nodded, looked down into the cooling stew. "I just wish I could do something."

"You can," I said. "Help Lula and Phon. Comfort people. Cheer them up if you can. You're family now, Zoe."

She looked up, blinking tears from her thick, black lashes. "Thank you," she whispered. "I miss family."

I left her there, helping some of the witches clean up, sending a quick message to Mom. *Take care of Zoe*, I sent. *She needs someone. Sic Sass on her, maybe?*

Hrumph, he sent. Why wasn't I surprised he was listening in?

Will do, Mom sent. *Where are you going?*

To see if the maji will talk to me, I sent. *I've just been handed a whole bunch of questions and its time they stepped up and answered.*

I didn't give her a chance to argue, reaching for the veil. Paused one last moment. *You'll watch over them?*

The Stronghold's rumbling answer made me feel so much better. *Like they were you*, he sent.

I'd heard that not so long ago from Charlotte. And felt just as confident in his promise as I had in hers.

I tore open the veil, conscience eased, and headed for Center. And was bounced back, as if I'd hit a soft, rubbery wall.

Oh hell *no*, they did not just do that to me.

I tried again, with the same result, staggered out of the veil in the cafeteria, swearing and stomping my feet as the family who hung out there stared with wide eyes. Maybe at full strength I would have been able to bully my way into the Light maji realm, but not in this state.

Damn it.

I stopped swearing and looked up, an idea popping into my head, along with a face I worried about all over again. Sebastian had been at the vampire mansion in Wilding Springs. Where the maji chamber was. Maybe I could reach Iepa from there. It was worth a shot and might mean getting a tracker line on my vampire friend and former bestie.

This time, when I stepped through the veil, there was no resistance. But the silence and darkness that greeted me made me shudder, much as the quiet of Castle DeWinter had. The mistress of the mansion, Anastasia, was one of Sebastian's most trusted lieutenants. She would never abandon this place.

Unless he told her to.

The mystery of the vampire king would have to wait, though I hated not knowing if he was all right or not. Instead, I headed down the left corridor, more memories trying to take over, good and bad. Of Demetrius, the night he stole my demon from me, when he was still the leader of the Chosen of the Light. To hunting her here, freeing her at last, in time to save Wilding Springs from the Wild Hunt. Of Mom's trial when Batsheva tried to put my mother to death, only to be thwarted by Gram and me. Rescuing Sebastian from near death and making him something different than he had been. And, my wedding day. When I married Quaid.

I drew a breath and pushed on the library door, slipping inside. The staircase leading down to the underground was closed and it took me a frustrating couple of minutes to find the right combination of wall stones to press to make them appear. Charlotte was way better at this than I was. I finally managed, though, the grinding sound as the floor shifted and the stairs came into view ending my irritation and I made my way down into the dark.

I really needed sleep, but that would have to wait. The long, cold corridor of stone led me to the entry to the surface chamber, walls covered in glyphs. I smiled into the dark at the recollection of Liam, the first time he entered this room. I had a different experience, forced to watch Gram and Pender resurrect the echoes of fallen witches to defend Mom, calling up Alison's ghost on the same night. But when Liam came here much later, we had no idea there was more to this place, until his investigations proved otherwise.

I rested one hand on the pedestal in the middle of the room, the familiar tingle of magic rippling around my fingers. Again, stone ground, the floor dropping away, exposing the spiral staircase descending into the ground. I knew this whole place was an archive, held the history of my family and all magic families. But I'd never had time to study it. And Liam…

Neither did he.

Witchlight flared as I touched down on the bottom step in the breathless silence under the earth. This place was so full of memories too, but I couldn't get lost in them. My eyes avoided the spot on the floor where Ameline died when I stopped her heart. To save my son and the Universe.

I wouldn't go there, not right now. Instead, I crossed to the bedlike slab of rock in the middle of the round chamber, the walls etched with the names of my bloodline, and laid both hands upon it.

Iepa. I sent her name out into the ether. *I need to talk to you.* Not that she was reliable. In fact, notoriously the opposite. But I had come to believe, despite her lack of support, she truly cared and wanted to help, only to be stopped by her people and their non-interference policy.

Again, I sent her name out. And was met with silence. I leaned against the slab with a sigh, finally hoisting myself up on it, elbows on knees, head in hands.

"Damn it all to hell," I whispered into the stillness. "Now what?"

"Finally," a familiar voice said. "I've been waiting for you."

My head whipped up, shot around, eyes huge, mouth hanging open as I caught my breath and held it. And stared into the quiet, watchful gaze of Ameline Benoit.

TWENTY-SIX

I almost jumped out of my skin. "You're dead."

She laughed, a tinkling sound. I remembered her laugh. Used to hate it more than anything in this world. But now, it felt different. Light hearted, without malice.

What the hell?

"I assumed you'd show up long before now." She drifted toward me, looking solid and as real as ever. It had been seven years since I killed her. How was she standing here, perfect black bangs shining in the low light, ice-blue eyes sparkling, flawless, porcelain skin ghostly? She wore the same robe she was wearing the night I killed her.

I did kill her. Right?

"Been a little busy living my life." This was impossible. And yet, when she pulled herself up beside me, I reached out and touched her hand.

Solid. Real.

Oh. My. Swearword.

"Don't worry," she said with a wink. "I'm not going to attack you or anything." She laughed again, swinging her feet. Shock ripped through me. I'd never seen Ameline wink, let alone do something as carefree as swing her feet. "In fact, I'm really happy to see you. I've been down here alone so long, it's nice to have company."

"This is... what the... you're not..." I simply couldn't complete a sentence. My poor, weary brain was about to explode.

Ameline, once my nemesis who only ever wanted, in her sad and twisted way, for me to love her, set one hand on mine and fell serious, nose bare inches from my own, clear blue eyes locking me in place.

"I'm dead, Syd," she said, softly, with sorrow. "You did your job. It's over."

I nodded, unable to do anything else.

"But," she said, looking away, around at the walls of the chamber, "while my body died and my ego was devoured by your ghost friend, Alison, my soul became trapped down here." She waved around us. "That, I've discovered, was part of the point. The maji chamber needed a soul and mine was up for grabs."

I shuddered as I realized it could have been me, had she won. "Are you... okay?" Such a silly question to ask, all things considered. And did I really care? But I found I did. Time and distance and the new, fresh look on her face made me pause. Was this the same person who killed Liam? Who kidnapped my son and made me believe he was dead like his father?

"The part of me that was broken is long gone," Ameline said. "Alison saw to that. And I thank her for it." She paused, smiled as I recalled the ghostly girl devouring Ameline's furious echo. "And you, Syd. You might not want to know it, but you saved me from myself." Ameline squeezed my fingers. "I wasn't a very nice person, was I?"

I shook my head. "Not even close."

Ameline laughed.

"I rather like this place," she said, looking around again. "So much information. And I'm tied directly to the maji, so I'm not really bored or anything. Just a little lonely." A hint of girlish loss colored her voice. She turned to me with a faint smile and a hopeful expression that left me shaking as I tried to reconcile this Ameline with the one who murdered my grandmother, Ahbi, and caused so much destruction. "I'd like to think," she said, "I had the potential to turn out like you, had I the benefit of a Hayle family upbringing." Her brow creased slightly. "Instead, my lot was far different." The Dumonts. Even I didn't wish that evil family on anyone.

Was Ameline right? I sighed out my old animosity and let it go.

"I'm sorry," she said at last. "For your demon grandmother. For hurting you with Gabriel." She stopped and lowered her head. "And for Liam, Syd. For him, most of all. His soul was so kind. He tried to befriend me, to understand me, just before you arrived, just before I killed him. And, were I as I am now, things would have turned out so differently."

My heart constricted, his loss though long past still aching inside me.

Could I forgive her? It didn't matter, now.

"I need to ask you something," I said, if only to change the subject. Her head lifted and her little smile returned. I rather liked her openness. It made her delicate beauty all the more stunning. "I found out my heritage, how I was able to become maji."

Her smile widened. "The drach," she said.

"But you don't have drach blood." Or did she?

Ameline shook her head. "No," she said. "Mine is pure maji. From long ago, one of the dark maji fathered a daughter with a witch. And so, you see, even from the very beginning, at the core of us, you were always meant to be stronger. You have the blood of the first race. But I only had that of the second. Which, if you think about it, is really unfair." She grinned, though, as though she found it funny.

Like she was teasing an old friend.

I laid back on the slab, closing my eyes, not sure I could handle much more. "Do you know what's happening in the world?"

A breath of air movement alerted me just before Ameline's voice sounded in my ear. "I do," she said. "Through the maji."

I turned my head to stare into her eyes. "They know everything?"

She nodded, sadly and with regret. "I'm afraid so."

I looked away, up at the ceiling, anger bubbling. "Typical," I said. "They'll just leave us to die and not lift a finger. When it was the power of one of theirs that gave the Brotherhood the damned advantage in the first damned place."

Ameline's hand crept over mine again. "I'm sorry, Syd. But you don't need them, you know. You never did." I met her eyes again and wondered what the hell I was thinking taking comfort from Ameline Benoit while realizing I could really come to like this version of her a lot.

"You know what?" I sat up, her beside me. "You're absolutely right." Screw the maji. I'd deal with them eventually. And right now I was prepared to start pissing off everyone in any kind of authority I could get within hearing range. Maybe I was tired, and maybe my power wasn't at full strength. But I was a Hayle and a maji and the damned Light One and all that crap.

They'd better just look the hell out.

I hopped down, Ameline at my side, and turned to face her. "Sebastian and Alison were here a few days ago," I said.

Ameline nodded, suddenly shy. Shy? Seriously? "I felt them arrive, but they left and I didn't make myself known."

"Do you have any idea where they went?" Maybe I could solve one mystery at least.

But Ameline shattered that hope with a shake of her head. "I'm sorry," she said. "I have no idea."

Okay, maybe not. I drew a breath. "Do you know Belaisle's true aim?"

This time, she nodded. "The maji are aware he had Gaia. And that he is looking for a replacement."

"Me," I said.

Ameline bit her lower lip. "I fear so," she said. Hearing such things from her gave me the heebie jeebies while my heart softened and wanted to believe her. I was such a sucker. "But, Syd, the maji are afraid. Not of Belaisle. But of the one he serves. The one they call his dark master."

"Who?" Belaisle served no one, was far too arrogant for that.

Again, Ameline shook her head. "I don't know. But I do know it's not good. They won't speak directly of him, only in whispers I catch from time to time. You must be careful." Her hands caught mine. "You can't give him the power he requires to fulfill his master's needs."

"Not in the day planner for this week," I said.

"Thanks for the warning." And paused, considering. "Have you heard anything about the drach?"

Ameline's brow puckered again in a tiny frown. "No," she said. "Nor have the maji, as though something prevents them from being in contact." She shrugged her narrow shoulders, perfect bangs shadowing her eyes. "You're worried about them."

I was, but without help or knowing where to look, I was at a loss. And if the maji were clueless… well, no comment. Since they were usually clueless—

Okay, so it wasn't like me to keep my opinions to myself. Time to go. I looked around, feeling suddenly awkward. "Can you leave the chamber?"

Sad eyes belied the smile she gave me. "No," she said. "My life is here. As the keeper of the chamber. It's been too long without a soul to give it voice. That's my job, now."

Which meant I had to just leave her here, right?

"Syd," she said, fingers brushing over my arm, "ask the Stronghold about Creator."

Um, what? "What do you mean?"

Ameline's frown was back, deeper this time. "I don't know," she said. "But the maji are chattering about Creator and something to do with the Stronghold." She finally sighed and shrugged, stepping away from me, a small wave and a hopeful smile her farewell. "I hope you'll come back again, soon," she said.

And vanished into thin air.

I released a huge gust of air and shivered in the coolness of the chamber, not sure what to think. But I paused at the bottom of the stair and looked back. "I'll be back to visit," I said in the stillness.

No response. But I was sure she heard me.

The long, slow climb to the surface took me longer than usual, thighs aching from the exercise, whole body ready to drop. I reached the top only to have to climb one more flight, out from under the ground. I suppose I could have just torn open the veil, but I needed the time to work through things in my head, to shift my thinking about Ameline and absorb my anger at the maji.

Besides, I wanted a look around upstairs to see if there were any clues as to where Sebastian and his people had gone. I was so tired as I cleared the last step and turned to slap the protruding stone on the wall to close up the staircase, I failed to realize I wasn't alone in the room. In fact, I was half-turned toward the door before the shadowy shapes surrounding me registered at all.

My power rippled, though sluggish. It turned out my weariness saved them from a quick and painful death. Considering the young woman who stepped out of the shadows and came to hug me had a face I loved, I was happy for once to be this worn out.

"Syd." Trill Zornov embraced me, dark, curly hair tickling my nose. When she leaned away, I mustered a smile.

"Trill." The human born maji and her sorcerer brothers had helped me in the past. Trill worked through Max to draw me out of the veil when Batsheva drained my blood, saved me from an endless prison and possible death. And we'd fought together to tackle the Brotherhood, so I knew I could trust her and relaxed. Though when her small band of friends closed in, my natural caution kicked in once again.

"These are maji, like me." She turned and gestured to the young man in the front, about my height with a thick black beard and dark eyes. His were narrowed as he approached, but his handshake was firm and warm. "Sydlynn Hayle, Cable Noonan."

"Any friend of Trill's," he said.

"Has to prove himself," I said, only half joking. Okay, not joking even a little bit. Not after the last few days I'd had.

Trill's face fell a moment as he scowled, but I ignored him and pulled her aside. "You know what's going on?"

She nodded quickly. "We came to Wilding Springs as soon as we understood the magnitude of what happened." Her hand shook as it squeezed my arm. "I was so afraid for you and the family. Especially when the house was empty, everyone gone."

"They're safe," I said. Why was I being so short with her? This was Trill, my friend.

"We came here next," she said. "Wilding Springs is crawling with Brotherhood and Enforcers. I figured if anyone knew where you were, it would be the vampires." She looked around. "But they're gone, too."

I felt her frustration like my own and finally eased out of suspicion. Too wound up for your own good, Hayle.

"I know," I said, leaning back against a chair, rubbing my face with one hand. My eyes burned with weariness, body aching. But I had a meeting to go to and a long way to travel before I could sleep. "They're missing from Europe, too."

Trill gasped softly. "Sunny?"

"No." I turned toward Cable and his group. "Just the DeWinters." I gestured to the small group of maji. "Thanks for coming." There, now that wasn't so hard, was it?

Cable shrugged, black leather motorcycle jacket creaking. "Trill's idea," he said.

Okay. Asshat.

"We came to help," she said, glaring at him. "Anything we can do, Syd." Her intense eyes locked on mine. "Anything." Her power rippled around me and, for the first time since she'd hugged me a moment ago, I tasted her magic.

And recoiled. "What have you done?" I didn't mean to whisper those words, staring at her in shock. She felt totally different, her maji power warped somehow. Black now instead of shining rainbow light.

Trill grimaced, glanced at Cable who shook his head at her.

"It's a long story," she said. "But it's worth listening to, I promise."

She felt like a sorcerer. That wasn't possible, was it? And suddenly all the trust I had for her flew out the window and went South for the winter. Still, this was Trill.

I had one way to find out if she was trustworthy. The Stronghold would let me know the minute they tried to enter its borders.

"Come with me," I said, offering my hand and a small smile. She took it quickly, gesturing to her friends to gather close. "I have a safe place to go."

"We need to make a stop," Trill said. "Owen and Apollo."

At least I knew her brothers were okay and not on the missing list like so many of my friends seemed to be.

"Show me," I said. And carried them through the veil with me, heart beating just a little too fast.

TWENTY-SEVEN

Trill's odd new sorcerous feeling guided me to the center of Wilding Springs. I stepped out in the narrow space between the corner drug store and Johnny's, the local teen hangout. I'd spent quite a few Friday and Saturday nights there when I was younger, took the kids for burgers at least once a week now I was an old married woman. Being here, in the middle of my town—so eerily quiet and empty of power—made my skin crawl.

Trill pushed past me and stopped at the sidewalk, her friends waiting behind the dumpster the two businesses shared. I ignored them, concentrating on my shielding. This was a foolish place to be, though part of me longed for a fight with the Brotherhood, especially if I had allies with me. But a big battle in the heart of Wilding Springs would draw too much attention, especially now the normal residents didn't have the blur of embedded power to keep them from noticing.

The sound of pattering feet on pavement made me tense, two figures darkening the end of the alley. I relaxed a little as the smaller one waved at me and waved back. Owen slipped forward on sneakered feet to hug me. He'd grown tall, as tall as me, though I doubted he'd ever be as big as his brother, Apollo. Brilliant blue eyes—the bluest I'd ever seen in my life—smiled at me as Owen let me go, but there was something of worry and even fear in them, making it past his happiness to see me.

"Syd." I still thought of him as a kid, the boy I'd met so long ago, he and his sister on the run from the Brotherhood. His deep voice and the shadow of a beard on his face reminded me he'd grown up with the rest of us. "You're safe."

"You, too." I looked up as Apollo joined us. His typical smirk was missing, handsome face serious. I'd always liked him, though I would never tell him, only because he had this arrogant, misogynistic attitude for which I sometimes wanted to smack him. But all of that was gone from his demeanor as he hugged me tight, smelling of fresh air and fabric softener.

That created a swirl of memories in my head, of Liam. Damn it, I didn't have time for this.

"We have to go," Apollo said, releasing me. He looked genuinely afraid, glancing back over his shoulder.

"This place is stacked with Brotherhood."

I nodded, reached for the veil, the exact moment a blast of black rolled down the alley and slammed into all of us. My shields held, but I staggered, cursing my continuing weakness, drawing on the family magic a little more than I would have liked. It responded as best it could shoring up the gaps in my wards as my sorcery blossomed and went hunting.

Multiple shadows blocked the light from the street, back the way Trill had gone. She whistled to her people and we all turned at once, only to see our exit the other way had been cut off.

Trapped. Well, not for long.

The veil felt sluggish, my demon doing her best. I wrenched at it, sweat breaking out on my forehead while the others crowded around me, backs to me to protect me long enough for me to save them. I just hoped their faith wasn't misplaced.

I'm sorry, my demon grunted. *I'm trying*.

Shaylee threw her earth magic into it, shaking the ground, but it was a minor tremor, barely enough to make the oncoming Brotherhood stagger.

"Syd." Trill's hiss of worry reached me from over her shoulder. "What's the holdup?"

I didn't answer her, gritting my teeth and jerking at the edge of the veil. Blackness poured over us while Trill and her people pushed back. I could feel their power rippling around me, waves of darkness devouring other waves of darkness. My blossom of sorcery wanted to join them, but I pulled it back, hand reaching desperately into my pocket to retrieve my crystal.

It pulsed in my hand, the tiny life inside it as weary as I was. But, with a soft gasp that sounded like the ringing of a tiny bell, it shoved power at me, the last of its reserves. Enough to open the veil.

On this end, at least. I would just have to worry about getting us back out when we had left the Brotherhood behind.

The veil parted at last, the gaping hole beckoning. Panting, I turned to Trill only to see her gather a giant mass of black. My senses felt what she was doing before I could stop her or even fathom what she had planned. Creation energy channeled into the sorcery, feeding it, making it swell and grow, seeding it until it became something I'd never seen before.

She hurtled the mass forward, into the approaching Brotherhood. I could only stand and stare in horror as it hit them, engulfed them. And began to suck the very life from them. Creation power was meant to create, not destroy, and yet Trill had finally found a way to combine the hunger of sorcery's need to devour with the bursting, life-giving energy of creation magic.

The results were devastating. Flesh melted from bone, blood running black, bodies collapsing into puddles that used to be tendon and meat only seconds before. She spun on me, eyes jet black, before gesturing at the hole I'd made.

"Are we going?" She half laughed, exhilarated, clearly, and full of power.

I turned, realized what happened on one side of me was repeated on the other. Cable and his friends had squeezed past when I was otherwise occupied and dissolved their opponents, too. Sickened, unable to speak, I met Owen's troubled eyes. He took my hand without comment and led me into the veil.

I feared becoming trapped, though the moment I entered the place between planes, I felt a resurgence of energy and wondered where the power drain had come from. Yes, I was tired, but surely I wasn't that tired. Which made me wonder about Trill and her new friends and this ability they seemed to possess.

Had it affected me in my weakened state? I didn't want to think about it. Besides, if they weren't on the up and up, the Stronghold would let me know. Though I hated taking the risk bringing them there in the first place, I wasn't trusting my own power or cognition at the moment.

The veil parted before me, the main hall of the Stronghold a welcome sight. I stepped out and turned immediately, still holding Owen's hand. Apollo was next, on his brother's heels, dropping his grip on Owen's fingers the moment he was free. But I wasn't worried about the Zornov brothers being accepted.

I wanted to see what the Stronghold would do about Trill.

She leaped out with full confidence, looking around her with a grin. Her maji friends entered in a group, Cable at their head. His attitude pissed me off immediately, how he seemed to claim the place with his gaze.

I needn't have worried about anyone thinking in terms of ownership about the Stronghold. Not ever again. His power pressed down on Trill and the others, a bubble of shimmering, rainbow magic pinning them in place as the veil slipped shut.

Syd, he sent, anger in his mental voice, a thundering earthquake in my head. *Who are these?*

Not Brotherhood, I sent. *But. What do you think? I'll trust your judgment.*

He grunted, the whole room shaking from it. Trill finally looked afraid, eyes meeting mine.

"Syd, what's going on?" She raised one hand, touched the barrier. It didn't harm her, but the Stronghold wasn't letting her through, either.

"It's not me," I said. "This place has a soul, Trill. He's deciding if you're welcome or not."

Cable glared at me, his little pack of whatever they'd become sharing his nasty expression. Trill's face fell, but she stepped back, into their midst. She'd made her choice, apparently.

Agreed they are not Brotherhood, the Stronghold sent at last. *But they are of maji blood, Syd. And have corrupted their creation power, their gift, with the darkness of sorcery. I have never encountered their kind before.* He paused. *I am wary of them. Still, if you speak on their behalf, I will allow them to remain.* The Stronghold sounded troubled and I agreed with his concern.

"He says you've corrupted your creation power," I said to the group. "And from what I saw in that alley, you're not afraid to use it."

"Should we be?" Cable bit off the words like explaining anything to me was a waste of his time. He turned to Trill, gripped her upper arm in one hand, dark hair falling over his face, the scruff of his beard. Apollo and Owen both leaned forward, as if to protect their sister, but from their expressions they knew they'd lose even if they could reach her through the shield.

"Syd, please listen." She jerked free of Cable and stepped forward again, both hands pressed to the inside of the shimmering wall between us. I moved forward on aching legs, heart weary, mind exhausted, wanting to believe my friend. "We're tired of the Brotherhood always having the advantage. You are strong, able to fight them." She didn't sound bitter, just frustrated. "But you're not always around. And you need foot soldiers who can handle themselves." She looked back over her shoulder at her glaring companions. "We can be your army."

I didn't respond right away, knowing we were gathering a bit of a peanut gallery. I could feel witches watching, Mom and Dad among them, but thankfully they kept their distance and let me deal with this.

What do you think? I sent to my alter egos. *She kind of makes sense, doesn't she?* I'd longed for others who could step up and take on the Brotherhood, allies strong enough not to fall under the power of their sorcery. And while I didn't really like Cable, Trill was my friend.

This feels sketchy, my demon growled. *Something's off with this bunch. Like they have another reason for wanting us to trust them.*

Agreed, Shaylee sent in her soft and elegant voice. *And they feel dirty, Syd. Like they've been tainted.*

By sorcery. My vampire's sadness was clear in my head, in my whole body. *I don't think we can allow them access to us or to the Stronghold. Allies? Perhaps. But outside our safety zone. Until they can prove their worth and real goals.*

Syd, Owen's voice met mine, the darkness of his sorcery somehow cleaner than what his sister had become. *I love her. She's my sister. But I don't know her anymore.*

That decided me. I sighed and nodded before meeting Trill's eyes. It couldn't have been easy for Owen to speak against her like that. He only would if he was really worried.

"Trill," I said. "There are lines drawn we just don't cross. And I'm afraid you crossed one."

Her face darkened, anger finally showing as black crawled over her brown eyes. I watched it ripple with sorrow falling over me.

"How dare you judge me?" She slammed both fists against the shielding. "I've been out there, Syd. Alone, trying to make this work." Obviously her brothers didn't count. "Not all of us have the benefit of being pure maji." There was the bitterness at last. "And when I finally manage to figure it out, to come up with the means to fight back, you judge me." She barked a laugh. "You. Judging me. That's rich." She turned her back on me, joining her friends. "We offered you our help. Do you want it, or not?"

I needed to keep an eye on her. She was losing it, slipping away from the Trill I knew to the elements knew where. But I simply couldn't allow them to stay.

"Not," I said with real regret.

TWENTY-EIGHT

Trill spun, stared at me like I'd slapped her. Cable cursed softly and shrugged. A black tunnel formed and I gaped at them, though I could see a faint glimmer of Harvard Yard on the other side. So, they couldn't travel between planes, per se. The connection between Boston and the Stronghold must have given them something to latch onto.

At least, I hoped that was the case.

Trill continued to hold my gaze as her friends filed through and left the Stronghold. She lingered one last moment, sadness on her face before she turned to Owen and Apollo.

"Are you coming?" She held out her hand to her brothers, desperation clear.

Owen shook his head, refusing to meet her eyes while

Apollo sighed softly, hands in his pockets.

"Be safe, sis," he said. "We'll be waiting for you when you come to your senses."

Her teeth caught her lower lip, tears standing in her eyes. For a moment, I wondered if she might change her mind and ask to stay. Instead, she turned and stepped into the tunnel, the blackness collapsing behind her.

What do you wish me to do, the Stronghold sent, *if they try to return?*

Only Trill is permitted, I sent. *Let me know if she tries to come back.*

I pulled Owen to me, hugged him as he snuffled on my shoulder. When he met my eyes again, there was so much pain in his face I almost wept myself.

"We're so worried about her," he said, Apollo draping one arm around his brother's shoulders. "But she won't listen to us." Owen looked up at the taller Zornov. "We hoped seeing you would help, but she's still wrapped around Cable's finger."

"He's a real piece of work," Apollo said, lips a grim line, blue eyes snapping anger. "I don't trust him at all, Syd."

"Then, I don't, either," I said. "I'm sorry, I should have been there for Trill." Why didn't they come to me sooner?

"Our fault," Owen said, wiping his face with one hand. "We thought we could handle it." He exchanged a sad look with his brother. "We were working together, hunting Belaisle and the Brotherhood." I nodded, knew that part. "Trill had made contact with Cable and his crew a few years ago, but neither of us really knew much about who he was or what Trill's association meant, outside the fact they were maji blood." Owen sighed, one hand running over his mouth. "I should have asked more questions, but she dodged and I let her." His impossibly blue eyes shone with tears. "She grew distant, not like her. Then, one day, she took off with Cable, told us she'd be right back."

"She was gone for a week," Apollo said, hand on his brother's shoulder, a comforting squeeze making Owen's head droop. "We went looking for her, but she blocked us, even Nona." Their grandmother usually kept close tabs on Trill, so I was surprised—and not so surprised— she managed to evade the old maji matriarch. "Seven days later, she strolled back into our lives a different person."

"Different how?" I already guessed.

"Her power." Owen shivered, shook his head. "It's different, Syd."

I'd seen that first hand. "Do you know what she did? The Stronghold said she's tainted her creation power."

"With sorcery," Owen bobbed a nod. "But I have no idea how. It does mean I'm obsolete, at least in her estimation." That seemed to trouble him most, and I understood. The pair were a team for so long, it must have hurt him to have her cut him out like this. "I know that's petty," he said, "but I'm worried, really worried. With me controlling the sorcery side, she had a buffer against it. Now she's blended the two..." He met his brother's eyes before returning his gaze to me. "I have no idea what she's becoming. But it's not good, Syd."

Apollo nodded in agreement, rubbing one arm like he was cold. "We hoped you might be able to help. But I guess she's too far gone into Cable's control for that."

Maybe if circumstances were different I could have made Trill a priority. Now?

Yeah. Rugs and sweepings under and guilt.

Mom's soft magic brushed against me as she gently approached. Her kind, welcoming smile made both Zornovs smile in return.

"You two must be tired and starving," she said, linking arms with them. Apollo half bowed, but his douchebag self was nowhere in evidence.

"Thank you, Mrs. Hayle," he said before meeting my eyes. "Anything we can do to help, Syd. We might not be Trill, but we're sorcerers."

I nodded, squeezed his hand. I liked this new, reserved Apollo much better than the arrogant player he'd always portrayed. "I'll put you to work, don't worry." I frowned, shook my head, thinking about his past and how he'd grown up in the underworld of normals. Gambling, stealing, grifting. "Maybe you can be more helpful in another way." The family fortune. We might not need it this minute, the Stronghold taking care of our needs, but if we were going to reclaim Wilding Springs, we'd need our money back. Or a new fortune made.

Apollo listened carefully as I explained what happened. His eyes lit up and he grinned at me, a little of his old self showing as he winked and clucked his tongue at me, shooting me with an imaginary gun.

"I know just the badass," he said, stepping away from Mom. Owen joined him. "Thanks for the offer, Mrs. Hayle," he said, saluting her with a jaunty wave. "We'll take you up on that as soon as we get back."

She let them go as I fished in my pocket and handed them my mirror shard. "Be careful," I said. "And thank you."

The Zornov brothers, both invigorated by the thought of helping from the grins on their faces, took off at a jog for the now shimmering giant mirror, disappearing through it. I hoped I hadn't sent them into fresh danger, but if they could really help, I'd be forever grateful.

Mom hugged me gently from the side, chin on my shoulder. "You have a lot to tell me, I take it?"

I woke with a start, body quivering in the darkness. It took a moment for my demon to wake, grumbling and complaining. My vampire nudged me gently.

It's my turn to rest, she sent as my demon stretched and yawned. *Shaylee will wake shortly and take over.*

I'd learned long ago they took turns watching over me as I slept. *How much time did I get?* I yawned, too, jaw creaking. It felt like I'd just closed my eyes.

About an hour, my vampire sent. *I'm sorry, it's all the time we had. You need to be in Europe shortly.*

Right. Message in from Femke to Mom told me the meeting was almost ready, if a few hours later than the European leader would have liked. Trying to force the world council leaders to move at speed was like herding cats on high test catnip.

I turned to sit on the edge of the bed, elbows on knees, face in hands. The room Quaid picked for us was nice, carpeted floor soft on my bare feet, the bed that perfect mix of soft and hard I loved. Too bad I couldn't sink into it for about a week.

My bones moaned as I stood and stretched out the kinks of this endless night. So much had happened in the last two and a half days. The story of my life. But it was time to put an end to this, even if I had to force the other world council leaders to step up and take action.

I made time for a five minute shower, emerging from the steaming water feeling a little better. My power was still low, but much more ready, willing and able than it had been just an hour ago. If I could have managed another hour, I might have been able to refresh completely, but I'd take what I could get.

As I left the room in my clean jeans and t-shirt, sneakers squeaking on the stone floor, I dodged a pair of running children before being tackled by my own. The two who skimmed past me stopped and waited, bouncing on impatient feet while Galleytrot came to a halt, sinking to his haunches to watch me with his tongue lolling out.

At least someone was having a good time. Ethie's little cheeks glowed pink, her eyes bright with laughter and Gabriel was pretty much the same.

"Mom!" Ethie clapped her hands in excitement. "So much fun!"

I grinned, kissed her, sent her on to her friends. Gabriel hugged me.

"Are you okay, Mom?" His natural empathy reminded me of Liam.

"I'm fine," I said, tousling his strawberry blond hair. "Now, go play with your sister."

He beamed me a smile and took off running, the pack of four joined by two more who burst out of a side corridor to a chorus of giggles and shrieks. Galleytrot's low chuckle turned me around to face him.

"Enjoying yourself, are you?" He came to my side, my hands digging into the fur of his mane, making him groan in happiness.

"They've kept me on my toes," he said. "But they are safe, and that is all I can ask for." Red fire flickered in his eyes. Gwynn might have freed him, but Galleytrot was still a wild hound. "Do you need me?"

"You are doing exactly what I need you to do already," I said, hugging his big head, planting a kiss on his soft ear. "Thank you."

"Galleytrot!" Ethie's piercing voice summoned him with imperialness from the end of the hall.

"It appears my presence is required," he said with laughter in his voice. "Keep me posted?"

"Of course." I let him go, watched him bound off after the kids and hugged myself, grateful for this little slice of happy.

When I turned to go the other way, I let out a shriek of shock. The silver Persian at my feet glared up at me with glowing amber eyes.

"Warn a girl," I said, bending to scoop him into my arms.

"I take it you have news." His fur shivered. "Report."

I laughed. I just couldn't help it. He was so pissed at me, and that always tickled my funny bone. It wasn't funny, but all the stress and worry and rushing about had made me a little punch drunk, so laughing was my only option.

That or collapsing into tears. I'd take the giggles.

Sassafras rolled his eyes at me, batting my face. "Just tell me," he sighed.

I filled him in on everything I knew as I carried him

toward the cafeteria. By the time I was done, we were slipping inside, my eyes huge at the number of witches gathered, chatting and eating.

"Is it just me," I said, "or has the family gotten a whole lot bigger?" There had to be at least two hundred and fifty people here, pushing up the numbers of my normally one hundred or so coven into bursting.

"More refugees arrive every hour," he said, soft and sad. "With horror stories and death following them. I'm just glad they're finding us."

"So the rescue teams are effective?" I liberated an orange—or what I guessed was an orange with its thick skin and deep red color of local fruit— a small carton of milk and a bottle of water from the buffet style table before turning and leaving the room for the main hall. I sat on one of the benches in the empty space, grateful for the quiet, setting the silver Persian down beside me. I cracked open the carton for him, pulling down the sides to make a small bowl before peeling my breakfast.

"It would appear so." He lapped a few tongue swipes before looking up at me, a bead of milk hanging from his chin. "You're leaving soon?"

I nodded. "The world council should be in Oxford by now." I checked my watch, amazed it was only seven in the morning, Wilding Springs time. That meant noon in England. She said 1PM. I'd have to hurry.

The mirror shimmered as I stuffed the sweet sliver of

citrus into my mouth, Piers striding through. Behind him came a string of witches, soot-covered and stumbling from shock, but alive and well. Mom hurried forward at once, appearing out of nowhere, and suddenly the main hall was as crowded as the cafeteria. I stood, sweeping my breakfast behind me, to greet my friend as he came to hug me.

"Big haul," he said. "We found them hiding out." His voice vibrated with weariness, but the hint of success. "Most of them made it."

"Thank you." I pulled away from him. "You need sleep before you go out again."

"I can't," he said, shaking his head so his silken hair moved like a wave. Zoe appeared, worming her way under his arm. He smiled down at her, kissed the tip of her nose. "But, breakfast would be awesome."

The mirror shimmered again, catching my attention. A young man stumbled through, his sorcery hitting me like a blow. But it wasn't an attack, not from the shocked look on Piers's face, the way his whole body crumbled when the sorcerer lurched toward him and fell into his arms.

"The Steam Union has fallen," the young man gasped. "We need you, Piers."

TWENTY-NINE

The sorcerer collapsed, Piers easing him to the floor. I crouched with him, Mom rushing over to check on us. My friend's face compressed in grief as he finally looked up and met my eyes.

"Syd," he choked. "She's made her bed."

I know he was talking about his mother, but I couldn't leave it there. "We can't let the Steam Union just vanish," I said, pulling him to his feet. "We're going. Now."

Piers followed me as I jerked open the veil and reached for the young man's mind at the same time. The image of an underground tunnel was all I had to latch onto, that and the feeling of danger.

"This could be bumpy," I said as Piers and I leaped through the gap I'd made. A moment of weightlessness followed, then the other end opened and dropped us into overly fragrant dimness. My feet splashed into water, stone tunnel roof overhead making me crouch, though it only appeared low. Piers grunted beside me, the bottom of his longcoat soaking in the stinking fluid washing past us.

"Sewer," he said, a hint of relief in his voice. "This way."

The fact he knew where we were and where to go made me wonder about his hiding habits. Instead, I plugged my nose with one hand and followed him down the tunnel. He hoisted himself up onto a ledge at the T-junction of the tunnel, pulling me up beside him. His nose wrinkled in disgust as he shook out the bottom of his coat, me examining my squishy and vile sneakers. A little push of magic cleaned them, giving me dry socks and jeans again, Piers's sorcery devouring the mess and cleansing him, too. Still, there was no ignoring the stench. We both shrugged and carried on.

I followed his tense shoulders down the narrow ledge, my magic probing ahead of me, finding nothing, just blank emptiness. Piers stopped at one point and lowered his head, chewing his bottom lip, face scrunched into a scowl.

"Where are they?" I wound up tighter. This could be a trap. But Piers shook his head and spun, slipping past me, going back the way we came.

"Sorry," he murmured. "Wrong turn. This way."

I let out a gust of frustrated air and followed.

Ten minutes of disgustingness later and Piers paused, glancing back at me over his shoulder. I caught the pressure of sorcery ahead, just the barest hint of it, right before his shoulders slumped and he nodded.

"Stay close," he said. "She's going to be pissed."

At what? Because we were here to help? Or because he was showing me their secret hideout in the nasty sewers?

Or, my vampire sent, awake again, *because he left her and she's still angry.*

Oh, yeah. That. Wasn't always about me, was it?

Piers stepped forward, two figures melting out of the darkness to greet him. I caught their murmured conversation, the sounds of it at least, then moved ahead with him when he gestured for me to keep advancing. I glanced to the right, at the sorcerer knee-deep in crap below, then to the left, shimmying past his partner. Both had desperate looks on their faces, full of fear and loss. My heart contracted as Piers turned toward the wall and pressed against the stone with his magic.

The rock ground together, moving inward, shifting to one side. He stepped through without hesitation, into the light and I went with him, not nearly as confident of our welcome.

The door wound its way shut behind me, but I wasn't paying attention to it. Not when I had more important—

and painful—things to focus on. This appeared to be the main entry to some kind of bunker, almost like a small version of the great hall at the Stronghold. Bodies lay scattered around, though not from battle. It appeared the Steam Union made it safely here and could go no further. The sounds of soft snoring and the near-comatose feel to some of them screamed pure exhaustion.

A young woman detached from a small knot of people and hurried forward, throwing her arms around Piers. I recognized his sister, Clover, just as she leaned around him, her thick, black braid dangling between us and offered me a sad smile.

"Be welcome, both of you," Clover Southway said. "I'm so glad you're here." And burst into tears.

Piers comforted his sister while I looked around, horror growing by the minute. Damn it, I shouldn't have just abandoned the Steam Union like this. I let my dislike for Eva Southway put an entire group into danger.

We have stretched ourselves to our very limits, my vampire sent in a chiding tone. *Don't you dare say we were slacking even for a second.*

I know, I sent, guilt easing. *It's just hard to see this.*

Commotion stirred, the tall, severe blonde with the furious face who stormed toward us making me take a step back. Not out of fear, but out of a renewed sense of guilt. That was, until Eva Southway opened her damned spiteful mouth and spoke.

"What are you doing here?" She glared at her son before shooting me one of those "if looks could kill I'd be dead ten times over" stares. "Neither of you are welcome."

She had to be kidding. "We want to help, Mum," Piers said, the sound of his heart breaking in his voice. "We have a safe place to offer, where you can regroup."

He might as well have told her to go to hell, the way her face constricted in fury. "How dare you?" She strode the last few steps and jerked Clover out of Piers's grip. Her daughter trembled, lower lip vibrating, looking up at her mother with grief so powerful I wondered how this woman had managed to have two amazing kids. "We don't need your handouts."

That did it. I'd been through quite enough crap in the last little while, thank you, to take flack for offering to help a band of clearly undeserving creepzillas with a death wish.

"Good to know," I snapped. "Have fun keeping your mess together." I stared around with open disdain. "Looks like you have it handled."

She spun on me, practically spitting fury. "This is none of your concern!" Her power slammed into me, but even in my weakened, tired state, she was no match. Her magic was depleted, on the edge of starvation and I jerked out of my rage and into sympathy. And back again as she went on. "Considering the fact this is all your fault, oh high and mighty Maji Sydlynn Hayle who cares about no one but herself." Eva shook so hard I thought she might break apart, even as my anger spiked.

"My fault." I laughed in her face. No one was allowed to blame me for disasters that went down but me. She didn't qualify. "So, the Brotherhood taking over the world is my fault. Got it."

"Mum." Piers glared at me, though his eyes weren't angry but pleading. "You have to listen. We need the Steam Union to survive. Don't let your anger stop you from saving our people."

She whipped her head around again, temper focused on her son. A tall, dark haired man with a beard wearily stepped forward, one hand on her shoulder, but she shrugged off. I recognized Pier's father, Felix, even as his sad, dark eyes met mine.

"You gave up the right to claim the Steam Union as your family," she spit in her son's sad face. "You're part of the problem, Piers, not the solution. The Steam Union has taken a blow to the core, but we will survive." Her words seemed to put backbone in those who listened, though they all looked and felt so weary, ready to quit. "We're tired of being the weak cousins of our great enemy." A few murmurs of agreement rose. "But we're also tired of keeping watch for those who could care less about us." I almost snorted and replied. Something along the lines of since freaking when, but she was still rattling on so I held my tongue. "Now, if you two are done, I have my people to care for. While you deal with the mess you've made."

Fine. Whatever. I saluted her with my middle finger and turned, not caring if Piers followed. I couldn't drag her, kicking and screaming, into caring that there was a whole bunch of others out there dying and suffering. Because, clearly, the Steam Union were the only freaking group that mattered even a little. They and their sacrifices.

I was so mad by the time I was out in the sewer again, I let Shaylee out. She shook the stone, the water sloshing around the startled guard, rocks and dust falling from the ceiling.

Please be more careful, my vampire sent in a pained tone. *I'd rather not dig out from a ton of rubble because of your childish temper.*

Shaylee sulked, but I sighed and nodded just as a hand settled on my shoulder. I turned to face Piers, saw the tears on his cheeks and hugged him, my own anger forgotten.

"She's going to get everyone killed," he whispered into my hair.

"I'm sorry." I pulled away. "What do you want to do?"

The patter of chasing feet turned us around. Clover threw herself into his arms, his white blond hair stark contrast against her black braid, but their gray eyes and aristocratic, angular features a perfect match for each other. "I'm so afraid," she said, almost wailed. She looked like she was barely holding it together. "Please, Piers. You have to stay. Mum will listen to you once she's calmed down."

But my friend shook his head. "I left two years ago," he said, "because she'd stopped listening to anyone, Clover." He touched his sister's cheek with one trembling hand. "Come with us."

It was her turn to say no, backing away, hugging herself inside her dark gray coat. "I have to stay," she said. "If only for Dad." Her eyes met mine. "Take care of my brother," she said, before spinning and running past the sentry and back into the bunker.

I grasped Piers's arm and pulled him around to face me. "What do you want to do?"

"Nothing," he said, trying to push past me.

"Piers." I stopped him, with physical force and with magic. "If the Steam Union does fall, it creates a vacuum in power and I'm not sure that's a great idea."

"She doesn't want to have anything to do with us," Piers said, eyes glittering with anger and hurt. "It's not like she's going to be much good anyway."

I sighed and let him go. "Okay," I said. "We'll tell Femke and let her deal with it."

Why did I get the terrible feeling, as we retreated through the veil, I'd just made the wrong decision?

THIRTY

I did my best not to fidget in my seat while the others in the room whispered among themselves. Our arrival at Oxford was just in time, the veil delivering Piers and me to Femke's office where Danilo and Sunny sat talking with the European Council Leader.

Femke walked over to me and hugged me, though the wrinkling of her nose as she came close made me sigh. A burst of power cleared the air, though the stench of the sewer still clung to the insides of my nostrils and left me with a bad taste in my mouth.

It took us only a few minutes to fill her in on everything that happened since I saw her the night before. Femke, the vampire queen and werewolf king all listened carefully, Danilo's expression of anger at Eva's reaction joined by a pulse of irritation from Sunny and a heavy sigh from Femke.

"I've been trying to reach her," the tall Swede said. "I feared she and her people were gone."

"They might as well be," Piers said, disgust replacing his sadness. He rammed both hands into his pockets, head down, brow furrowed. "Let her implode. I just hope she does it fast and without taking too many of the family with her."

I squeeze his arm, the only comfort I could offer and changed the subject. "Are the leaders here?"

Femke nodded quickly, though the look she cast at Sunny and Danilo made my temper fire. "I was just about to call to order," she said.

"Let me guess." I jerked a thumb at the vampire and werewolf, both stone faced. "Shortsighted, old fashioned, irritating witches only."

Femke opened her mouth and closed it again before laughing weakly. "Oh, Syd," she said. "I needed that." She cleared her throat before speaking. "I'm sorry, we're just going to have to tolerate it." One hand came up, though no one had protested. "For now. Until this crisis is over. But I intend to ensure this never happens again." Whether she referred to our present predicament, or the exclusion of Sunny and Danilo, I had no idea.

Ten minutes later I squirmed in the large, overly carved wooden chair around a large circular table in a back room warded so heavily I didn't think even a nuclear bomb could make a dent in the protections. I was half tempted to argue on Sunny and Danilo's behalf, but Femke's blue eyes begged me to behave. Besides, there was so much fear in the room, I figured I'd give them their private meeting. But only if I got the result I was looking for.

Femke's power formed a shining blue hammer which she used to strike the table. It vibrated with song, the normal sharp thudding a bell-like tone that nonetheless penetrated to my bones. I shivered and focused, while the rest of the assembled turned eyes on Femke. I took the opportunity to examine their faces. I hadn't seen most of them since the world conclave in Wilding Springs, and that was about eight years ago. It looked like none of the leaderships had changed, at least. Now, if I could only remember their names.

"Thank you all for coming to Oxford for this meeting," Femke said in her smooth, diplomatic voice.

"It was kind of you to host." Sumiko Himura, leader of the Asian territory, said, her dark, quiet eyes turning to me and back to Femke. "We are all concerned about what has happened to seal off the North American territory." She did a good job hiding fear, that one. And had called me a goddess, once. Maybe I could use that to my advantage. "The fact Sydlynn Hayle is in our midst does not bode well." I wasn't sure if I should be flattered or insulted.

"I wouldn't be here," I said, keeping my voice as level

as possible, "if it wasn't life or death."

They murmured, even the Enforcer leaders standing behind their council counterparts. Femke let them. *Nicely done*, she sent. After a moment, her bell-tone hammer struck the table. "I will now ask Coven Leader Hayle to show us what is happening behind the power blocks."

I rose to my feet and called on my maji power. It rose before me, forming a sphere that burst outward, turning the air in the middle of the table into a holographic, 3D space. "Council Leaders," I said as I showed them my former Council, Belaisle smirking among them, "North America has been taken by the Brotherhood."

They gasped as one, staring as I increased the size of Belaisle's face until it dominated the view. I'd thought carefully about how to present this to them, what kind of theatrics they might require. And decided to throw all in at once. Better to hit them as hard as I could.

One Syd fastball, coming up.

"Council Leader Plower has betrayed all witches," I said. "She has signed a law giving full control of our territory to the Brotherhood, including policing and justice. And they have used that power to crush our covens." This was the difficult image to show, but I lived it again as I projected the fire, the stakes, seen out the door of the Rhodes coven house, the writhing bodies collapsing into the flames.

The leaders were silent this time, but their outrage

and grief hit me like a wall as a single tear made it down my cheek. I showed them the death of Violet Rhodes, the soot-covered refugees being comforted by my people, even the collapsed and weakened Steam Union I'd just left behind.

I shut off the image abruptly, to a few shrieks of shock. "We need you," I said. "Like we have never needed you before."

So much fury in them, washing around me, aimed at the Brotherhood, their anger carrying in their whispered conversations. Could it be? Would they actually step up for once and do what was necessary?

Could this be all over in a matter of hours? I could only hope.

"Sydlynn Hayle." Sumiko's cool voice was the first to speak up. "My territory would be honored to accept the Hayle coven and offer you sanctuary."

That triggered a landslide of such offers that warmed my heart. They were practically fighting over my family by the time I raised my hand with a smile.

"Thank you," I said. "Such generosity is unnecessary but much appreciated. If you truly want to help, you will instead assist me in taking back my territory." I paused. "For the good of all witches."

And there it was, the first glimmer of retreat. I felt them pulling back from me even as Bindi Braylen, the Council Leader from Australia, spoke in her heavy accent.

"What would you have us do?"

"The law states," I said, "only a unanimous vote of the world councils can disband and render void a rogue council and their laws." Anxiety stirred in them. What the hell were they so afraid of? "If you were to vote in favor of declaring the present North American council rogue, the laws they created granting power to the Brotherhood would be null and void and the Enforcers could regain control."

"What you ask," Yamini Dhavan, the quiet, statuesque Indian Leader said, "is a massive request." Her brown eyes told me nothing of what she was thinking, dark skin red-toned in the light. "You understand this?"

My nostrils flared. "I'm asking you to protect the witches of my territory from a council that has handed them over to the enemy," I said, flashing the image of the burning stakes again. She flinched from it, but shook her head, silken, black hair shimmering

"We are well aware of the situation," Yamini said. "But, might I play Devil's advocate a moment." No, she damned well could not. But she went on anyway before I could shut her the hell up. "You say Erica Plower was not coerced, nor was her council. That they made these decisions on their own, by choice, with full disclosure."

"Not to the covens of my territory," I said through clenched teeth.

"Which, according to law," Sumiko continued for her

counterpart, sleek black bob barely moving as she tilted her head, "is their prerogative, correct? They are not required to gain the permission of all covens to pass law."

And this was exactly where I feared this conversation would go. "So you'll stand by and allow the Brotherhood to slaughter witches and do nothing about it, is that it?"

Ife Maalouf, African Leader, smiled sadly, big hands flat on the table, skin so deep in tone she matched the stain of the wood. "Our hands truly are tied," she said, sitting back while the others nodded. "Perhaps if we had proof she was coerced. But it is not our right to judge or control a council leader who has the support of her council. It sets a terrible precedent." She leaned forward again, intent and focused. "What about the next time a council leader makes a decision with which the others disagree? Will this become an epidemic of crushing the free will of witches?" They were nodding and chattering among themselves like they were so freaking clever. "I cannot support such an action."

"I demand to hear directly from Erica Plower." Ana Maria Diaz, South American Leader, nodded to her right and left, a smug look on her face, Latino beauty failing her as she aged. Just my irritated opinion.

What the hell? "This is a terrible idea," I said, desperation and fury spinning around like a tornado inside me.

But Ana Maria was already acting, her rich, soupy

power reaching out toward the wards. And Femke, frowning, head down, let her do it.

I barely had time to feel the crushing blow of my friend's compliance when the air sizzled with blue magic and Erica appeared.

Her eyes locked immediately on me, scowl so deep it aged her years. "I shouldn't be surprised to find you here," she snapped before looking around at the others. "Though, I am shocked by this betrayal."

"Not at all," Sumiko said in her smooth voice, gesturing gracefully in spare motion for a seat to be brought forward. "We asked you to join us for a reason." Her glittering black eyes settled on me. "We've been told the Brotherhood have been given control of your territory, by design."

Erica grunted as she hit the seat hard. "They have formed an equal partnership with us," she said, face smoothing out, her Council Leader persona taking over. "And though there has been some unrest, we are in the process of restructuring. Some dissent is expected in these times of change."

They were buying it, this slick act she offered them. Femke met my furious eyes, her anxiety on her face, but remained silent.

"How forward thinking of you," Bindi said, sounding like she meant it, even a little cheer in her voice.

Erica bowed her head. "I'm certain my allies would be

willing to discuss a similar arrangement with you."

Bindi gulped visibly and looked away, tanned face paling to ashen gray. So did the others, to a witch. Which meant they didn't believe a word Erica was saying. The contrary, back stabbing, weak willed bitches.

"Yes," I said. "How forward thinking." My power flared as hot as my temper, casting the image of the burning at them one more time, the loss of the Rhodes coven sharp and real, my magic even filling the room with the harsh scent of burnt death.

Erica's power sliced through the image, cutting it into shards that dissipated with soft moans like the departing souls of lost witches. All eyes turned to her. She didn't even bat an eye, stern face tight with contempt.

Erica's face lifted, eyes meeting mine again. "I'm not surprised to find you've been bad mouthing me and the North American Council to the rest of the world," she said. "Your little display makes that clear." Display? Executing witches was a display to her, now. "But, did you also tell them you declared the Hayle coven autonomous?" Gasps of shock met that tidbit, enough the Council Leaders spun on me. She'd given them something to focus on, to shake free from what I'd shown them and they took the bait. Of course they did. Why did I ever expect any of them to do otherwise? Erica's triumph glistened in her eyes. "No? You failed to inform this august assembly you no longer wish to claim any territory as your own?" She knew that wasn't true, but it gave her ammunition against me, didn't it? Their wary eyes probed me.

"I think it's obvious why I took that action," I said as coldly as I could manage. So I wouldn't freak out and lose my damned temper and maybe tear her into itty bitty bite-sized pieces my demon could eat with tartar sauce. "To protect my coven."

"You doomed your coven," Erica snapped. "And removed yourself from this great alliance in an effort to undermine everything we have tried to do. To stop our progress." She gestured around herself. "I hope now you see how futile that effort is."

I didn't need to look around me. Her smug satisfaction was enough answer anything I said in response would fall on deaf ears. While I didn't expect them to jump up and defend me, the Council Leaders remained stonily silent, their quiet, stern gazes telling me she had more of their support than I did.

Why the hell did I bother again?

"Now," Erica stood, "if you'll all excuse me, I have a territory to run. As I'm sure you do, too." She glared at me. "Sydlynn Hayle," she said. "I tell you this with all the world leaders of our people as witness. If you try anything, do anything to harm me or to damage this alliance, the entire world will hunt you down for the rest of your days."

THIRTY-ONE

I've always been hot tempered. It was so hard not to lunge across the table at Erica, my body trembling with the effort. My vampire held me still while Shaylee whispered a dig I could offer instead.

I grinned, tight and furious. "That's okay, Erica," I said. "You have your little moment of victory. While my family found a place where we can be safe and not be harvested by the Brotherhood for our power." Maybe it was stupid to tell her, but it wasn't like she or Belaisle could do anything about it. And I needed a scrap of success or I'd go mad. Her eyes narrowed, face tense as I laughed at her growing understanding and frustration. "That's right," I said, grinding in it. "He may have rejected you and your Enforcers, kicked out the Brotherhood because of their evil. But right now, at this moment, the Hayle coven and all the witches we've managed to rescue rest in comfort and under the protection of the Stronghold." Erica's anger cracked her veneer and she snarled at me. "Such a shame he saw right through you," I said while the other council leaders looked suddenly less sure of themselves. The Stronghold had long been the second home of the North America Enforcer order, its power once taken over by the Brotherhood to the worry of all witches. Only my battle with Belaisle had freed the first plane created and returned it to the Enforcers. A powerful advantage.

One she'd lost.

A single glance around the room told me the other leaders might have been shocked, but they weren't about to budge. My jaw ached from grinding my teeth, but there was nothing I could do to force them to listen. "Just so you know," I snarled. "I'd trust a building's instincts over anyone here." I refused to look at Femke. I was just too angry with her at the moment. "What does that say for what we've become?"

"The law is the law." Erica's blunt statement put an end to my protest. She swept the circle with her gaze, power crackling. "If any of you try to enter my territory uninvited, if this creature," she points at me, "somehow convinces you to break the law and do so, I will consider it an act of war." Blue flames engulfed her. "You don't want to test me or my allies." And then, she was gone.

"And that," I said, "is where the world is heading. To

puppets controlled by the Brotherhood." I gusted out a frustrated breath of air. "Are you all happy now?"

The spluttering and anger started instantly, but I was done with their small minded pettiness. "If you don't learn to work together," I said, leaning over the table with both fists planted on the surface, "you are done."

They all stared at me, silent but unmovable.

"What will it take?" Femke's voice broke the silence. I glanced at her at last, her own fury as hot as mine. "Seriously, tell me. What will it take for all of you to see the real threat here?" She met my eyes. "And it's not Sydlynn Hayle." She looked back. "Perhaps one of our territories being attacked?" They squirmed, silent. "No? Will you sit back and watch our Councils fall, one by one, relying on your assurance that it's not your territory and none of your business?"

I couldn't have said it better myself. My anger toward Femke faded, died off. I knew better. She was on my side and always had been.

"If I've learned anything," I said, softer this time, with feeling, "from combining all these personalities in my head," I tapped at my temple while my demon, vampire and Sidhe princess all murmured their agreement, "it's that all of us, working apart, are a mess. But when we got our crap together and finally joined up, nothing could— or will—stop us." I sagged, knowing I'd lost, but unable to stop myself. "How long do you think it will be before the Brotherhood comes after you? How long before you're under their thumb, your families and those of your territories burned, their power stolen? Your loved ones consigned to the fire of this ridiculous false future they are trying to pass as whole cloth?" Still didn't have them. They were so closed I doubted they heard a word past their own quivering, fear filled mental voices. But I just had to finish. "The Brotherhood is winning because no one will step up." My shoulders pushed back, chin rising. "Well, I'm stepping up, with or without you. And when the day comes when the Brotherhood invade your territory, you'd better damned well hope I'm willing to take your call when you come running."

I couldn't stand them anymore, their staring faces, their silence and reticence. With my anger tightly clenched around me, I spun and stalked out of the room.

I heard the door slam behind me when I was barely halfway down the hall, the patter of feet running toward me turning me partially around. Femke embraced me, breathless and shaking, as I hugged her back.

"I'm sorry," she whispered before leaning away, blue eyes intense with regret. "But the moment I felt them turn, I knew it was a lost cause. I wish I could have saved you that heartache." She dropped her arms. "Please don't think I abandoned you in there. You were brilliant." Her voice was steady despite her shivering. "And they are, as they have always been, impossible."

I shrugged and turned from her, still stinging no matter her excuses. "Whatever," I said.

She jerked me around, voice dropping in volume, looking over her shoulder before sighing. "I tried to coerce them." Her eyes were huge, the pupils drowning out the blue suddenly as I drew a breath. "I know, I know." She bit her lower lip. "It was so wrong and if anyone ever found out… I pushed so hard, Syd. But they just wouldn't take the bait."

I hugged her again, understanding now her failure to speak up. She'd been a little busy. "I wish I'd thought of that," I growled in her ear. "Stupid, Femke."

She nodded against my shoulder, letting me go. "I know. I just…" she looked back down the hall toward the door, sudden fury flashing over her face.

I took her hand, pulling her along, linking my arm in hers as she drifted, listless, beside me. "Yeah," I said. "I know. Don't do anything like that ever again." Bad enough the Brotherhood were burning witches with no provocation. If the other Council Leaders found out she'd tried to coerce them, she'd be killed on the spot. Damned risky and I didn't agree with her tactics, but her frustration? That I understood.

She coughed a laugh. "Yes, Mummy."

I glared at her as we paused outside her office door. "I mean it," I said. "We've all been pushed to our limits before. I don't want to worry you might cross the line into something you'll regret and will get you killed."

She nodded, shoulders stiffening, but not with anger. "I know it was a foolish thing to do," she said. "And a waste of precious time and energy." She shook out her short, blonde hair. "I learned a valuable lesson, Syd, and not about them, either." Her breath whistled between her teeth as she exhaled. "About how far I'm willing to go."

"And?" I waited for her to go on. Damn it, I really didn't want to have to worry she might crack and lose it. Femke was the one solid ally in the witch world I had right now.

"And." Her blue eyes cleared. "They're all rubbish. And not worth giving up my beliefs or pushing me past the point of no return."

"Damned right." I growled the words. "No one is."

She hesitated, touched my hand. "Syd, you are."

I shook her, grasping her upper arms in my hands. She was older than me by at least a decade, but I treated her like someone younger at times. "Listen to me," I said, voice low and harsh. "No one. Not even me. Promise."

Femke swallowed audibly. "You're our only hope," she said. "I'll do anything to protect you."

"I can take care of myself," I said, letting her go. "You know that. And I need to believe you're not going to do something we'll both have to pay for later because you think I need help."

Femke stared at me, mute and hurt before shaking it

off. I'd never seen her so vulnerable, probably a byproduct of the coercion attempt, leaving her open and defenseless. When she met my eyes again, my friend was back, grim smile in place.

"You're stubborn and ridiculous," she said. "And I love you for it." She didn't wait for me to comment, pushing her office door open and walking in. I followed her, head down, heart pounding at how close we came to her breaking.

If anything happened to Femke and the Councils stood by, I'd clean house myself. They had no idea, none. How thin a line I walked, how easy it would be to crack myself, to become an avenging angel, a rogue with no conscience, only revenge in my heart.

Except for us, my vampire sent.

We will never let you fall, Shaylee whispered.

Never. My demon's power crackled. *Though I'd be in for a little constructive ass kicking in the name of education.*

I laughed shakily, running one hand over my mouth as a cold sweat engulfed me. So easy to just let go and let the power take over. But they were right and I was so lucky to have them.

By the time I'd pulled it together and stepped through the door, Femke had clearly filled in the waiting Sunny and Danilo, because they were both furious. While the vampire queen's came across as icy calm, the werewolf king looked about ready to go on a rampage.

You have to present the right example, my vampire sent. *For their sake.*

Appearances could bite me.

"I have a question." Sunny's blue eyes found and held mine. "When you came to see me, asked about the dull feeling that Sassafras uncovered, did you make the connection to Belaisle?"

I froze a moment and stared at her. "What connection?" But, yes, of course I had. I'd just forgotten the instant of understanding, just as Zoe left, when the Brotherhood first attacked. I just hadn't thought of it since. Been a little busy.

"Think about it." Her rigid shoulders and perfect posture made her look like a statue of a stunning, angry woman. "How ever did Belaisle manage to take over so slickly?"

"He bound his sorcery to the council's magic," I said, sinking into a chair. "Yes, I assumed the lassitude had something to do with it, but I figured it was just to make everyone look the other way."

"Wherein lies the problem," she said. "We agreed with you, did we not, we felt it, too?" She looked to Femke and to Danilo who both nodded. "If we are to assume he inflicted this feeling, and that we in Europe felt it as much as you in North America, does it not carry that our entire plane is affected?"

Femke hesitated. "Maybe not," she said. "He knows

Syd has allies here in Europe. It could be he tried to influence us just to keep us from noticing anything or asking questions."

"Why then," Sunny said, "am I still feeling it, if subtly, in my mind?"

I didn't. But Femke's startled expression and Danilo's sudden bout of swearing told me they did.

"If he has no desire to spread his hold to other territories," Sunny said, "he would have dropped his little naptime routine when he took control of North America, correct?" I nodded, numb for another reason. "The fact he hasn't can only mean one thing."

"He plans to attack other territories." Danilo surged to his feet, pacing as his mouth formed a wolf's muzzle before retreating again. "Surely the other councils will act with this knowledge."

"Only if we can present proof of it," Femke said. But she was sounding hopeful so I latched onto that. Was there a way to make them see and pay attention? To show them they were all at risk right now?

That might be enough to make them act.

"Let's run with that," I said, standing again, needing to get out of there. The three nodded to me as I opened the veil, reaching for the Stronghold. "Keep me posted."

"What are you going to do?" Femke's hesitation was gone, my friend fully returned.

"I don't know," I said. "But when I figure it out,

you'll be the first to know."

I didn't have the heart to tell them I was running away as I stepped through the veil and reached for the Stronghold. Okay, not exactly. But I needed time to think things through, to shake off the disappointment of the same old same old. And, I wanted to talk to Mom. She'd help me figure this out.

The moment I set foot in the Stronghold I was practically assaulted by two young sorcerers. The Zornov brothers grinned at me like they'd found some delicious way to exact revenge on their most hated rivals. I hoped that was good news for me.

"Syd," Apollo said with a grin, "we have a way to get the family fortune back."

My eyes flew wide, heart pounding as I beamed. About time I had some good news. "How?"

He hooked his arm through mine while Charlotte approached, eyes narrowed. I didn't know she was back, waved at her to join us. She did as the sorcerer gestured toward the mirror.

"I have someone I want you to meet." He bowed at the waist. "After you."

THIRTY-TWO

I let him take the lead, pulling Charlotte along next to me, happy to have her with me.

Where have you been? Her tone was almost accusatory, like she wasn't off rescuing witches or anything without me.

Council meeting, I sent as the mirror flowed around me.

Result? Her tone softened, though there was little hope in her mental voice.

Predictable, I sent, breathing in fresh night air as we crossed out of the portal and into a darkened street. The light over our heads was burnt out, only the one at the far end flickering with illumination, scent of asphalt cooling biting my senses. A car passed us at speed, roaring by with its headlights flashing in our faces, the catcalls of young men garbled by the night air and their car's engine. I ignored their rude behavior and followed Apollo as he

291

turned and led us away from the light, toward a small building on the right side of the street. I looked down the small grade into the city below us, pebbles harsh under the thin soles of my worn sneakers, wondering where we were. Not that it mattered if whoever Apollo had lined up could do the job.

So, as usual, Charlotte sent, *we're on our own.*

I grinned at her in the dark, sadness in my expression. *Think we can handle it?*

Her eyes flashed with the wolf in her, face stony and serious. *As you're so fond of saying, they'd better look the hell out.* She sent those words with so much conviction my heart sang.

Apollo circled the building, coming to a small side door. His sorcery made short work of the lock, the metal portal ringing a little on its hinges as he pulled it open. This time he led the way, not waiting for me to go first and I let him, following Owen and his brother with Charlotte beside me.

The interior was dark, some kind of warehouse, I guessed, stacked with dark, bulky shapes. A single, white toned light glowed on the right, leading us that way as much as Apollo's long strides. I had to push myself to keep up, weariness catching up with me again and was panting a little by the time we reached a smoked glass door leading to some kind of office.

The silence was unnerving for some reason, broken

by the whoosh of air as Apollo opened the door, the sound of humming coming from the interior. I stepped through after the Zornovs, Charlotte behind me in protective stance, and ran my gaze over the banks of computer backs facing me, sharp tang of hot plastic and too much electricity making me want to sneeze. The sound of tapping on computer keys paused, a chair creaked.

"Lo," a voice I was sure I'd heard before muttered. "That you?"

"Brought the client I mentioned," Apollo said. "Sydlynn Hayle, I want you to meet my friend, Si. Better known as BitsnBytes."

My heart dropped into my feet as a young man, his glasses flashing in the lights of his computer monitors, stood and stepped around the desk, mouth drawn into a thin line.

"Oh," Simon Clement said, my old friend staring at me like he wanted me dead, "Syd and I have met."

I hadn't seen Simon for years. My sweet, kind hearted and slightly socially awkward friend had gone off to college early, attending Harvard. I only ran into him my first year, but too late. He'd been sucked into the Star Club, a private group led by Darin Mavore, who turned Simon over to vampires and Ameline Benoit. The resulting trauma ruined him and, grades dropping and soul shattered, Simon disappeared.

Why had I never gone looking for him again? Guilt rose and this time none of my alter egos even considered mentioning I shouldn't feel bad, their own concern and regret as powerful as mine.

Apollo looked back and forth between us, smile fading. "How do you two know each other?"

"We're friends," I said, meaning it.

"We were." Simon's coldness hit me, crisp and harsh. He crossed his arms over his chest, still staring at me, though I couldn't see his eyes past the glow of his glasses. He looked good, if pale, dark hair short and spiked, a fandom t-shirt hugging his narrow chest. He'd grow into himself, no longer the nerdy, tiny kid who was far too smart for his age, far too smart for his own good. I wished I could reach him somehow, but the rigidity of his stance, the closed feeling of his mind, told me this wasn't the time.

"It's good to see you, Simon," I said. "How have you been?"

"Just dandy," he said, bitterness crusting his words. "Heard you ruined Blood and Pain's lives, too. And since Al committed suicide, I guess you're three for four." His body shook. "Seen Beth lately? Heard she's doing great. You missed one."

My jaw clamped shut. None of that was my fault, but what was I supposed to say? Our little gang of friends was scattered, true enough. Mia—formerly the Goth girl,

Pain, the heir to the Dumont family—dead. Blood, her boyfriend, now Rupe, had been lost to the Brotherhood, then madness as the werewolf infection he purposely inflicted on himself tried to destroy him. Alison, my ghostly friend, had found some happiness at least after her death. Thinking of her made me worry all over again where she and Sebastian had gone.

And, finally, Simon. But he was right. Beth made it out, the scholarship Mom gave her taking her away from me, from everything.

I hoped she was happy. And worried maybe Simon was right.

"What do you want?" My former friend turned from me, sank into his chair. I circled as Apollo did, to scan the computer monitors. Code and flashing images and other things raced across the four huge screens, so fast I was nauseated almost immediately.

"Syd wants to hire you," Apollo said, not sounding so sure of himself anymore.

Simon shook his head. "Not interested."

I frowned at Apollo with a tilt to my head. "What's the deal?"

"My dude here," he said, "is one of the country's greatest hackers. If anyone can get your money back, it's him."

Simon stopped typing, turned to face me as grief struck again. He was brilliant, and this was how he was spending his life?

"What kind of money?" The flat question made me pause, but I answered.

"Family fortune," I said. "Stolen by a corporation called Coterie Industries." No way was I dragging him into the magic world further. I had no idea how much he remembered from his time with the Star Club, but I wasn't about to make matters worse. I figured it was safe enough using Belaisle's old cover.

I needn't have worried about protecting Simon. "The Brotherhood." He turned back to his screens. "Who'd you piss off that they targeted you?"

How much did he know? Apollo looked hopeful, nodded at me to continue, so I shrugged.

"Liander Belaisle and I go way back," I said.

Simon stopped typing again, turned to face me. This time, there was shock and a bit of respect there. "When Coterie fell," he said. "That was you?"

I did my best not to grin. "I had a hand in it," I said.

Simon sat back in his chair, long fingers laced over his chest, elbows on the arm rests. He'd really grown, was probably taller than me now, with that lean and lanky geekboy look so many girls fell for these days. "Okay, I'm impressed," he said. "I'm expensive."

"I can pay," I said. "Once the money is returned."

"How much are we talking?" His expression didn't change.

"I don't know exactly," I said. "In excess of a billion, thereabouts."

Apollo whistled low, eyes huge. "You're kidding me."

Simon nodded once, turned away, focus back on his computer screens. "I'll do it," he said. "For twenty percent."

Apollo grunted, opened his mouth. I knew this probably should have been a negotiation, but it was just money to me. And, even if his present life wasn't my fault, I owed Simon.

"Done," I said. "How long?"

His fingers paused, then resumed. "I'll be in touch."

Apollo led me away while I glanced back at the serious, hurting young man I used to know, one more burden for my heart to carry.

Simon's face still hovered in my mind as I exited the mirror and came to an abrupt halt inside the main hall of the Stronghold. No longer was I thinking about him, about the council members. About anything. Not while a small knot of furious sorcerers, Enforcers and one raging Erica Plower stared at me from the other side of a shimmering rainbow bubble.

I stared up at them in shock, Mom striding smoothly to my side with a small smile on her face. Her arm hooked through mine, voice bright as the witches of my family—and some of those rescued—came to gather and glare, their mood decidedly dark while Mom led me forward.

"Sydlynn, dear," she said in a bright, cheery voice. "Look, we have visitors."

I almost choked on my mother's evil delight because I wanted so much to laugh in Erica's furious face. Belaisle wasn't with her, more's the pity. I could have ended everything right here and now if he'd been stupid enough to come with her. As it was, she'd offered me a wonderful opportunity.

"Welcome to the Stronghold," I said. "It would appear he's not happy with your presence at the moment."

THIRTY-THREE

Indeed, the Stronghold grumbled while I grinned at Erica, the stone hall rumbling with his discontent. *I am not pleased to see her or feel the taint of her power. But I waited for you, Syd. In case you had instructions.*

How kind of you. I gestured at Erica. "So, your little warning about me not coming into your territory clearly was a one way threat." It was hard to decide if I was more amused or furious. "Classy."

"This Stronghold is the property of the North American Enforcers," Erica said, words crackling with power and anger.

Actually, the Stronghold boomed through all of our heads, though from the wincing and cries of pain from those inside the bubble, I could only assume they took the brunt of volume, *I belong to myself.* The giant circle of shielding began to compress, forcing the group closer and closer together. Erica's desperation made me sigh. She'd brought this on herself, but I wasn't feeling vengeful anymore. Just sad for her and for the rest of us.

The other witches in the hall weren't so forgiving. "Let her go." Karyn came forward, the Barrett witch's finger jabbing at Erica. "We'll deal with her personally." The angry mutter from the others sounded dangerously like a mob. "Show her what we think of her new laws." While I hardly blamed them, I wasn't interested in turning them loose on her.

"You're not exactly welcome here," I said. "But you knew that already. So, why did he send you, Erica? And not come himself? Hmm?" I glanced at a few of his sorcerers, their fear dominant. "He threw all of you at me to see what I'd do. To test my resolve." Or... did he? "Is it power he's after?" I shrugged, crossing my arms over my chest. "I guess that means the souls of all the witches he's killed so far aren't enough for him."

Erica quivered, for the first time since this began showing a flicker of remorse. "You don't understand," she said.

"Try me." Mom pushed forward, stepping in front. "Erica, tell me. You're my oldest friend." Sassafras snorted at my feet and I looked down, surprised to find him there, watching. I knew Mom didn't mean it, that he was my mother's oldest friend, of course, but he held still, obviously understanding she was trying to reach the woman being slowly crushed by the bodies of the magic users she brought with her. Power flickered inside the bubble, blue shields pressed together as the Enforcers circled her, trying to keep her safe while the sorcerers laid hands on the inside of the wards only to be thrown back again, crying out with hands singed and blackened. Mom ignored all that, eyes locked on her former second. "Tell me why you've betrayed us all."

She didn't get to answer. The Stronghold grunted at me.

I'm sending them away, he sent. *The sorcerers are trying to siphon my power.*

Can we keep her? I wanted to talk to Erica more closely.

I'm afraid not, he sent. *Either they all go, or they all stay.*

I reached out, laid my hand on Mom's shoulder. As much as I hated missing the opportunity, I needed to protect the family. "Mom."

She half turned to me, tears on her cheeks, just as the bubble burst and Erica and her people—sorcerers included—were gone.

Mom flinched, hands over her open mouth, but I hugged her tight.

"She's still alive," I whispered into her hair. "The Stronghold sent her back. That's all."

Mom turned and hugged me back. "I'm sorry," she said. "I know I should hate her. But, Syd…"

"I get it, Mom." I kissed her cheek, leaned away. "I

really do."

The gathering grumbled, began to disperse, but not before I blocked off the exits. They turned to me as I raised my voice to get their attention.

"Listen up." I didn't mean to take my anger out on them. That wasn't my intent. But I'd had enough crap in the last little while and my family wasn't going to turn into some mindless mass of vengeance on my watch. "We will not—and I repeat, will *not*," I stressed the last "not" with a burst of power that made them jump, "become *them*." I jabbed a finger where Erica and the others had recently hovered in their prison. "We cherish life. We protect it. And if one of us is found guilty of a crime against the rest, we hold a fair trial and we let justice prevail." Yeah, I was a good one to talk, right? Still.

"She killed our families." Karyn choked on a sob, supported by one of her people.

"I know," I said. "And I wish I could go back and save them all. But I can't. And hate will only eat you up and turn you into someone who can't ever think of rebuilding." I raised my voice again. "And we will rebuild. We will destroy the Brotherhood once and for all. But we will not turn against our own until they have been tried and sentenced. Agreed?"

Murmurs of ascent. "So the sorcerers are fair game?" That was Quaid. Why wasn't I surprised my husband had a bloodthirsty streak? But as I saw the others turn toward him, their anger easing as he spoke, I realized how brilliant he was.

"The Brotherhood," I said, "will never recover."

The cheer that met my little pep talk brought tears and laughter among the watchers. This time when I dropped my shields and they moved to leave they were smiling and hugging each other, grim though the situation was. I might have taken Erica from them—a clear and present danger—but they still had a group of enemies to focus on.

Best I could do on short notice.

Quaid came to my side, kissed my mom, then me. I leaned into his strength, the warmth of his arms. "I take it things didn't go as planned with the council."

I rolled my eyes and sighed. "Don't even want to go there."

Mom brushed tears from her face. "Stubborn and useless as usual?"

I booped her on the nose. "Get the woman a cookie." I waved to Apollo and Owen who joined us. "At least, we may have solved the family fortune problem." I left the boys to fill Mom and Quaid in, a thought passing through my head I needed to explore before I forgot.

Stronghold. I passed into the hallway on the right, hopping up into the windowsill and looking out over the lush green scape. *Do you know who I mean when I talk about Ameline Benoit?*

I do, he sent. *The Dark One.*

The former Dark One, I sent, feeling oddly protective of the soul I'd encountered. And quickly explained what I found out about her so I didn't have to think about why I felt that way.

Interesting, he sent. *But what does this have to do with me?*

She told me to ask you a question, I sent. *To ask you about Creator. Does that mean anything to you?* His sudden silence shook me, making me sit up, tense and afraid. Not just quiet, but as though he'd run away, gone from my mind. *Stronghold? She said the maji are afraid.*

His voice was soft and distant when he answered, presence retreating from me. *As they should be.*

Okay, that didn't sound good. *I need to know*, I sent. *Just in case.*

I can't tell you, Syd. Real regret under the sound of grinding stone as he pulled further away. *My deepest secret, one I've held since my birth. No one can ever know.*

Clearly, someone does, I sent, not wanted to get pissy with him, but seriously. *The maji must, right? Or they wouldn't be afraid.*

They might know the generalities, he sent. *But not the specifics.*

I sighed mentally. *You do realize secrets and half-truths are part of the reason we've almost fallen in the past, right? If I know what to expect, maybe I can plan for it.*

I'm sorry, he sent. And was gone.

Well, that went about exactly as I figured it would. Considering my track record and everything.

I hopped down from the ledge and tried to let it go. I'd chase him down after, see if I could persuade him to help me when this was over.

As usual, one giant mess at a time, thanks.

Mom came looking for me, composed all over again. "Your grandmother wants to talk to us," she said. I joined hands with her, crossed to the hall and down to the cafeteria. The room was huge, massive ceiling of stone lit with wide rock chandeliers glowing with witchlight. I sank onto a bench, accepting a plate of spaghetti which I attacked with a sudden ravenous hunger. Giant bites entered my mouth while I stuffed garlic bread after it and chewed myself into bliss.

Gram slid in across from me, Demetrius at her side. Charlotte and Sage joined us, Dad and Quaid, Piers and Zoe, while Sassafras hopped up and helped himself to a meatball from my plate.

Shenka finally tacked on the end, looking drawn, but offering me a little smile. I gulped down my food, suddenly remembering Tallah.

"How is she?" I sloshed a drink of milk while Shenka's smile deepened. Good news, then.

"She'll recover," she said, picking at the muffin on her plate with no obvious intention of actually eating it. "The Kennecotts are fabulous."

They really were. We were lucky to have them.

"Syd," Gram said while Sassafras pawed free another meatball, "I was talking with Sass about the numb feeling." Funny she mentioned that.

"Had the same conversation with Femke, Sunny and Danilo," I said. "That we were afraid it was worldwide and not confined to North America and Europe."

She nodded, glancing at her husband who looked grim for one of the first times ever. Even in terrible situations Demetrius managed to maintain his cheerful, cherub look. Right now he seemed ashen and very worried.

"We think we know how Belaisle is doing it," she said.

I stopped chewing. "How?"

"The world is a vast network," Demetrius said in his soft voice. "Connecting all living things together." His fingers made a webbed circle, fingertips touching before sliding together to lock in place. "Sorcery is the glue that binds us as one."

The first magic. I knew that already.

"That's what he must have used," Gram said. "Somehow tapped into the very energy that holds us all in a circle."

Piers frowned. "But how? That network is vast. It would take a ton of power to control it."

"Not necessarily," Gram said. "Not if he wasn't trying

to control it per se, but to influence it. To bend it slightly."

"You're saying Belaisle coerced the whole plane," I said. Unfreakingbelievable.

Demetrius nodded, leaning around Gram to smile at Zoe. "It was Miss Helios who gave us the idea," he said while Zoe tilted her head in surprise. "Consider this. Belaisle had access to a maji, correct?"

Zoe nodded. "Gaia," she said with sadness.

"The power of the maji would be enough," he said. "To infiltrate and influence."

"But she was almost drained," Zoe said. "By the time I found her."

"Not the strength of her power," Gram said, patting her hand. "The source."

What was it Liam had said about the maji all those years ago, when I'd first met Trill and Owen, first encountered Iepa? "They are outside spirit," I whispered.

Gram nodded. "Exactly," she said. "Outside everything. Having that kind of power at his disposal could have given Belaisle the in he needed to influence the entire network of magic on this plane and nudge it in the direction he wanted it to go."

"And with Gaia gone," Zoe said, "he needed a new power source to maintain it."

Demetrius met my eyes, his sad. "Which is what we think he's really after," he said. "Why he's draining witches. To maintain what he's begun."

"And when he has enough momentum," Gram said, "he'll sweep across the plane and no magic race will be safe from him."

A dim figure flickered behind Gram, drawing my eyes. I stared in shock at the sight of Iepa appearing and disappearing, face drawn and afraid. Zoe let out a little gasp of fright, turning to look at what caught my eye.

"Iepa!" The Oracle spun on me. "Help her!"

My power locked onto the maji, but she wavered as though someone fought her presence here. I could guess it was her own people, as usual. They despised any kind of interference.

Syd! Her mental voice barely reached me. *The drach!*

Iepa's face twisted and she vanished.

I didn't even realize I'd stood up, my friends and family rising around me. "Max is in trouble," I said, shaking suddenly. Quaid slipped his arm around my shoulder.

"Can you help?"

I shook my head, sinking back down while the others joined me, but we were all jumpy.

"I don't know how." I wrung my hands. "No one can find them, including the Stronghold. And there's no sign of them in the veil." How could I just abandon them, though? I needed to try.

As I looked around at the sad, worried faces at the

table, I let myself sag, exhaling.

"They'll have to fend for themselves for now," I whispered. Coughed softly. "The family comes first." Sharp need, the pressure of sudden hurry boiling in my stomach, drove my head up, my eyes catching Gram's. "Can you prove any of this?" If she could show the Council, it might make a difference. And the faster I cleared this up, the faster I could go looking for Max and the drach.

Gram paused before nodding sharply. "I'm sure I can show them," she said. "He has to be preparing to move into a new territory shortly. If he leaves this hanging too long, he'll lose his advantage."

I stood quickly, gesturing for her to follow me. "Then, let's go see if we can do the impossible and make the witch councils work together for once."

THIRTY-FOUR

The European Enforcers standing outside the meeting room door knew better than to get in my way. In fact, one of them, grinning under his thick beard, opened it for me, half bowing while his companion struggled not to laugh, both of them sending me a gentle nudge of approval.

Nice to know someone's Enforcers were good guys.

The circle of Council Leaders looked up as I entered, but before any of them—Erica included from her place at the table—could interrupt, I stopped them with a raised hand.

I hadn't expected Erica to be here, not after threatening everyone like she did. Aside from Femke's tense expression, they all looked like one big, happy family. I was, however, about to show them the black sheep they had in their midst was a wolf in disguise.

Danilo crowded in behind me, Gram on my right, Sunny sweeping forward with her perfection shining ghostly white. Demetrius held back, but I could feel his sorcery against mine and knew he was preparing to help Gram in whatever way she needed. I just hoped she could be convincing, because if this didn't work we were screwed as a race.

"Welcome, Coven Leader Hayle," Femke said, rising and gesturing for me to join them. But Erica was already scowling in protest.

"She needs to be arrested, not welcomed." At least none of the other council leaders had the courage to agree with her. And who knew? They might only have been hobnobbing to gain information or to try to stay on Erica's good side. A pathetic attempt to be the last to fall?

"Liander Belaisle and the Brotherhood are preparing to attack a new territory." Lying through my teeth? Check. Doing a bang up job? Check. Able to back it up?

Yeah, about that.

Gram, bless her, had my back, as usual. While the Council Leaders gaped and Erica opened her mouth to scream blue murder at me, my amazing grandmother tapped directly into the sorcery in the room. I only knew because I was right there with her, her magic taking me along for the ride.

She showed them the connection between the Council Leaders, the pulsing ropes of darkness that was sorcery.

"You might not want to believe," she said, "but I know you've been told. Every living thing has the capacity for sorcery." Finer threads linked the table, chairs, even the pens and paper, light fixtures, their clothing, until the entire room was a spider's web of connections. "That is how sorcerers are able to draw on the power around them, through those points of shared energy."

"Irrelevant," Erica muttered.

"Not so," Demetrius said, joining his wife. "Untouched, the magic that binds us together serves as the heartbeat of this plane, maintaining balance and relative peace in weather systems, eco systems, and the health and wellbeing of all living creatures."

"Too much of a draw on that network," Gram said, "and everything falls apart." She held the web another moment before letting it collapse with a sigh of black mist. The Council leaders got the point from the horrified looks on their faces.

"You are a sorcerer," Erica said. "Why should we trust you?"

"I am Ethpeal Hayle," Gram told her with so much pride vibrating in her voice I wanted to cheer, "former Enforcer, Coven Leader and now Steam Union representative. I have, I would say, a unique perspective. Wouldn't you, Erica?"

The Council Leader didn't respond. In fact, from the flicker of panic on her face, she knew where this was going and I desperately hoped the rapt looks on the other Leader's faces meant we were going to win this round as Erica feared.

"Speak, Sorcerer Hayle," Femke said. "I for one am interested to hear what you have to say."

The others nodded—with one obvious exception—and Gram went on.

"Does this feel familiar?" Gram intensified the dullness Sassafras had first mentioned, tweaking it slightly. Everyone nodded, shivered as she let them go.

"I've been feeling rather bored of late," Yamini said, glancing right and left.

Bindi rubbed her bare, tanned arms with both hands. "As have I," she said. "Bloody unexciting."

More murmurs of assent. Gram's magic sketched out the entire world before them in glowing lights, while the darkness of her sorcery formed the web that was the borders of our plane. "That feeling," she said, "is everywhere." Okay, we hadn't checked that, but I trusted Gram. And as I watched the pinpoint of its beginning form at Harvard and race around the world, I knew she had, if only just now. And there was no denying this wasn't real. I felt Gram touch each and every one of the souls present, opening her sorcery to their inherent dark power.

No denying it as she dragged me along with them. Not a single person spoke, everyone staring as the tracery of control finally completed its race around the plane and back to Harvard.

Erica lurched to her feet. "I demand their deaths," she said, desperation clear on her face. "Clearly they are conspiring against a Council Leader."

"Do be still, Erica," Sumiko said, face pale. "Go on, Sorcerer Hayle."

We had them. We really had them. It took supreme effort to hold in my surge of nasty joy at the look of horror on Erica's face. I kept her locked to me, our eyes holding equal stares, hers afraid and mine vengeful, no matter what I told my coven.

Do as I say, not as I do.

The black lines of power sketched their way across the Atlantic, into Europe. Sick fascination held me still, my eyes—and those of everyone in the room—tracking across the globe, from territory to territory, over the mass of continents. Like a dark spider's lair, the sorcery net expanded outward from every direction, covering Africa, Asia, the south Pacific, circumnavigating the entire plane until it settled its noose of magic around South America and the circle was complete.

Gram's face tightened, her magic pulsing once in shock. "It's begun," she said. "See there." We all looked, even me, releasing Erica from my gaze, staring in shock at the giant wash of sorcery heading south toward a new territory.

Ana Maria freaked, pushing her chair back, almost falling into her Enforcer leader's arms. "Save us! Please, I beg you, save us."

South America was already pulsing with more power, more control. If they were going to act, to stand as one, it had to be now.

I drew a breath, held it as the group stared, frozen and unsure. Until Femke slammed both hands down on the table.

"This isn't just a North American problem," she snapped, jerking her thumb at Erica. "We are all at risk. And we must act immediately."

Her words set them free in a torrent of shouting, their rage so powerful I took a step back. Erica's fire flared, blue glow surrounding her. Ana Maria lunged, but too late, Albert, Femke's Enforcer Leader, latching onto nothing as she vanished.

Sumiko finally called for quiet, shaking and red faced. She bowed to me, ceremonial and slow.

"Sydlynn Hayle," she said. "We beg forgiveness." Nodding all around, terrified weeping from Ana Maria. "You have our attention at last."

Sunny sat beside me, Danilo across from me, Gram and Demetrius squeezed in, too. I'd already asked for Meira and the Sidhe to be included, as they had been for conclave, but even Femke said no, though I think she would have agreed if the wave of denial had been less.

"We must focus on our safety," Sumiko said. "That of this plane. No others are at risk at this time?"

I shrugged. "I have no idea," I said. "But no, not as far as I can tell."

"Then we deal with the threat," she said, "before they are."

First lick of sense I'd heard from any of them yet. Besides, the fact they were all working together at all was the biggest step. The rest would have to wait.

"Might I suggest," Gram said, "there have been many mitigating factors that have led us to this unfortunate crossroads."

How diplomatic, I sent. *You can certainly turn a phrase.* Okay, so I was a little giddy with relief, not to mention worried about Max and the drach, about what Erica was telling Belaisle and, quite frankly, wiped out to the edge of exhaustion.

All the better to manipulate them, my girl, Gram sent.

"Agreed," Femke said while the others nodded.

"It is my thought," Gram said, "that a World Paranormal Council should be formed at once. One that carries the strength and power to enact law and provide protection—not to mention forewarning—should anything like this brew again."

Wow, I sent. *Ambitious.*

Hush, girl, she sent, eyes twinkling as she met my gaze, face flat and precise.

They were stunned, clearly, no one saying or projecting a thing.

"And excellent idea," Femke said.

"Indeed," Sunny agreed. "It's not just witches in danger under these circumstances. The blood clans of my people will also be targets—if we aren't already."

"Agreed," Danilo said, deep voice rumbling like the wolf he was, making a few of the Council Leaders shift in discomfort. But he was eloquent when he went on, though his animal core glowed in his angry eyes. "All paranormal races are now at risk. No one is safe unless everyone works together to ensure universal protection against threats like this one."

Sunny nodded to him with her exquisite grace. "We, too, have felt the lassitude that plagues you. Which means it is only a matter of time before Belaisle's plan devours all magic on this plane. We, as the leaders of our communities, have an obligation to protect all paranormals who stand to be harmed by such greed." She turned to Femke. "It is our wish to eliminate segregation, to unite the races and allow for all paranormals to have equal protection from threats of this nature."

What would it take to convince them? I could feel the Council Leader's continuing hesitation, but didn't give them a chance to back down now.

"Consider it done," I snapped. "You want my help?" They nodded as a group. "You say yes and be grateful for it."

I worried as the last word left my mouth I'd gone too far. Wouldn't be the first time. But Sumiko bowed her head to me.

"I would be willing," she said. "If you were the leader of such a council."

Did I mention I was tired? Yeah. Laughed in her face. Long and loud, compulsive, hands clutching my ribs as it went on and on. I couldn't breathe, could barely squeak out anything, silent hilarity driving tears from the corners of my eyes.

When I finally pulled in a breath, I gasped for air, grinning at her.

"Worst." I tapped the table top with one finger. "Choice." And again, for emphasis. "Ever."

Sumiko looked stunned by my response. But I had a better suggestion anyway.

"You do not want me leading anything," I said. "Not on this scale." I shuddered at the thought. Seriously, with my temper and penchant for throwing myself at problems like a bull in a china shop? Hell no. "But I do have a suggestion for the perfect person." My eyes went to Femke, all humor gone, feeling suddenly sorry for her though I knew she was the only choice possible. Her blue gaze widened and she started to shake her head, too late.

"I nominate Femke Svennson."

So much pressure to put on her shoulders. But, as the other Council Leaders turned to her, murmuring their agreement, I knew she could handle it.

We'll talk about this, she sent, an edge to her voice.

I'm sorry, I sent. *But I'm not wrong.*

Her gaze dropped from mine and she drew a breath. Smiled gently, professionally, bowed her head.

"I would be honored," she said. And cut off their mutters of congratulations. "As interim leader. Until such time as a permanent choice can be duly voted in."

They seemed okay with that, and so was I. Because I knew, in the end, they'd never let her go.

"Will I be required to give up leadership of the European territory?" She spoke slowly, steadily, voice light but firm. Which meant she was probably freaking out.

"No," I said. "Not yet. We'll hammer all this crap out once the threat is taken care of."

She nodded once, brusque. "Very well then," she said. "As the leader of the new Paranormal World Council, I decree our first order of business is to march on the North American territory and deal with Liander Belaisle." Her eyes flashed blue fire. "I don't know about the rest of you, but I've had it up to here," she cut a line above her head with one hand, "with the Brotherhood. It's time they knew what taking on witches really means."

THIRTY-FIVE

I had a clear view of the gathering forces in the courtyard below from the big window on the back side of Femke's office. While I knew they would stand little chance against the Brotherhood alone, it was a good feeling to see so many witches of so many territories coming together for a common cause.

Each of the councils agreed to commit a small group of twenty or so Enforcers including a representative of the councils. Danilo and Sunny immediately volunteered their own people, too. I worried a little for the vampires, since it would still be daylight when we arrived in Harvard, but she assured me the experiments Sebastian performed should protect them as long as they stayed indoors for most of the time.

I didn't plan to be outside at all. In fact, my goal was to pick up the lot of us and land us right smack dab in the middle of the council chamber, win big touchdowns and mop up the remains, hopefully in a very short time period. While I knew the likelihood of such success was slim, I hung onto the idea anyway.

I could dream, right?

At least it took a few hours to assemble the forces, leaving me time to run back to the Stronghold and fill everyone in before collapsing for another two hours of sleep. I didn't normally need much, thanks to my advanced power and immortality, so that two hours did me a world of good. I was even smiling when I returned to Oxford, the magic inside me as refreshed as I was.

Femke looked up at me from the courtyard below. *Ready when you are*, she sent.

I slipped through the veil and down to her side. *I'm really sorry about this*, I sent at her cool tone.

She didn't respond to my apology. "You're taking care of transport?"

I sighed inwardly and nodded. "Everyone together, now." The six groups of Enforcers looked awkward as they shuffled closer. "Don't be shy. Hand holding is not a sign of weakness." They slowly did as I said, linking together like a giant daisy chain of different kinds of magic. When the last werewolf grasped the hand of the final Enforcer, I turned to Femke and offered my hand. She slipped her fingers over mine, closing them softly.

I know you did what you thought you needed to, Femke sent

as I tried to decide how wide to open the veil to accommodate everyone. *I just wish you'd said something to me first.*

It was my turn not to comment. "Ready? Remember, we're walking into a hostile environment. I'll shield you as long as you stay within this circle." I let the shielding crackle so they could see the dome of power protecting them. "If you choose to leave it, you're on your own." I nodded to Piers who nodded back, Gram and Demetrius scattered among the group. "Stay with your sorcerer leader," I said. "And listen to their orders. They are your safety net if things get ugly." I'd never really played the role of general before, but had spent enough time as a coven leader and with Max—not to mention in ugly situations—it felt almost natural to give orders like this. "Our first priority is to capture Liander Belaisle. Second is to take Erica Plower alive." Justice had to prevail, I guess. "And last, the Brotherhood and council members. But as long as we have the two ringleaders the others should fall into line."

Nods all around, eager, anxious paranormals watching me, waiting for my signal. I recognized faces as I looked around the anxious group. Isabelle and Maksym, the vampire and werewolf lovers I'd first met when I came to Ukraine to rescue Charlotte smiled and nodded to me. Finlay and Gwendolyn, Enforcers under Femke did the same. Those two had almost foiled my plans to save my werefriend, though had proved allies in the end, and not just to me.

No time for a scoot down memory lane. But it was nice to know I had those around me I could trust.

"It's time," I said. "Stay together, stay focused and don't lose your temper."

Ha, Gram sent to me. *I dub thee black, pot.*

And you, kettle, I sent with a burst of love.

The veil sighed open, a massive gap wide enough for the gathering to pass through shimmering around the edges with rainbow light. I felt their nervousness and embraced them with my power.

"I'll keep you safe," I said. "This will all be over soon."

Hoping I hadn't just lied to them, I stepped through the veil, the sound of over a hundred pairs of feet marching behind me.

The moment I hit the veil I felt resistance and starting swearing in my head. My demon snarled, thrashing against the pressure of power trying to tie us down. With a hiss and a slice of spirit magic, my vampire cut us loose, my sorcery joining Shaylee as the family magic pounded back whoever was trying to stop us.

Together, we flared with iridescence, sending a wave of light up and away from the bubble of people I protected. For a long moment the power pressing against me fought, writhing in anger, but finally released and fled.

But not before I felt the familiar tang of maji. And knew who it was that tried so hard to keep me from succeeding. I didn't have time to deal with them at the moment. But they'd be having a visit now I was at full power again.

Oh, my, yes.

All is well, I sent back along the line through Femke as a pulse of nervousness reached me. They must have sensed the blockage. *Count down in three*. They tensed. *Two*. Mass inhale. *One*. Mass exhale.

And I tore open the veil.

My shields pushed back the handful of sorcerers scattered around the council chamber main floor, sending them sliding backward with frightened shouts. We landed as one on the tile, facing the council bench and the staring faces of the witches who didn't seem as shocked as they could have.

So they knew we were coming. Of course they did. Wouldn't save them or anything.

On cue, Piers locked all the doors with whips of black energy, sealing the exits with sorcery. I quickly scanned the place for my targets, easily spotting Erica perched on her seat as Council Leader, staring down at me with a tremble to her lower lip. She looked less certain of herself, much more fragile than she had only a few hours before and I wondered what had changed.

Not that it mattered.

Gram strode forward, her small group of Enforcers behind her, vampires and werewolves fanning out on Demetrius's command. They pushed the shielding outward, sealing the entire room while I allowed my own sorcery out. I hated to hurt them, but I had no choice in the matter. The blossom bloomed wide, drew in the energy stored in the Brotherhood sorcerers and dropped them to their knees.

The council panicked to a witch, scrambling to escape, only to be controlled and brought to their knees by the Enforcers now free to act. Erica remained where she was, face in her hands, shoulders shaking, but I couldn't bring myself to feel sorry for her.

Not when I realized Liander Belaisle was nowhere to be found.

"Where is he?" I stalked to the front of the bench, looking up at Erica who dropped her hands and met my eyes with her bloodshot ones. The sound of sorrowful moaning from the captured council kept a counterpoint to her shaking voice.

"Gone," she whispered. "Long gone. He's abandoned us and left us to be arrested."

The moment she finished speaking I felt the bubble burst. Not the shielding I'd used to protect my people, but the coating of filth holding Harvard in control. The recoil bounced off me with the distinct touch of Belaisle, but, worse, with the trapped power of the Council in its grasp.

Erica wailed her horror as the magic of the North American witches was ripped from her, pulling her forward as it flashed free and disappeared, dropping her prone over her desk, unconscious.

Shaken and furious, I ground my teeth together in frustration. He planned this from day one. And now he had what he wanted, didn't he?

The power of the Council was gone.

THIRTY-SIX

I sat on the steps leading up to the Council bench platform and stayed the hell out of the way. Femke was amazing, had been since the moment the Council was secured and Belaisle's disappearance with the power of the witches gone with him was made apparent.

She stepped in immediately in her role as leader of the new alliance, ascending to the leader's seat and using her bell-like magic gavel on the table top.

"As the duly appointed leader of the new World Paranormal Council, I declare, under the authority of all magic races, the North American Witches Council is now defunct."

Erica's unconsciousness had only lasted a few moments. She watched from where Enforcers had dragged her down below, on her knees next to her Councilors, with dead and weary eyes. I expected some kind of resistance from her, but instead she seemed almost vacant. I could only imagine the damage Belaisle had done stripping the Council's power from her and wondered if she was even in there anymore.

Not that I cared much.

I'm going after Belaisle. Piers's fierce message spun me around as the final toll of Femke's bell had rung.

I'm coming with you. I was already on the move to his side, but he shook his head, dark tunnel formed and ready.

Femke is more important, he sent. And left me behind. Fuming, I considered going after him. He couldn't take on Belaisle alone. Besides, we really, really needed to take that bastard into custody and I was sure I was the only one who could take him down.

Syd, Femke's mind touched mine. *I need you.*

And that, as they say, was the straw that broke the camel and the cart and about three dozen eggs with one tiny message of need. I joined her, then, listened as she spoke.

"A new council will be assigned," she said. "From among the surviving families. For now, an interim council will consist of three witches in the spirit of expediency."

Don't you dare, I sent to her in a sharp poke of power.

You're kidding, right? She laughed in my head. *I know better. You were right when you said you'd be a terrible council leader.*

Thanks for that, I grumbled. *Who, then?*

Femke hesitated. *That's what I wanted you here for. Suggestions?*

This is temporary, right? I met her troubled eyes.

Yes, just until the families can be brought together and a new council chosen.

Then pick three, I sent. *Who cares who they are? Let's just get the ball rolling.* Her eyes widened at the suggestion, but I prodded her gently with power. *We'll be here to watch over them*, I sent. *Besides, they're powerless at this point.* I really had to go after Belaisle. The elements knew what he wanted that magic for and sudden worry for South America heated up my blood. *Pick three*, I sent to her, opening the veil. *I'm going to do some checking in with other territories.*

She let me go. Over the next hour or so I moved around the world, stopping in for visits with each of the leaders, now returned to their own territories. Ana Maria hugged me tight and whispered promises I knew she'd never keep while the other leaders seemed relieved and slightly shocked things had gone so wrong so fast. I just hoped they wouldn't try to renege on their agreement to support the new World Paranormal Council, but time would tell.

When I returned to Harvard, Femke had things firmly in hand. I sank to the step and watched her as she swore in three young and frightened looking witches. I recognized Philip, Erica's secretary, his hazel eyes flashing nerves and excitement as he gave me a thumbs up. I grinned and returned the gesture as Femke stepped back from the now black-robed witches.

"I declare you the interim North American Witches Council," she said. "Lead with integrity and honor for as long as you hold your posts." A pulse of power left her, a chunk of the magic she carried with her, but more than that. It came from the Enforcers, too, the ones the other leaders sent, and I realized Femke just created the seed of the new Council power from all sources of magic, werewolves and vampires included.

Interesting choice, I sent to her. She turned to meet my eyes even as the three, stunned a moment, finally turned to mount the steps and take their places.

Not much of a choice, she sent. *I couldn't leave them with nothing. It's not much, but something to build on. Until we get the power back from Belaisle.*

If we do. I had no illusions about that. *Everyone is filled in. I really have to go.*

Belaisle. Femke nodded to me. *You think you'll find him?*

Part of the reason I wasn't feeling anxious about going was my doubt I ever would. At least, not until he was ready to be found. *What did you do with the old Council?* They were gone when I got back, Erica included.

Under arrest awaiting trial, Erica sent. *I'll guide the new group on writing some laws as stopgaps. But Syd, this is a damned mess.*

Tell me about it. I rose to my feet. *If you don't need me, I'll trot off to the Stronghold and let them know all is—*

SYD! Piers appeared in a blast of black, hitting the ground at a run right for me, gray longcoat billowing out behind him. The panic on his face drove me forward toward him, Gram and Demetrius joining us at a dead dash.

Piers didn't speak, instead flashed an image at me. And terror drove me to slice open the veil and hurtle myself through it, the three following behind.

The Stronghold. Under attack by the Brotherhood.

I leaped through the other side in to chaos. Smoke filled the main hall, a large cluster of Brotherhood pinning witches and draining them right in front of me, Mom and Dad doing their best to fight them, a losing cause against sorcery. My feet hit the ground hard, a roar of pure rage rumbling up from my lungs, rainbow power rippling around me.

Everyone turned, the fear on the Brotherhood's faces as they realized they'd made the biggest mistake of their lives lasting one heartbeat. Just as long as it took for me to let out my fury. The power of the maji, fed by my absolute need to protect my family, pulsed outward in a blast of magic so strong I staggered when it left me.

It passed over the witches without harming them, rippling through and around them in sparkling light. But, the moment it hit the Brotherhood it turned to knives of light, slicing through them with power, cutting off their magic, sucking them dry and sending them crashing to the floor.

I gasped a breath, bent over with my hands on my knees as Gram, Demetrius and Piers split up and ran forward, presumably to check and make sure I hadn't missed anyone. Moans and weeping from the family filled the space, but didn't last as a weak but enthusiastic cheer rose and their love and gratitude hit me hard.

Mom. I reached for her, heart pounding. *From this moment on every one of our witches has their sorcery wakened and damned well learns to use it.*

Consider it done. She came to me, face lined and tired, and hugged me as Dad kissed the top of my head. Sassafras scampered forward, leaping into my arms.

"What happened?" I scanned the room in a moment of panic, spotting Quaid helping some witches to their feet, Shenka doing the same, Charlotte and Sage alive and well. "The kids!"

"Safe," Mom said. "Galleytrot took them all away when the Brotherhood came." She looked off, as if into the distance, then nodded. "He kept them out of harm's way down one of the corridors. They're fine."

I exhaled my relief, shaking a little. "What happened? How did they get in?" The Stronghold promised me.

Mom's shrug seemed slightly dazed. "One minute we were celebrating your victory and the next we all felt the

Stronghold shudder, as though attacked. We had that moment of warning only. And then the Brotherhood came."

Something was horribly wrong. I reached out to the Stronghold to find out what. *Are you okay? Did they hurt you somehow?*

No answer. Not even a breath of a hint of a sniff of anything. Fear came back with a vengeance. *Stronghold*, I sent, digging deeper. *Where are you?* Was he still mad at me for pushing to share his secret? No, that wasn't it. There was just nothing. But that was impossible, wasn't it? How did the consciousness of an entire plane just vanish?

It wasn't until I sank deep, deep into the heart of the Stronghold I felt him. But, when I tried to speak to him, he remained silent and still. As if he'd somehow been put to sleep.

I pulled free and opened my mouth to tell my family what I'd found at the exact moment the air above me split open and five massive bodies fell through.

Dragon shapes plummeted toward me, shifting as they fell into human form. I barely had time to cushion their descent, the weight of them almost too much to bear. I'd pushed myself so hard, twice now, with little rest, I was almost used up. But a surge of power from everyone around me gave me the boost I needed, as all the witches and friendly sorcerers and two werewolf friends threw their magic into the struggle to lower the drach safely to the stone floor.

I ran to Max as he collapsed, diamond eyes closing, bending over him as he sighed two words.

"Dark Brother."

THIRTY-SEVEN

I hovered over Max as Lula and Phon did their thing, not knowing if he was hurt or just tired or what. They firmly kept me outside their little packet of shielding as they quietly went about the work they were so good at while I paced and fumed and worried.

Mabel and three other drach rested in different rooms down this same hall, all brought here gently and with reverence by the witches of my family and those we'd rescued. They knew who the drach were, clearly, and from the anxiety and true compassion on their faces understood what role the mighty first race played in their safety and how grateful they were for that protection, even through their own pain and suffering.

There was hope for witches. I was sure of it now.

Lula finally sighed and sat back from where she bent over Max's silent face, the shields keeping me away falling. I joined her immediately, on my knees next to the bed as the big drach leader's diamond eyes flickered open, his bald head turning toward me. Scales rippled over his skin, his power reaching mine, the infinite and expansive magic of the drach feeling weak and distant. That scared me more than anything I'd ever felt in my life.

"Max." I stroked his cheek, tingle of power exchanged.

"Sydlynn Hayle." His deep, rumbling voice sounded hollowed out, lacking its usual robustness. "We made it to you."

I squeezed his big hand, the pressure of his fingers returning my gesture. "You did," I said, tears tracking down my cheeks as my throat tightened around my guilt. "I'm sorry," I said. "Things are a mess on my plane and I had to fix it, but I was coming to find you, I swear—"

He cut off my rambling confession/excuse freight train of regret with a soft chuckle.

"Thank you." His eyes met Lula's then Phon's. "For your assistance." His entire body tensed as he heaved himself up and spun sideways, feet on the floor. His bare toes were scaled more heavily than the rest of him, gray robe shimmering a moment as the bed creaked and groaned under his massive weight. "Mabel and the others?"

"Safe," I said. "I'll show you where."

"No." Max stood, a surge of power driving him to his

feet. He obviously felt better by the second, magic returning, though nowhere near his usual gigantic presence. "We have work to do, Syd. And very little time for it."

I followed him out the door, leaving the healers behind with a squeeze of hands and whispered thanks. Max strode with confidence down the corridor, me trotting to keep up behind him. I barely remembered coming here, I was so worried about him and the drach, it took me a minute to orient myself as he turned and took us up and then down stairs, covering ground with his massive strides.

"Mind telling me where we're going?" I tugged at his elbow and he slowed just slightly, bowing his head to me.

"You have tried to reach the mind of the Stronghold?" I nodded. "As have I," he said. "With the results I feared."

"He's asleep." I whispered it, in awe a little of what this could mean. "Not like before. I could talk to him, even when the Brotherhood had access, before the battle."

"Yes," Max said. "Something has changed. And I fear I know what."

I smacked his arm. "You know I hate secrets." Immediately the memory of my conversation with the Stronghold surfaced. "He told me he had something he couldn't tell me," I said. "To do with Creator."

Max sighed, sad and deep. "We are almost there," he said.

I followed in silence, realizing as we entered a round room with a staircase on one side I knew where I was. "This leads to the tower," I said. I knew it intimately. Had been kept prisoner there, as had Ameline. "The Stronghold called it his heart."

"It is, indeed," Max said. "Though only the crust of it. Observe." He crossed to the far wall under the stairs, big hands stroking the stone. His face twisted as werewolves sometimes did when they were emotional, but Max's transformation seemed calculated. His bones morphed, the face of his dragon shape appearing on his human neck and shoulders, diamond eyes swirling as he opened his muzzle and fire emerged. But not the flames I was used to, tinged with blue from the heat. This fire almost floated, as iridescent as the rainbow power we both shared. It washed the wall with light, slipping between stones, the entire section before him glowing, pulsing, and, finally, vanishing in a breath of superheated air.

A set of stairs led down into the dark. I stayed on Max's heels as he descended, wondering why my entire life seemed to be about finding secret hiding places in the bowels of the earth.

But, we didn't have far to go. Six steps down, a turn to the right and six more narrow stone stairs deposited us into a massive chamber. I looked up into the darkness, shivering at the quiet, buried power now sleeping inside this room.

"The hollow rises to the top of the tower," Max said, pausing with me. "It was created to protect and support what we seek. Come." I went after him as he crossed the shiny stone floor. It didn't look manmade or anything, more as though some natural power had polished it to a sheen. My eyes adjusted to the faint glow coming from the walls, my demon's sight seemingly useless here. Max's diamond eyes glowed, leading the way. It wasn't until we were almost in the middle of the room I realized something huge loomed there.

Its shadow cast long, broad darkness back from the glow of Max's eyes, towering over us. We circled slowly, until I made out the shape of a throne from behind, then the side, a massive arm resting on the edge. But as we finally reached the front of what I now knew was a statue of some kind, I felt a pang of nervousness born from years of watching horror movies.

Not that it was particularly horrific. Just that I had the impending feeling something terrible was about to happen and I was the cheeky genius girl who got an axe in the chest for being so clever.

"Behold," Max said, voice barely carrying in the muffled quiet of the giant room. "Creator."

He said what? I stared up at the headless statue and could barely breathe.

"What I'm about to tell you," Max said, "no other soul in this Universe was meant to know. Creator left the secrets with me long ago. And I had thought I was the only one who knew the truth." He shook his big head. "I should have realized the consciousness tied to the Stronghold was from this source. But I never made the connection until my people were almost destroyed."

My feet pulled me closer slowly, carefully as I studied the massive, headless figure before me. It had to be the height of a three story house, as wide as the same, the carved shoulders rising into the dark. One of the hands was missing, the opposite arm, as well and a giant chunk of stone was gone from the center of the chest. One foot had been removed, the rest of the masculinized female shape clothed in a robe of stone.

I stopped and gasped at the sight of movement, both hands pressed to my chest and ready to run despite the power I held. This felt like nothing I was prepared for, could handle on my own, and I had no idea why.

A shining, slippery thread of sliver fell from the chest cavity and slithered into the lap of the statue before shimmying down over one knee and trickling across the edge. I stepped back as it spun its way to the floor and collapsed in a weak and hurt puddle on the top of the one intact foot. A song like I'd never heard, full of agony so powerful I was weeping and wanted to fall to my knees and sob my heart out rose around me.

The only thing that saved me was the sound of Max's voice.

"The song of the drach," he said.

I looked up at him, wiping tears away as his power softly masked the music from the thread. And then I remembered, the ribbons of power I rescued from the rooftop in Miami, from the crystal machine Belaisle used to strip the Dumont family magic. I'd shattered the crystals and let them go, only to have them warn me and keep me safe later.

The souls of dead drach in their purest form.

I stared in softly easing grief at the tiny puddle of silver, going to it, lifting its weightless slipperiness into my hands. It curled around my wrist and sagged there, listless as its song finally went silent. I turned to Max, cupping it in my hands, holding it out to him.

"What happened?" I coughed through the last of my tears. "This is different."

"It is," he nodded. "This is one of the nine drach who gave their physical forms to protect Creator's body when the Universe was made."

My mind didn't want to grasp what he was saying. "I don't understand."

"There is no time to explain now," he said. "We must go speak to Fate. I have the answer I need, Sydlynn. Now I must know where this answer will lead us." He gently took the ribbon from me, deposited it on the foot of the statue again. "I will explain everything, I promise. But we have to go."

I nodded, feeling vacant, like my poor brain was on a time out. My alter egos seemed equally as stunned, the four of us still struggling to get past the terrible grief of the drach soul. Even my sorcery felt blunted and sad, recoiled tightly beneath me as Max took my hand and opened the veil.

We both felt the resistance the moment we entered. It triggered my anger, but what I felt was clearly nothing compared to Max's rage. With a roar he burst into drach form and tossed me at the same moment. I landed firmly on his back, weakened power more than enough to anchor me to him.

Let me, I sent. *You're still tired.* Like I wasn't.

The hell I am, he snarled in my head, magic surging around him, violence in his power. I'd never felt him angry before and it scared the crap out of me.

Remind me never to piss you off, I sent as he smashed through the barrier with a burst of fire and a heave of his broad wings. I heard the screams of fear from those who opposed us, their failure echoing into the veil even as Max slashed a giant hole in the rubbery membrane and hurtled us through it.

Instead of shifting to human shape as he usually did, the giant drach skimmed low over Center, the maji city barely ten feet below us. His shadow sent the white-robed residents running, screaming as his power preceded him. A back wash of his wings sent a few flying, tumbling away as he landed us in the central plaza, at the foot of the steps to the main hall and where Light Fate resided.

Four rows of maji stood in our way, all terrified but refusing to back down. And, at their head, stood the old leader, Zeon. He held up both hands, Santa Claus face a mask of command, though I could tell from the shaking of his body he was as anxious as his people.

"You may not enter!" His voice boomed, making visible ripples in the air.

Max roared again, power shaking the ground, sending the maji stumbling and falling from the steps they guarded. Zeon caught himself in time, but he still looked foolish to me.

"Get out of my way, maji," Max growled, smoke and a hint of fire puffing from his massive muzzle. "Now."

Zeon's eyes flickered to me. "She may not accompany you," he said, pointing at me. "She's done enough damage."

Max snorted more smoke. "She's with me."

"She is maji!" His shriek totally blew his whole master of the Universe routine, revealing his fear clearly at last. "She will obey my commands!"

"Zeon," I said, slipping from Max's back as he shifted to human form and began a firm, deliberate stride toward the maji leader, "take a flying leap already."

I didn't have to do anything. The drach leader's power—the magic of the first race of the Universe—even weakened was more than a match for the frightened maji. With a wedge of shielding shoved in front of him, Max sent our opposition scrambling out of the way while Zeon, face alternating between rage and terror, followed us.

I ignored him. Who cared what he had to say? Max didn't seem to and, from the ineffectual way the maji had handled pretty much every major disaster in my life—that is to say they didn't lift a freaking finger—I was pretty much ready to trust Max on it.

"Drach!" Zeon wasn't about to quit as we strode up the steps, growing, as we were always forced to, to meet the size of the place. I pushed upward until the main hall looked less like I was an insect and more like I belonged there. "Any crisis that befalls us because of your meddling with Creator is on your head. Do you hear me?" Max kept walking. "Do not come crying to the maji when the servant of the Dark Universe unleashes hell!"

Max spun suddenly, stopping so fast I caught my breath. He glared down at Zeon who cowered a little. Just for a moment, but the rage and resentment that flashed in his eyes told me he hated Max for making him feel small.

"Stay out of this," the drach leader said, "like you always do, maji. Whisper your lies to each other, your old dreams never realized because you were too weak and afraid to act. Pronounce your judgments on those who choose to act. But leave the salvation of the Universe to your betters."

I could have jumped up and down and cheered and made na-na-na boo-boo sounds at Zeon. Could have. Decided to be a grownup and just shrug at him with an arched eyebrow.

Sucked to be him.

Together, Max and I spun on our heels and left Zeon behind.

THIRTY-EIGHT

I wasn't surprised to find Fate waiting for us, though I was a little shocked to discover her dark brother was with her. But the moment the two heard our footsteps, I realized things were way worse than I'd ever imagined.

Light Fate's face was sheathed in tears, her white, blind eyes wide and staring. Usually, she seemed to be able to make her way easily, as though guided by what she could see internally. But even her brother looked drawn and frightened, Dark Fate's anxiety and lack of poise pulling me to a halt.

Max didn't falter approaching Light Fate. I knew he loved her, though the origins of their first meeting and what they truly meant to each other was lost to me. They didn't talk about it and I didn't ask. Besides, this was no time to bring it up, not when she stumbled and almost fell, feet tentative beneath her, Max's strong hands catching her and lifting her to him.

She cried out and buried her face in his chest, sang the song that was his name while he sang softly back to her. Whatever he said made her sag as he guided her to the fountain where I'd first met her, sat her down beside her staring and desperate brother.

"Tell me," Max said.

"Is Sydlynn here?" Light Fate felt around with her hands and I realized, for the first time, she and her brother were truly blind. I caught her fingers in mine, Dark Fate's in my other and watched them both shiver but ease in their fear.

"My love," she whispered. "We can no longer see the future."

Her brother bobbed his head, blond, wavy hair hanging around his cheeks. "For days now," he said. "Since Zoe Helios became a phoenix."

She became a what? So that was how she survived the flames. But what did that mean?

"It wasn't supposed to happen like this." Light Fate's voice cracked and warbled. "She was meant to heal the Oracles, to cleanse them of the taint of the Brotherhood and reset their abilities. To prevent further damage to the future."

All caught up now, I hoped.

"Be we didn't foresee this." Dark Fate's hand fell from mine and he slouched, looking more like a teenager with a terrible secret then an all-powerful Fate of Creator.

"Zoe can't see anything either," I said. "Her power is gone."

Light Fate hiccupped, nodded. "Then, I fear the worst has happened," she said. "That somehow Liander Belaisle has found out a way to move outside Fate and, in doing so, has rendered us helpless."

That had to be impossible. They were the Fates, weren't they?

"I worried for Syd," Max said, "when I was unable to reach her almost three days ago." Wow, had it only been three days? "I suspected the Brotherhood when I tried to find her, the feeling of their foul sorcery everywhere. But, I was forced to leave that investigation to her." He nodded sadly to me. "I traced Belaisle's power, you see. Not to Gaia or the council. But to the edge of the Universe."

The sound of running feet whipped my head around and I barely had time to brace myself before Iepa threw her arms around my neck and hugged me.

"Syd," she said, backing away, her face mirroring the Fate's fear. "I tried so hard to help. But they wouldn't let me go." Frustration burst through her power.

"You're here," I said. "Thank you." I paused, frowned. "You're responsible for Ameline's soul being trapped in the maji chamber."

She gulped and nodded, sinking down next to me

beside the bubbling fountain. "And for what little information she told you," she said. "I could only hope you would find her at last and she could point you in the right direction."

There had been a time I didn't trust Iepa, that she'd betrayed me, or I thought she had. Only to discover Fate was in control of everything. But now, in this moment, I saw clearly just how much she'd done, what she'd risked and fought for, to help me. And I hugged her for it.

"You did great," I said before turning back to Max with her hand in mine. "Keep going."

"Your effort was most valiant, Iepa," the drach said. "But, I fear, no manner of support from you or even all the maji could have helped against what Belaisle has already done."

I almost didn't want to ask. "What would that be?" Like it would be me if I didn't look down the rabbit hole.

"You already know, Syd," Max said, showing us all a vision of the drach caught in a spinning maelstrom of what looked like power and the veil and darkness all woven together. "I've already spoken his name. Belaisle has made a pact with the other Universe. His new master is Creator's Dark Brother."

We all sat silent, lost in what Max had said.

"The rest of the drach?" I should have known better than to let that burst of panic go anywhere.

"Safe," he said. "On Demonicon, resting. It was a

close thing, but we managed to escape the vortex and partially reseal it. But Syd, I was mistaken all along thinking we'd closed the way to the other Universe." He shook his big head, eyes sparkling with regret. "I now understand once the way is opened it can never be closed again."

Something Gabriel's actions triggered seven years ago. There was an "unless" hanging in his voice, but I was too afraid to ask him what it might mean. Because I was positive whatever he would tell me would have to do with my son and I refused to put Gabriel in harm's way.

Max knew that. Maybe he held back on purpose, to save me. But, then again, I needed to know.

"Tell me something," I said, though I knew he might see my question as shifting blame. I never intended it that way. "If your race created the two Universes, why can't you just fix the hole?" Way to prod your drach friend with the fun fact this was all his fault.

He sighed, shrugged. "It's always easier to destroy than create," he said. "And though we had the power to segment the Universes by creating the new magicks, we were unable to undo the damage once it unfolded. Only the power of Creator was strong enough to keep both Universes from being destroyed by the very forces that broke them in two."

Gotcha. Sucked, but made sense.

"What's made things worse in the long run," Max

went on, stifling my unhappy ponderings, "is the fact Belaisle has linked himself to Dark Brother. Perhaps if he hadn't the schism would have remained small and gone unnoticed. But with his interference, by permanently bonding himself to the other side, he has created the potential for growth of the crack. Please understand," he said to me, as if I was the only one in the dark , "the way between Universes is a veil of its own, but nothing really like what separates the planes. It is, instead, the exact moment the two Universes split, held in stasis. Time, an instant of it, formed into a thin band of limbo. Life goes on around and on both sides of it. But that hair-thin barrier was always meant to be impermeable and has been, in the history of all things, the strongest force known to any magic."

"Because time itself is immovable," Light Fate said, regaining some of her poise as she spoke. "Fluid and under constant motion, but always the baseline of everything in the Universe. The pulse of life."

"When Creator realized what was happening," Max said, "when she discovered the new Universe had sprung up, in reflection to this one due to the creation of the new magicks, she forced time to stop and create a barrier to forever keep the two apart."

"In doing so," Dark Fate said, young man's face serious, "she was forced to give of herself—

her being and all her power to this Universe, to

abandon her physical form to create the time seal and save us from destruction."

"What will letting Dark Brother through to this Universe do to us?" I had to force myself to breathe, so tense my lungs ached with each inhale and exhale.

"Were that his purpose," Max said with grim anger, "I would worry less than the true goals in his dark heart."

"What has happened?" Light Fate clutched at his arm.

"Creator gave up her being to protect us," he said. "But her physical form wasn't destroyed, was impossible to eliminate. And so, she instructed the drach to break apart her body and protect it, scattering nine pieces around the Universe to keep them safe. No one knew of their locations but the drach who guarded Creator's pieces."

I did not like the sound of this. "The Stronghold," I said with a soft gasp. "The statue."

"No statue," Max said. "But the final resting place of Creator."

Oh. My. Swearword.

"Her heart was left with her body," Max said, "that much we were allowed to know." The Stronghold called it his heart. That made total sense to me now. Creator's own heart beating in the deepest soul of the first plane. "Protected by the soul of one of the drach." Max was sad about something, and I wondered what could make any of this any worse than it already was. "My mother," he said.

Wait. What? I thought he was the first drach ever? While I pondered that anomaly, my own heart crumbled. "The silver thread?"

He nodded. "I lead the drach," he said. "But only because my family gave of themselves in the beginning. They no longer exist, not as we understand existence."

I leaned into his shoulder, my forehead against the soft fabric of his robe and I cried silently for the drach who had birthed him, the remains I'd held in my hands and the song she'd sung, the last of her legacy.

When I leaned back, snuffling, tears ran down his cheeks, though he smiled at me. "She was proud to answer Creator's call," he said. "As were my father and brother." That made three of the nine. "The rest were chosen specifically for their strengths and their dedication to Creator." Max's words became hesitant and I wondered why he wasn't chosen. He was the best of them, as far as I knew.

"But our visit to the chamber has now proven to me someone else knows about Creator's form," Max said. "And is actively seeking to assemble the pieces separate from her body."

The hole in the statue's chest. The falling thread. "Her heart is gone."

Light Fate gasped so loud I jumped. "To where? Who has stolen it?"

"We don't know," Max said. "But it bodes evil for us all. With the loss of Creator's heart, Fate has stopped, holds its breath. What Gabriel began is evolving, thanks to Belaisle and his pact with Dark Brother."

"And that is why," Zeon's voice cut through our conversation, making me lunge to my feet with a snarl of rage on my lips, "the abomination you mothered must be destroyed."

Over my dead and desiccated corpse.

My power hit Zeon full in the chest, not holding back my anger even a little. He staggered, fury on his face. Let him be pissed. He had no idea what anger was.

About to find out, though.

"You come near my son," I snarled, "and the maji will regret your decision for generations to come." Zeon opened his mouth and I shut it with a blast of magic. "You do not want to find out if I'm kidding. Trust me."

But Light Fate was openly weeping. "He may be right," she whispered.

I turned on her, spitting fire. "Don't even think about it."

"Syd is right," Max said. "It's far too late, now. And Gabriel's existence was necessary to fulfil the prophecy. Which ended with Syd victorious. His continued health and wellbeing is of no concern to us. The damage is done and cannot be unmade." He glared at Zeon. "Or do you now challenge the prophecy Creator herself put down for us to follow? I have heard no thanks from you since its completion at great personal risk to Sydlynn and her son seven of her years ago."

The maji leader backed off a bit as my white-hot temper cooled to bubbling lava.

"I'm afraid," Light Fate said. "For the first time in creation, there is no guidance, nothing to show us the path." Dark Fate nodded with her.

"Maybe that's a good thing," I snapped. Okay, maybe not. But I was tired of being the only one who didn't have a damned clue. Nice to have company for a change.

"How did Belaisle know to take Creator's heart?" Iepa turned her back on Zeon, speaking quietly while her leader glared with his arms crossed over his wide chest. He looked more like an angry Zeus than Santa Claus, but I still didn't respect his dumb ass.

"Dark Brother must have told him," Max said.

I shook my head, sinking to the fountain's edge again. "He couldn't have done it," I said. "Stronghold kicked all the Brotherhood out. There's no way Belaisle made it past his defenses."

"Then, he had an ally," Max said. "Who the Stronghold trusted."

I shuddered. That meant someone I knew was a traitor.

"With Creator's heart gone," Max said, "the Stronghold's personality is sleeping. It must have developed separately, out of the presence of Creator's heart."

"Maybe we can appeal directly to Creator." I had no idea how, but wasn't it worth a try? Normals prayed and stuff all the time to their deities, didn't they?

"There is no cohesive personality to appeal to any longer," Max said. "Creator is all around us, in every part of the Universe. The body is simply dense with magic because it bore Creator. But the essence of the one who made us is long absorbed."

"But Dark Brother is still aware, I take it?"

Max nodded. "He wasn't forced to take the same path and remained a solid entity, from what I know."

"Good," I said, gut churning but determined to end this any way I could. "If he has solid form, we can destroy him."

I might as well have told them I was going to have a baby roast and eat their little brains with some vintage red wine and a square of dark chocolate.

"Blasphemy!" Zeon's face turned bright red then darkened to purple, eyes bulging out of their sockets. "You dare suggest attempting to destroy a force of creation?" He shook wildly, jabbing fingers at the Fates, at Iepa and Max. "And still you tell me she isn't dangerous?"

I stared at him, blank faced and out of give a craps. "You don't know me very well," I said, voice quiet and cold. "I will do anything—anything—to protect my family. And my son." I turned my back on him, focused on Max's troubled diamond eyes. "Any guesses what Dark Brother is after?" Trying to ponder the needs and wants of something—I couldn't bring myself to call him a some*one*—made my head ache worse than ever. "He has to have a goal, right?"

Max's distant frown told me he was thinking about it, but when he dropped his chin almost to his chest I knew he was at a loss. "I can't imagine he would want to destroy the Universes," he said. "It's possible he craves Creator's form to gain her power. Though what that would do to the crack in the time veil I have no idea."

Light Fate shuddered beside him. "He is Dark Brother," she whispered. "It's possible he doesn't care if everything is destroyed as long as he is the master of the result."

That kind of ginormous insanity I couldn't fathom. Best to focus on what I could. Like taking out a certain sorcerer who I should have dealt with ages ago. "How about killing Belaisle?" That would be the simplest answer, if the wretched blighter would just sit still long enough for me to do the job.

But Max's sigh told me that was a bad idea. "He is now a keyhole," Max said. "Doing so might open the way further and leave us exposed completely. Dark Brother will have no choice but to cross himself and seize the pieces personally. I'm sure he'd rather not do that, since it could tear apart both Universes. As long as he has Belaisle doing his dirty work, there is still a chance to stop this."

"How?" And then it hit me. I almost smacked myself in the forehead even as Light Fate spoke.

"You must track down and protect the other pieces," she said, real hope in her voice for the first time since we arrived. "Make sure Belaisle does not gain access to any more parts of Creator."

"Agreed," Max said. "For if all nine pieces are found and brought together, the one in possession will have access to all the power of creation."

I stared up at him while he patted my hand like a kindly uncle.

"Reassemble the statue," he said, "and you *are* Creator."

THIRTY-NINE

Of course. "Belaisle's endgame," I said. "And just like him to think he could play god."

"While I'm certain," Max said, "Dark Brother has other ideas for all that power."

"Like?" My brain was far too scrambled to put two and two together and get any food group but purple.

"I don't know," Max said. "But it's likely he'll try to use it to break the barrier between Universes in a way he can control them both." The big drach paused, brow furrowing. "You must know, it's highly unlikely Belaisle is in full command of himself any longer and probably hasn't been for some time."

It might explain his cleverness, even outside his cheating by using the Oracles to see the future.

"I'm supposed to mourn his poor, unfortunate soul?" Not in my lifetime. And I planned to live forever.

"No," Max said. "Just a warning. If he carries part of Dark Brother's consciousness, we are dealing with a vast mind capable of anything."

"However," Light Fate said with a hint of breathiness as she looked up. "That means we are also dealing with an arrogant and unstable presence that could perhaps be manipulated given the right circumstances."

I liked the sound of that. Zeon, not so much.

"You will bring down the destruction of all of us." His voice vibrated with righteous rage and I wondered if he had any other state of being these days.

"Regardless of Belaisle's possible possession," Max said, "we have a job of our own to do."

Right. "Find the pieces." I leaped to my feet, sudden worry making me ill. "Let's go."

Max's smile lit his diamond eyes, hand gently pulling me down again. "There is no immediate need," he said. "Our search has already begun." He tapped one temple. So he'd filled in the drach while we sat here, nattering. Good to know someone was on the ball. "My people will do what they can, but I assure you after all this time I have never heard of any one of us coming across a piece. Never. And, unless Belaisle has a way to seek them, he's in the same position we are." It was hard to hold still, to accept the reasonable tone in his voice. "No one knows where they are, remember?"

"Not even Dark Brother?" That's what worried me

most.

Max shook his head. "I believe not," he said. "Though I'm certain he's aware what Creator did to seal the two Universes from each other, if he knew where the pieces rested he wouldn't have wasted time on Belaisle attacking your council. The heart in the Stronghold must have been an obvious discovery, considering the personality of the plane itself."

"Belaisle needed the power," I said. "But why? Why doesn't Dark Brother just give him some?"

"It doesn't work that way," Max said. "And I doubt Creator's sibling is as generous as our beloved one. Belaisle is a tool, nothing more. To be used and discarded, much like the witches whom he drained for their magic." His gaze turned to Iepa. "I mourn the loss of Gaia," he said. "But fear Belaisle might target another maji to forward his plans."

"Let him try," Zeon said, puffing out his chest. We'd gathered quite the crowd by now, the maji come to whisper and watch. They reminded me so much of witches with their busybody nature and lack of conviction to act I clenched my jaw to keep from driving them off.

"I already know who he's lined up to take her place," I said.

Max's furrowed brow turned to a ravine, fury in his eyes. That was the second time I saw him mad today, curls of smoke escaping his nostrils. "If he comes near you, I will devour him."

I patted his arm with a grin. "No killing, remember?"

"Who said I'd kill him?" Max's eyebrow arched. "My belly is vast and an unpleasant place to be, but I could keep him alive in there. For a while."

The implications of that were just too disgusting to linger on.

"So, how do we find the pieces?" That was step next, I assumed.

"You want to be Creator now, is that it?" Zeon's scornful snort made the gathered maji flinch. I wished he'd just shut the hell up already.

"We must do something," Max said, "to start Fate again. And that could happen simply by retrieving one of the pieces." Light Fate nodded quickly, Dark Fate along with her.

"The Universe is not meant to operate without us," Light Fate said. "We are adrift and pathless. Anything could happen."

I took it from her shudder and the one her brother mirrored that was a bad thing to think about.

"I swear to you, Sydlynn Hayle," Zeon pontificated while the maji huddled behind him, "if you attempt to assemble Creator's form, I will do everything in my power to stop you."

He really had to learn to get over himself. "Bring it," I said.

Zeon stormed off, his people following, though some looked afraid, others focusing their worry on Iepa who waved them off. Maybe the high and mighty leader of the maji wasn't as popular as he thought he was, nor were his policies.

"I fear we will face hard opposition in our fight to save the Universe," Max said. "Zeon has forever held himself apart and, in tune with him, the maji. If they choose to actively come against us, I don't know if we will be able to repel them all."

Didn't matter, not when I was struck with another facepalm moment. "That's it, though, right?" I grinned, kind of lopsided, feeling giddy with relief. "All we need is one piece. Go in, nab it, keep it from Belaisle and he's screwed." I was so clever I could just kiss myself.

If that was true, why was Max looking at me like I'd lost touch with reality?

"These are pieces of Creator, Syd," he said. "Even having possession of one means holding the source of creation in your hands. With each piece he acquires, Belaisle will become stronger and stronger. We must beat him to the chase and return the pieces directly to the statue."

"And then what?" I shrugged in frustration, standing to pace past the four of them. "We put Creator back together—does she come to life again? Fight Dark Brother for us?"

Max spread his hands before him, face sad. "I have no idea," he said. "But hiding them again, keeping them in our possession or assembling the statue are our only options."

"Not destroying them, I take it." His headshake shattered that idea.

"Hiding them is out," he said. "There is nowhere safe once Belaisle starts looking. Keeping them is just as dangerous. Who knows what possession of the pieces could do to us, immortal or not?"

Iepa nodded. "I agree with Max," she said. "We must put Creator back together."

They were grasping at straws, my favorite. Not like I had a better idea.

"What about the dark maji?" They hadn't made a peep. Wasn't that odd?

"I don't know," Iepa said. "All has been quiet and I've not been able to enter Core." The dark version of Center had always seemed more open and welcoming to me. Funny, considering I'd been called the Light One.

"I was here with my sister, focused on Zoe Helios, when our visions failed us," Dark Fate said. "I haven't been able to reach them."

"Worth investigating," I said. "Maybe they'd be willing to give us a hand against Zeon."

More gasping. Even Max looked horrified.

"Syd." Light Fate stood, stumbled toward me and I

caught her. "Don't say that."

"Say what?" We needed help, didn't we?

"It's too late," Dark Fate whispered. "It's in motion and you know it."

Oh crap. Now what did I do?

"The end of the Universe is upon us," Light Fate said, voice cracking as she wept against me. "When maji turn against maji and the drach are caught in the middle."

Shudder. Why did I feel like someone just walked over the place where my grave should have been a million times over? I pushed her back, refusing to let her terror affect me no matter my visceral reaction. I had stuff to do, damn it.

"I thought the prophecy was over?" They said so, didn't they? But, hang on. Light Fate told me once I'd be called on again. This sounded like I was in the wrong place at the wrong time without a choice in the matter.

"The final vision," she said, tongue tripping over the words as though her very mouth fought against them. "The last foresight."

To hell with that. I'd had it up to here with seeing the future. Like it ever did me one damned bit of good. I'd been on my own, no matter the stupid prophecy. That was Belaisle's department, stealing the power and visions of the Helios Oracles. And I'd beaten him, hadn't I?

"I don't care what you saw before now," I said. "Until you two are back to normal, let's hold off on the doom saying, okay?"

She turned from me, fell into her brother's arms as Max stood and joined me. Iepa rose but held her place, looking down at the Fates with gentle concern.

"I'll care for them personally," she said. "And I will be your eyes and ears here for as long as I am able."

"You let us know if Zeon is being an asshat," I said. "We'll come give him hell for you."

"Be safe," she said, one hand raised as Max opened the veil.

First, your home, he sent as we stepped out into the place between planes. He held his human shape for once as we traveled. The drain on his power must have cost him if he didn't shift into drach form. *We must ensure your people are safe.*

And then the pieces of Creator. I nodded into the darkness. *Got it.*

Just another life and death, end of everything day at the office. Had to love it.

FORTY

I brushed back my dark hair from my shoulders, refraining from my usual ponytail in favor of leaving the wavy heaviness hanging loose around me. Though it rankled to conform, I'd carefully dressed in a dark blue silk blouse and floor length, black velvet skirt, a pentagram patterned silver chain belt hanging around my waist.

I touched the matching encircled star around my throat, staring into the restored mirror of my dressing table. Quaid had worked hard and expended a lot of energy to bring everything back to the way it was before the Brotherhood attacked, right down to the tiny nick in the edge of the tabletop I'd accidentally made the first day he gave it to me.

My fingers traced over the tiny sliver of missing wood and I smiled. The sounds of the kids laughing down the hall made everything seem surreal, as though the last week had been a terrible dream we'd all shared, but thankfully woken up from.

Well, some of us anyway. I sighed and stood, turning toward the door, not wanting to think of the loss of life our race had sustained. It was just too sad and horrible to contemplate.

Ethie and Gabriel raced from his room, Galleytrot loping along behind them, with, "Hey, Mom!" thrown at me from the pair while the big, black hound winked on his way. I let them go, smiling, heart tired and sore but healing.

"It's nice to be home." Sassafras exited Ethie's room and joined me as I descended the stairs, a fistful of my skirt in my hands so I didn't trip. At least my shoes were comfortable, even if this getup made me feel like a fraud.

He was right. We'd returned to Wilding Springs, family magic and all, late the night after the Council's mass arrest. I'd managed to reestablish the power controls over the town, though it felt different without the constant, humming presence of the Wild Hunt. Made me wonder how effective the glamour would be in the end, but I wasn't willing to give up our home again just yet.

I had noticed the funny way the locals seemed to look at us these days, though never with malice. More with curiosity, as though they'd only just realized we were there. I couldn't help but wonder if Belaisle's tampering had left behind more than I thought. After all, he'd used the network of all sorcery of all living things. Could he have wakened their magic somehow?

I only hoped that wasn't the case. Though, if a rash of sorcerers started showing up I'd deal with it somehow. So far, so good.

Sassafras beat me to the kitchen, where Shenka sat at the table with her eyes far distant and a little smile on her face. I let her be, going for a cup of coffee. She sighed and shifted behind me just as I turned.

"Almost settled," she said. "The coven has grown by more than double, did you know that? We're doing our best, but it's a bit of a struggle to find enough places for everyone on short notice." Some of the refugees had begged to be allowed to join the coven and I couldn't turn them away. A few still waited at the Stronghold while living arrangements were hammered out here in Wilding Springs, the rest returned to their former homes in an attempt to put the pieces of their lives back together.

"Good thing then," Sassafras said, leaping up onto the table, "there are so many for sale signs out there." His amber gaze flickered to the door. "Who knows, we could eventually make this place a witch town. Now, wouldn't that be a novelty?"

Would it ever. And turn us into targets. Though, the idea had merit. It would be nice to not have to watch every single thing we did at all times.

Something to think about.

"Considering," Shenka said, rising to join me at the coffee pot, "witches are still arriving every day from all across the continent, that idea might be reality before we know it." Her brown eyes caught mine with a hint of amusement and worry twined together. "Can we handle it?"

I hugged her gently. "I know we can."

The kitchen door opened and Mom entered, looking every inch a witch leader. She smiled at my outfit and winked at me before hugging Shenka and turning to kiss Sass on the top of his head.

"Ready?" Her steady gaze made me nervous.

"I guess so," I said, setting aside my coffee. "This sucks, Mom."

She nodded, taking my hand. "We've been here before," she said. "And will be again, more than likely. But we're Hayles, Syd. We'll be fine."

Not that I was worried we were in trouble. But these trial things always seemed to end the same way. Only Mom's had a happy result. And, no matter what she'd done, I wasn't looking forward to watching Erica Plower burn.

Sassafras joined us, Mom lifting him into her arms as I opened the veil and waved half-heartedly to Shenka who returned the gesture while Mom, Sass and I went to Harvard.

The moment we arrived outside the council room, two Enforcers approached, bowing deeply. They were young, probably too young to be elevated out of training, but they seemed eager and serious so I just nodded back.

"Coven Leader Hayle," one said, voice squeaking a little, the barest scruff of a beard on his chin as though he was trying to look older. "Former Council Leader Hayle," he bowed to Mom. "Um, Sassafras," he stammered the finish.

"Get on with it, boy," my demon cat snapped.

"She's ready to speak with you." The Enforcer's flustered blurting made me smile a little.

"It's okay," I said, one hand running down his arm. "Just show us where."

He bobbed his head in gratitude, turning and walking down the hall. I trailed after him, Mom beside me, reaching out to Sassafras.

You didn't need to be mean to him, I sent. *They're just kids, Sass.*

They have to grow up fast, he shot back. The majority of the Enforcer order had been decommissioned and would stand their own trials. They had been obeying orders, but the new council wanted to ensure no one duplicitous went unpunished. I figured at the worst they would be banned from rejoining the Enforcers and relegated back to their families. Who, likely, needed them far more than the order did. Femke had been nice enough to lend out some of hers, as had the other councils, so we weren't unprotected, at least. And there were enough excited young witches who wanted to join, to give back after the conflict, I figured they'd be restocked in a few short years.

Still, I sent as the door unsealed, magic rippling down its sides and the young Enforcer opened it so we could walk through, *they've been through as much as we have. Cut them some slack, okay?*

He grumbled, but I wasn't listening to him. I was too focused on the woman sitting in the chair in the center of the small room. Mom kept a firm hold on Sassafras as she brushed past me and I waved off the Enforcer who closed the door behind us. The tingle of magic resealing the exit I ignored.

Not like Erica was going anywhere. Not from the all gone look on her face, the loss of her dignity as clear as the departure of the power she held for the last seven years. She looked up, slightly dazed, into Mom's eyes.

"Miriam?" Her voice faltered, one hand going to her blonde bob, a question and distance on her face before she looked away, frowning, as if trying to remember something from the way she tapped one finger on her lips. "Now, where did I put it?"

We both knew what she was looking for. The Council's power. I remembered the ache of missing my magic, and I knew Mom had to be reliving being stripped of the coven's power so long ago. My mother turned her back, hands tight on the silver Persian who began to purr. I met her blue eyes just before she began to silently weep and held her gaze until she was able to pull herself together, my power holding her firmly but gently while Sassafras soothed away her hurt.

She handed Sass over to me before wiping impatiently at her face, finally turning to sit next to her old friend. Erica's weak, wobbly smile increased as she touched Mom's cheek.

"You look lovely today, Mir," Erica said. "Always so lovely."

I couldn't help but remember another day like this one, when a friend of mine told me the brother she couldn't remember liked me before brightly and emptily going to the stake to be burned. I still missed Mia and regretted her passing. Wished I could somehow go back in time and make things all right again. But she was gone and, soon, so would Erica.

There had to be a way to shield Mom from this. But no. Like me, this was her guilt to bear, though it wasn't her wrongdoing, not really. She'd wanted her freedom from the council, to be with Dad. That didn't make it her fault the council insisted on another Hayle witch while Mom and I both knew Erica wasn't strong enough.

No one's fault. But from the tight smile on Mom's face, the way she handled her friend so delicately, she blamed herself. Of course she did.

She was a Hayle witch, after all.

Erica's face twisted, her jaw jumping as she turned away from Mom. "Not fair," she muttered, still lost to whatever dream world she'd retreated. "So perfect, so Miriam Hayle. Everyone loves you." She pouted. "And I'm always second best."

I bit my bottom lip to keep from speaking. This wasn't my conversation to have.

Mom turned her around, forced Erica to face her. "Is that why, Erica? Why you betrayed us to the Brotherhood?" Anger found its way into Mom's tone, into her words and her magic. Erica cried out, tried to wriggle free, but Mom wasn't letting her go just yet. "Answer the question!"

Erica sagged, sobbed once and seemed to come back to herself for a moment. "He said," she whispered. "He was so sincere. Said I could be greater, bigger, more than you ever were. That I had a destiny." Erica looked up, blinking, broken. "They compared us all the time," her words dragged out. "All. The. Time. You and Syd and you and Syd. Always telling me I wasn't you and Syd." She shook her head, wiped her nose on the back of one shaking hand. "He wanted me to show my potential." Erica sat up straighter. "It made sense, Mir. His plan." She sagged again. "At first. But then it started going wrong and witches died." She choked on the words, sinking against Mom, mouth gaping open, a thin line of drool falling to the floor beneath them as grief so powerful I had to shield against it washed over me. "They died, Mir. Because of me."

Mom held her, a mix of disgust and old love on her face. "Oh, Erica," she whispered.

Her former second pulled herself up, clawing her way up Mom's arm until they were face to face. "I thought this was right," she said. "I only ever wanted to be worthy."

Mom held her as Erica cried.

FORTY-ONE

Sassafras perched on my lap, looking down over the heads of the gathered witches as the new Council came into session. It was weird how packed the place was considering how many witches we'd lost. But it appeared no one wanted to miss putting Erica and her council out of their misery and I guess I didn't blame them for that.

The new Council members filed in, Femke sitting off to one side with a handful of representatives of the other councils watching silently. I had no idea what deals they'd made or how the new Council had been chosen after those initial first steps, but if Femke was watching over them I knew I had nothing to worry about.

I settled back into the wooden bench seat and scanned faces around me. So odd how many I knew, at least in passing, including a pair of men I hadn't seen in quite some time. Jean Marc and Kristophe Dumont were on their own, though, their father and coven leader, Andre, conspicuously absent. I wondered how hard their family had been hit, though not out of compassion. If Belaisle had wiped them out, I would have gleefully cheered him on.

No you wouldn't, Sassafras sent. *But I would have.*

I turned away from their pinched expressions, normal arrogance gone. They survived, like cockroaches usually did. I was sure I'd hear from them sooner or later.

Odd, I only now noticed the center seat of the Council was empty. Where was their Leader? A sickening feeling rose in my chest and I clutched at Mom's hand even as the Councilor on the end rose.

Marigold Santos, Mom sent, sadness leaking through her magic. *I heard she was supposed to take over as coven leader, but she volunteered to sit on the Council instead.* A huge sacrifice, considering. If I was her, I'd want to be home with my people, rebuilding. Respect for her tough decision rose as the young, slim and dark haired woman addressed everyone, the sound of her voice commanding silence.

"We are the new North American Witches Council," Marigold said, voice shaking slightly, young face tight but calm. "But we are incomplete. Hard days have come to our people, and more will pass before the scars and burns of this terrible time have fully healed. If ever." She paused as I prodded Femke.

This better not be what I think it is. She shot me a glare I threw right back at her. She didn't respond, turning away, leaving me to break out into a cold sweat. If they asked me, I would implode. Or run.

Ah, hell.

"We require powerful leadership, tried and true, trusted by all." The young woman gestured toward me and panic bloomed. No. Freaking. Way. "Miriam Hayle," she said as my heart contracted and I opened my mouth to tell her where to go. "We need you now, more than we ever have. Will you take your place at our helm and lead us where we need to go?"

Mom sat frozen next to me while I tried to restart my brain. I turned to her, eyes wide, as Mom sighed softly.

You knew, I sent.

I suspected. She turned her head a fraction, a tiny, sad smile on her lips. *And I understand their need.* She stood as I gaped up at her and nodded.

"I accept," she said. "And can only hope to serve you well and truly from this day forward."

And then she was moving, and I had to bend my knees sideways to let her out of the row because I wasn't sure I could stand, that those same knees would hold me up. Mom calmly and quietly stepped down to the main floor before alighting the steps to the council dais, nodding as she went to each of the Councilors before bowing to Femke and the representatives.

"I am honored you have asked me to take on this role," she said, a blue glow surrounding her, whirling with light, forming a draped, black velvet robe settling on her shoulders like an old friend. "The trust you've shown in requesting my return will not be betrayed. I am and always will be at your service."

Femke nodded to Mom as the power she and the other Councils gave up swirled in a tiny tornado around my mother. It used to be vast, and would be again with Mom's careful management, I had no doubt. The funnel of magic slipped inside her and my mother sank, slowly and gracefully, into the Council Leader's seat.

Oh, dear, Sassafras sent in a hurt little voice. *Syd, I wish we could help her. This is going to be terrible. Beyond terrible.*

What are you talking about? I shivered when he turned his head to look up at me, amber eyes meeting mine.

"The first order of business," Mom said, answering me when he did not, "is the sentencing of Erica Plower. Bring her forward."

And then I understood. Erica's trial happened yesterday, the verdict predictable. And now, thanks to their selfishness and need to have Mom at their helm, these witches had knowingly put my mother in a position where she would be forced to sentence her former best friend to burn at the stake.

Rage rippled through me, hit Femke like a blow. She turned to stare at me, blue eyes huge and fear on her face.

What? She pushed back, but more out of reflex from what I could tell.

Did you know they were going to do this to her? My voice screamed in her head.

Femke fell back, face falling. *Oh, Syd,* she sent. *I'm sorry. This didn't even cross my mind. I approved their choice, but I didn't think...*

No, I snapped at her. *You sure as hell didn't.* And cut her off when she tried to reach me.

The bitches. All of them. Cowards not worthy of my mother. I would never, ever, forgive them for this.

Erica was led forward, left to stand, listless and wavering, in the middle of the room. Mom's face didn't twitch, her stern, formal expression level, voice calm as she spoke.

"Erica Diane Plower," she said, "formerly of the Hayle coven and leader of the North American Witches Council, you have been found guilty of all charges, including conspiring with the enemy, betrayal of your race, and murder. Are you prepared for your sentence?"

Erica bowed her head. But didn't get to answer. The doors to the council chamber rumbled and green fire forced them open. I spun, staring, as Gwynn ap Nudd, still dressed in his gold and silver armor, strode into the room, Galleytrot at his heels.

What is he up to? Sassafras perched on one paw resting on my hand so he could see over everyone's startled heads.

No idea, I sent as the Sidhe lord came to a halt. Erica turned to stare at the big, black hound who had once been Jared Runnel, the man she loved. Her face twisted in old grief and she covered her face in her hands while Gwynn spoke.

"You know who I am." The air rumbled with the scent of ozone, a faint clap of thunder shaking the room.

"I do," Mom said, still composed. "Gwynn ap Nudd, leader of the Wild Hunt."

Lots of gasping at that. I would have grinned, if I wasn't still so pissed off.

"You freed me," he said. "And, because of this, I owe you a boon." His hand fell on Galleytrot's shoulder. "This one has asked I consider a new hound to take his place. And I understand you have a likely candidate."

No one said a word, though even Mom's carefully groomed eyebrows shot up.

"I don't understand," she said. "The Wild Hunt is no more."

"The Wild Hunt will always be," Gwynn said, voice soft but deep, full of ancient sadness. "I may no more long for the destruction of everything to avenge the death of my true love, but I have worn the mantle of this position for far too long for the Wild to be disbanded. One day, my people and I will rise and scour the planes as we were created to do. Until that time, I am in need of a new hound." He turned and looked Erica up and down. "Only the most heinous of criminals, their hearts blackened by what they have done, will do to fill the role."

Mom stuttered before composing herself. "T-this witch is responsible for the deaths of thousands," she said.

"All the better." He gestured at Erica. "She will suffer endless torment in more lifetimes than you can imagine, forced to wear the skin of a hound and serve me until the end of time."

Galleytrot was condemning her to this? I didn't believe it. But his gentle mind reached mine.

What he says is true, he sent, a rumble of an old storm dying in the distance. *But what he doesn't say is that becoming a hound means a rewrite of your soul, Syd. She will eventually, like me, discover the good in herself again and be renewed and reborn.*

He shook his huge mane and bowed to Mom.

"Council Leader Hayle," Galleytrot said. "Even if you still deem this fate kinder than the one you had planned, haven't there been enough witches burned?"

That hit home. Everyone groaned softly, as though his words seared them like flame.

Mom finally nodded. "You will never grant her freedom?"

"She belongs to me until the end of time," Gwynn said.

My mother's face twitched, though I wasn't sure if it was in grief or gratitude. "Then take her," she said. "And begin her eternal suffering."

Erica wept, but she turned to Gwynn without protest. He reached out to touch her, one shining gauntlet glowing with green fire. Her eyes flashed blue one last time before they spun into darkness, her shape morphing as she trembled. I'd seen enough werewolf shiftings I knew what to expect, but this was far more gruesome. Instead of her body changing, she shed it to the sound of wet tearing, her howl of agony erupting as her skin split down her back. The black hound burst from inside Erica's flesh in a violent outward motion, flinging parts of her to the shields Mom quickly threw up to protect the gallery. The sounds of retching made me sick, but I was too focused on what was going on to let a little gore distract me.

Said a lot for who I'd grown into, didn't it?

Erica shook her new form, black eyes flaring with red fire before she settled on her haunches next to her master. Black fur so dark it absorbed the light shivered as she turned her massive head, looking up to meet my eyes, nodding ever so slightly before facing Mom.

"I will take my leave," Gwynn said, snapping his fingers at Erica. "Come along, hound."

No one said a word as the huge, black dog brushed past Galleytrot, nor did anyone comment when he head-butted her gently on the way by. Silence held until the doors closed behind the Sidhe lord and it was Mom who broke it.

"Gwynn is correct," she said, voice shaking ever so slightly, a tremor I'm sure only I heard because I knew her so well. "There have been enough burnings. All other witches convicted of their crimes attached to this matter will be imprisoned for life and their power stripped."

No one protested. I think we were all sick of death by now. And, as everyone began to file out, the trials and sentencings over, a pair of poor unfortunate young witches wincing as they began to clean up what remained of Erica's human form, I reached out to my mother gently.

Miriam Hayle, I sent. *Council Leader.*

Sydlynn Hayle, she sent. *Oh dear.* And sighed. *What am I going to tell your father?*

I couldn't help but laugh.

FORTY-TWO

Just when I thought I'd gotten my happily ever after. Yeah, wishful thinking, Hayle.

Mom's second act of power was to declare an official week of mourning while her new Enforcer order scoured the continent for the lost and the dead. Every day reports came in on partial covens who made it into hiding, more stories of horror and death to share. I spent as much time with Mom those first few days as I could, offering a shoulder to lean on, an ear as she struggled to keep everyone from losing it while the final numbers came in.

Of course, her third order of business was to declare any Brotherhood member who was seen in her territory would be summarily killed without trial and without question. I wondered at her choice, worried as I was last time other sorcerers might get caught up in the dragnet of anger, but a warning through Piers and Gram would hopefully keep any strays safe from harm as long as they kept their heads down.

Nice of her to accept my request for the Hayle coven to return to the fold. The small portion of Council power that came along with our reinstatement made me sad how far we'd fallen, but there was a new determination in the witches I met and spoke to, a shift in attitude away from blame and despair to a willingness to act. I hated it had taken this kind of a tragedy to create change, but at least something good seemed to have come from all the devastation.

Silver linings helped me find the bright side.

The new World Paranormal Council was going strong, despite my worries the Witch Councils might back off now that things weren't falling apart anymore. But, to my surprise and relief, that wasn't the case. Femke's position had been made permanent by unanimous decision, joined by Sunny and Danilo as well as a few prominent witches on other Councils. She was permitted to keep her place as European leader, fortunately, though I didn't envy her the workload.

We hadn't spoken since I lost my mind at her during Erica's sentencing. Neither of us had reached out and, I knew she was furious about being forced into the position of World Leader. I figured we'd both go through a cooling off period then hash it out. She was too good a friend to let this stand between us.

Besides, now more than ever I was firmly convinced she was the best person for the job.

She did call on me to come and speak to the World Council about the situation with Max and the Fates, though she did it through her secretary and only spoke to me in her official capacity. At least she wasn't mad enough at me she let it cloud her good judgment. And I felt better knowing everyone was finally paying attention to just how much trouble there was out there for us to get into.

Weird, everyone getting along and playing nice. Made me feel like the end of everything might be coming after all.

Max and the drach had fully recovered, and he sent his people scouring the Universe for clues as to where the pieces of Creator were hidden. A growing sense of urgency gripped me daily, but it was a game of hurry up and wait until we had a line on where to go looking. Considering I'm not the most patient person in the Universe, I think I was beginning to drive my family nuts with my mood swings and anxiety.

The drach were looking for nine shiny needles in about a gazillion haystacks. At least, from what he told me, if one of the drach grew near they'd sense the soul of one of the nine guarding the pieces, so that was something. But they had to get really close, so I wasn't holding my breath this particular tactic would pan out.

At least Belaisle didn't have a clue, either. As far as I knew. This kind of thinking was what kept me up at night. That and wondering over and over who in my family had betrayed me by sneaking into the statue chamber and stealing Creator's heart.

When not out flying around looking for chunks of their goddess, the drach were now permanently living in the Stronghold. Protecting it was more important now than ever before. Had I known the remains of Creator were at the base of the tower, I probably wouldn't have let anyone in, whether the Stronghold saved our asses or not.

Max had been kind enough—insert sarcasm here—to list off the pieces we were looking for. Like some cosmic shopping list, just great. The heart, naturally. We had to get it back. Eyes (shudder), brain (gag me), head, one ear, one arm, a hand, that missing foot and, though he had no idea how it was depicted in stone, Creator's soul.

Okay then.

I distracted myself from my endless worry by focusing on other things that would surely give me an ulcer. Like Sebastian and Alison and their entire missing blood clan. No one could find them, feel a hint of them anywhere and I was beginning to worry something horrible had happened. I mentioned it to Max, about what we discussed, losing whole races to the other Universe, but he didn't seem to think it would be possible for the transfer to be that specific.

I wasn't so sure.

I had, as yet, to find time to take Gabriel to see Ameline. But I would when things settled down further. For some reason it felt necessary to me to have him meet her, to understand what really happened the night he opened the gateway to the other Universe. I hoped it would make taking his talent seriously easier on him. His sensitive nature was lovely and all, but I needed him to truly see just how dangerous his gift was. And, when he finally did come to realize it, I needed him tough enough to keep things together. Just in case Max and I required his particular talent somewhere down the line.

Why did I get the feeling that might be sooner rather than later?

One happy bit of news. Lula and Phon, once free agents under the employ of the Council, were now official members of the Hayle coven. They'd asked and I didn't think twice, thrilled to have them. They seemed happy enough and the coven adored them, so I called it a win.

Piers was gone with Zoe, his sister's appearance the afternoon of Erica's sentencing finally convincing him to try to do something about his mother. I hadn't heard from him since, but I knew when he was ready he'd be in touch. Of course they added to my elevated blood pressure and worries. Eva was clearly at her breaking point. But he needed to do this and I wasn't about to stop him.

Family, right? Family was everything. Besides, I knew how she felt, in a way. Spending years on her own, without support, feeling alone. Just described my life. Without the family, I would have been a nutjob loner. So, I'd cut her some slack as long as she came around and didn't do anything stupid.

So far, according to Mom, all offers for Eva to join the World Council had been ignored point blank. Which meant I wasn't holding out hope for the "anything stupid" part.

Galleytrot wasn't acting as upset as I expected and there were times when I found him staring into space, a doggy smile on his face. But when I asked him about it he would just shrug his big shoulders and lower his head into his paws, closing his eyes. Ignoring me. Fair enough. Whatever he'd done, he'd saved Mom from having to burn her old friend. And I loved him for that.

Like I needed another reason.

The kids didn't even seem to realize we'd had a crisis, both of them still wound up about their days spent exploring the Stronghold. I let them have their happiness, just grateful they weren't scarred for life like the rest of us. Still, it was hard not to stare at Gabriel's sleeping face at night and wonder what might be coming for him.

Or who.

Tallah was back in California, prepared to rebuild and

I sent Shenka with her to do it. My second tried to protest, that the family needed her, but I could tell she really wanted to go. In the end, Quaid insisted, taking over her second's duties and I couldn't have been prouder of him.

But I had bigger plans for my husband and shared those niggling ideas with my mother one night over a quiet dinner with just the two of us. The stupid law that prevented Enforcers from marrying coven leaders had to go. And Mom agreed.

Quaid was just too good at being an Enforcer to let him waste his talents. I couldn't wait to see the look on his face when I told him he could have both of his true loves again.

Charlotte and Sage, Gram and Demetrius, all joined Tallah in California. I missed them like crazy, but was busy anyway integrating new witches and helping the coven adapt to their newly woken sorcery. It was going to take some time—and I was positive the normal townsfolk were going to notice the odd issue—but it was important everyone had the ability to protect themselves from now on.

I just wished I'd thought of it sooner.

My power resealed the cavern, emptied of the flotsam of our short time there. I shielded it yet again, just in case. Never knew when I would need a safe place to hide.

Mom recruited Varity Rhodes to lead her new

Enforcer order, and the older witch said yes. Though from the stoop of her shoulders she was looking forward to the day her replacement could be trained. Mom didn't say anything, but I assumed she had a certain chocolate-eyed man in mind for the job and I wasn't about to protest.

Time for Quaid to make a mark of his own.

The saddest part was the final headcount. Fully one third of all registered North American witches were either dead or still missing and presumed lost. According to most of the covens we talked to, they tried to surrender but were either killed outright and their power taken or herded into camps and siphoned over time. I stopped attending the meetings with Mom, hating to abandon her. But I just couldn't listen anymore or my head would explode.

I had to find Belaisle. Maybe I couldn't kill his keyhole ass, but I could make him suffer.

And suffer.

No sign of Trill, which bothered me. I wondered where she and her friends had gotten off to. But Owen and Apollo stayed with us, helping me to train the coven in their sorcery. It was nice to have them around, even if I missed their troubled sister.

Thankfully, the maji had decided to keep their nasty noses out of my business. I hadn't heard word one from Zeon and Iepa seemed to think things had settled down, though there was still no word from the dark maji and the Fates were still blind to the future.

I was working on it.

The best news, by far? Simon came through for me. The day we returned to Wilding Springs, I found a note taped to a laptop on the kitchen table. It read, *Fortune restored. Payment taken. Nice doing business with you.*

Now, if only I could find a way to restore our friendship, too.

Like what you read? Find out more at
pattilarsen.com

Here's a look at the first chapter of
Book Two of the Hayle Coven Destinies

STEAM UNION

ONE

I shifted uncomfortably in the wobbly folding chair, doing my best to keep the polite smile on my face though my lips and cheeks ached from it. Shenka hustled around the basement making last-minute adjustments, and I wished she'd just come sit down next to me already.

Bad enough I had over fifty witches staring at me, waiting for me to say something. I could use the support.

The space was better lit than usual, my chair on the edge of the pentagram, witches from covens all around North America crowded into the area in a rough circle, packed in layers of bodies. My toe scuffed over the painted white line, eyes roving over the old lamps Shenka dug out of the mess and set up to cast pale yellow light around the basement. We usually made due with the single bulb over the center of the room, and I found I kind of missed the shadows. This much brilliance seemed to dim the wonder I always held for this place, making it feel chintzy, somehow, almost like a carnival sideshow instead of the base of my family's magic.

So many memories down here. They crowded around me almost as much as the anxious, waiting witches. Of discomfort, unhappiness at first, sneaking my nutjob grandmother sweets to keep her quiet during coven rituals, welcoming Dad from his home plane, Demonicon, to ours. The anguish of forcing myself to use magic as a teenager though it often made me ill. Uncovering the truth of who I was, taking over my coven after freeing Gram's power from where she'd hidden it inside me.

The years pressed down on my shoulders, made me feel old suddenly. A funny concept for a woman who would supposedly live forever. I had no idea what old really was. And yet, sitting here with my hands fidgeting in my lap, tension mounting with the scrutiny of my witch peers, I felt every single second of my existence like a weight on my heart.

I knew why they were here, in Wilding Springs, in my basement. Why all the coven leaders—or, the majority of them, anyway—and their seconds perched with eager worry, arriving in pairs and quartets without notice until my basement was flooded with them and their nervous magic.

Thank goodness for Shenka. As she finally settled beside me, her own smile easy, more practiced than mine, I reached out and squeezed her hand in thanks before drawing a breath to speak. No idea what I was going to say. But I had to say something.

"I can guess why you've come." They bobbed their heads at me, pressure of their intense focus increasing. I shifted under the stress and went on. "Our people have suffered terrible losses and we're still afraid."

"We have the right to be." Karyn Barrett, new leader of the Barrett coven, nodded sharply, her dark hair in a tight ponytail, her thick, blonde bangs wavering over her hazel eyes. The first time we'd met had been under terrible circumstances, at the Stronghold, just after Lula and Phon Kennecott helped rescue what remained of her coven. "And no offense to the new Council, but we're not seeing a whole lot of progress to guarantee our safety."

Murmurs and more nods.

You need to cut this off at the pass. A silver ball of fluff wound his way through the chairs, accepting affectionate pats and full body strokes before coming to my side. The big Persian leaped into my lap, curling his thick tail around his paws, amber eyes scanning the crowd. *The last thing we need is someone suggesting mutiny against the Council.*

I know that, I sent, testy with Sassafras. The demon in the body of the cat purred softly, easing my tension a hair.

And I know you do, he sent, much more gently. *This is a tricky bit of business, Syd.*

Tell me about it. "I know the Council is working hard to find ways to protect us," I said out loud to the waiting witches. "But Liander Belaisle and his Brotherhood have gone underground again. We all know how hard it is to uncover sorcerers when they don't want to be found."

After the havoc he'd wreaked against our territory, killing off over a third of the witch population and stealing not only their family power, but that of the Council, Belaisle had more than enough to answer for. And that was just this time around. I had older hurts to lay at his feet.

"So they say," Tallah Hensley spoke up. Shenka's sister was thinner than the last time I saw her, leaned out face hardened, posture stiff. My second twitched next to me. Shenka had only just returned to my side after spending four weeks assisting her sister in rebuilding the Hensley coven in California. The last fourteen days Shenka had been home felt like walking on eggshells with her, but I hardly blamed her. We were all pushed to our limits these days.

"I have our Council Leader's personal assurance," I said. "She's working without rest to find ways to ensure our safety and that of our families."

"If only Miriam had been Council Leader when this

all fell apart." Dagney Rhodes choked a soft sob into the handful of tissues she clutched to her lips.

"It never would have happened in the first place," Paula Santos snapped at her, olive skin tight in anger. These were all new faces, their names coming to me slowly. I knew their mothers and grandmothers far better. But those women I'd once called my peers were dead and gone, lost to the takeover of our territory by the Brotherhood six weeks ago.

Six weeks. I still couldn't believe it had only been so long.

More mutterings, some of agreement, though Tallah spoke up again.

"Miriam Hayle is an excellent leader," she said, sounding like she didn't mean a word. "But, she herself has been thralled, under the influence of the Brotherhood. At this point, frankly, she just can't be trusted."

I wanted to slap her. How dare she attack my mother like that? But I held back, drew on the strength of my vampire essence for calm while my demon paced and snarled. The hitchhikers I carried in my head, their power mingling with mine, were a source of great comfort to me, now more than ever. The younger me would have lost her temper, flown off the handle, started a fight I'd win if it killed someone. But, thanks to Shenka, motherhood and my alter egos, I'd managed to mellow just a little bit. Enough I simply glared at Tallah instead of showing her just what I thought of her opinion.

Because, the truth was—and it hurt, oh, did it hurt—the Hensley leader was right.

Damn it.

"Our covens are depleted," Karyn said, young face pinched and aged beyond her twenty-four years. I'd gotten to know her a little, liked her a lot. She had a good head on her shoulders. I was more likely to listen to her than Tallah at this moment and gave her my full attention. "It will take generations to rebuild our numbers. But even if we were to replace every single witch we've lost, we're still at a terrible disadvantage." She swallowed hard, hands twisting in her lap. The scent of fear filled the room, a sharp tang of physical anxiety. "We're vulnerable and we know it, now."

I agreed with that much. Without sorcery to counter sorcery, the other paranormal races didn't stand a chance. The first magic could only be fought with more of the same. Which was why Belaisle and his Brotherhood managed to not only sway the old Council Leader, Erica Plower, into signing a treaty that gave them power over the territory, but to do as much damage as they did in such a short time.

"I'm sorry we just showed up." Karyn looked guilty, then, glancing sideways at the unrepentant Tallah. Was I going to have to keep an eye on Shenka's sister? The rage in her seemed to grow by the minute. And while I liked Tallah, had called her an ally in the past, she and I had fought over Shenka's choice to be my second and had butted heads over other issues that kept us from being true friends. The loss of the bulk of her coven to the Brotherhood hit her hard, clearly. Still, that was no excuse to abandon good judgment.

I nodded to Karyn, let it go. I was glad Quaid was out, frankly, that Dad had the kids at Harvard with Mom. This little impromptu meeting wasn't sanctioned by the Council and was making me more nervous by the minute. But what was I supposed to do when they just popped up out of nowhere in the arms of ex-Enforcers, returned to their families in disgrace, and dropped themselves in my lap?

"I understand your concerns," I said, reaching for all the diplomacy I'd absorbed from the responsible people in my life over the years.

"Do you?" Tallah was shaking a bit, jaw tight. "You didn't lose one witch, did you?"

They watched me with hurt and fearful eyes. But what was I supposed to say?

"We were fortunate," I said. "And grateful."

"We're not blaming you for anything, Syd." Karyn shot Tallah a glance and the Hensley leader looked away. "Please, understand that. In fact, we're happy at least one family survived intact. And that you were there to save us."

I'd spent most of my life railing against the closed-minded arrogance and head-in-the-sand attitude of witches. Her unexpected announcement made me pause and blush. But Karyn wasn't done.

"We came here outside the knowledge of the North American Witches Council for a reason." A small smile warmed her face, took away the taut bleakness. "We need your help."

I couldn't protect them all, if that was what they wanted.

Pay attention, Sassafras snapped in my head. *This is important.*

Dagney Rhodes pushed her blonde hair behind one ear, round cheeks pink with a flush of emotion. "We know discord is the last thing we need right now." At least someone understood it. We had to work together, to trust each other. Our separate ways, the privacy witches clung to, the secrecy, had to stop. At least to the point we could go to each other with problems and ask for help without losing face. "But our numbers are so reduced." The Rhodes coven had once been over two hundred witches, now down to just over twenty. I knew personally. I saved them from the Brotherhood the same day their beloved leader, Violet, was killed. "And we are helpless if the Brotherhood returns to finish us off."

"We're proposing a second layer of connection,"

Karyn said. "A shadow council to watchdog the NAWC. And we want you to lead it."

ABOUT THE AUTHOR

Everything you need to know about me is in this one statement: I've wanted to be a writer since I was a little girl, and now I'm doing it. How cool is that, being able to follow your dream and make it reality? I've tried everything from university to college, graduating the second with a journalism diploma (I sucked at telling real stories), am part of an all-girl improv troupe (if you've never tried it, I highly recommend making things up as you go along as often as possible). I've even been in a Celtic girl band (some of our stuff is on YouTube!) and was an independent film maker. My life has been one creative thing after another—all leading me here, to writing books for a living.

Now with multiple series in happy publication, I live on beautiful and magical Prince Edward Island (I know you've heard of Anne of Green Gables) with my very patient husband and multitude of pets.

I love-love-love hearing from you! You can reach me (and I promise I'll message back) at patti@pattilarsen.com. And if you're eager for your next dose of Patti Larsen books (usually about one release a month) come join my mailing list! All the best up and coming, giveaways, contests and, of course, my observations on the world (aren't you just dying to know what I think about everything?) all in one place: http://smarturl.it/PattiLarsenEmail.

Last—but not least!—I hope you enjoyed what you read! Your happiness is my happiness. And I'd love to hear just what you thought. A review where you found this book would mean the world to me—reviews feed writers more than you will ever know. So, loved it (or not so much), **your honest review would make my day**. Thank you!

www.ingramcontent.com/pod-product-compliance
Lightning Source LLC
Chambersburg PA
CBHW070353260626
47161CB00001B/130